A Slip of the Mask

"Derek!" Ada gasped. "You have news of my brother?"

"Yes, old fellow, I do."

Instinctively, at the joy in her eyes, Derek held out his arms.

Without thinking, Ada flew across the room and flung herself into them.

Exultant with her happiness, Derek lifted her in the air and whirled her with delight.

Suddenly Ada looked down at him. She was not behaving as her masquerade decreed. A *boy* would not have thrown herself at Derek. A *boy* would not be whirling about this way. *What* had she *done*?

————

THE LADY DISGUISED
A Regency Love Story by
ELIZABETH MANSFIELD

Elizabeth Mansfield

The Lady Disguised

CHARTER BOOKS, NEW YORK

THE LADY DISGUISED

A Charter Book/published by arrangement with
the author

PRINTING HISTORY
Charter edition/March 1989

ISBN: 1-55773-172-1

Charter Books are published by The Berkley Publishing Group,
200 Madison Avenue, New York, NY 10016.
The name "Charter" and the "C" logo
are trademarks belonging to Charter Communications, Inc.

PRINTED IN THE UNITED STATES OF AMERICA

10 9 8 7 6 5 4 3 2 1

Chapter One

The Honorable Stanley Farrington, aged eight, stood on tiptoe at the nursery window. His nose was pressed against the lowest pane, for Stanley was very small for his age and stood only a little higher than the sill. The view from the third-floor window of Farrington Park, located atop one of Suffolk's loveliest rises, was spectacular this October of 1816 (one could see miles of rolling English countryside from that vantage point, all of it bedecked in autumnal splendor), but Stanley was not taking any notice of the fleecy clouds that scudded across the bright, early-afternoon sky nor of the leaves of the oaks and maples that the early frost had turned to the most breathtaking yellows and glowing rusts. It was the sort of scene that made artists itch for their palettes and ordinary folk itch to be artists, but little Stanley was completely uninterested in the October splendor. His eyes were fixed on the middle distance, where a number of triangular pennons fluttered in the wind above a circle of gypsy wagons, a colorful caravan that had established itself on the far side of the home woods. To Stanley's eyes, the circle of garishly painted wagons, ragged tents and bravely colored flags was more romantic and attractive than any scene Mother Nature could paint. "Can't I go outdoorth now, Jollie?" he lisped, turning a pair of wide hazel eyes to his governess hopefully. "I'll read two whole chapterth tomorrow, I promithe."

The rotund governess, Mrs. Jolliffe to the staff but Jollie to her charge, sighed and shut the history book. "You'll be the death of me, Master Stanley," she muttered, rising from her chair with a grunt. "The death of me." She joined him at the window and, after brushing back a lock of his reddish-gold hair from his forehead, lifted his chin. "Why do you want to

1

see those gypsies anyway? They're nothing but a filthy lot."

"No, they're not. They're *exthiting*! They play the tambourine and danthe and wear ringth on every finger. And the ladieth wear shawlth with fringe thith long! And there'th a man there ath big ath a giant, with a red and yellow handkerchief tied on hith head and real cointh on a chain round hith neck and a big gold ring in hith ear. Pleathe, Jollie! I won't go too near to them, I thwear! I'll only peep from behind the hedge at the border of the north field."

The governess sighed again. She never could bring herself to refuse Stanley anything. One look from those wide hazel eyes, one little twitch of those full lips, one glimpse of the dimple that appeared in his left cheek when he was about to smile, and her heart melted in her ample chest. "Oh, very well, if your heart's set on it," she said, taking a wine-red wool muffler from a hook behind the door and winding it about his throat. "But be sure you don't go any closer than the north field. Those wicked creatures can't be trusted."

"Why, Jollie? Why can't they be truthted?"

"Because they're pagan, godless creatures, that's why."

Stanley, not understanding a word, didn't bother to ask for further explanation. He ran to the door quickly, hoping to make his escape before the governess talked herself into changing her mind.

Mrs. Jolliffe watched after him as he scurried down the hallway. "Keep your distance from them, as you promised, Stanley! Now, you *mind* me, boy! Those heathen have been known to steal little boys from their beds and cook them in stew!"

But Stanley was already halfway down the stairs.

He'd descended all three flights without meeting anyone, but as he was about to let himself out the east portico doorway, he came face to face with his sister, just coming in after her ride. "Stanley, love," she greeted warmly, "come here and give me a hug."

Stanley glanced up at her uneasily. "No hugth now, Ada, pleathe. I'm in a bit of a hurry."

He attempted to dart by her, but she caught him by the collar and pulled him round to face her. "Just a minute, young man," she laughed, a low, boyish laugh that Stanley normally loved to hear. But now she was bending down to ruffle his hair with one hand while she held on to his arm with the other, and he was in too much of a hurry to be off to enjoy her teasing. "Let me go, Ada," he said, squirming.

"You can't get away from me without so much as a how-de-do!" she said in her croaky, boyish voice. "Where are you off to in such a hurry?"

Ada Farrington, at nineteen, was still considered by everyone in the family to be a tomboy, but if a stranger had happened along at that moment, he would not have seen a tomboy at all. He would have judged her to be a lovely and stylish young miss. She looked very much the proper young lady in the dark coat and white neckerchief of her riding costume. Her rakish little riding hat sat on a head of magnificently glowing, long, thick hair as reddish-gold in color as Stanley's. Her eyes, also greenish-grey like her brother's, were shaped like half-saucers tilted up at the corners just enough to give the impression that she was hiding a mischievous secret. Her full lips and slightly pointed chin had in the past added to the boyish look that made the epithet "tomboy" so appropriate, but the family had not yet noticed that the boyishness was softening and maturing into delectable womanliness. Even her voice, which had been a tomboyish croak as a child, was now taking on the alluring timbre of a trained contralto. Nature was quickly transforming her into an uncommon but captivating young lady.

But Ada's metamorphosis into womanhood was something that Stanley would be the last to see. To him, Ada was as she'd always been—his best chum. Ada was the one who took him up on her horse and rode with him at breakneck speed, who taught him how to hunt grouse and who romped with him through the brambles and underbrush of the woods at the bottom of the north field. She was his favorite person in the entire world, but right now he was not glad to have run into her. She was his elder, after all, and elders were funny about gypsies. Even Ada might take it into her head to order him not to go to see them.

He brushed her hand away from his head but could not loose himself from her hold on his arm. He squirmed helplessly in her grasp and glared up at her. "I tell you I haven't time for you to be patting and petting me, Ada. Let me go!"

"I will, as soon as I get my hug and you tell me where you're off to," she said firmly.

"To the north field, if it'th any of your buthineth," he pouted. He really adored his sister, but he had to admit that she had one fault—she was eleven years his senior. Like all older siblings, she had a dismaying tendency to patronize him and order him about. And, what was even worse, she sometimes succumbed to the dismaying female habit of pinching his cheeks or ruffling his hair.

"What on earth do you want to go to the north field for?" the adored yet irritating sister demanded.

"I won't tell you," the boy said flatly. "It'th not your affair."

"If you're afraid to say," Ada responded calmly, "then you must be up to some mischief."

"I'm *not* afraid to say! I'll tell you if you promithe not to lecture me."

"Now see here, Stanley Algernon Farrington, that's much too rare and thick! Since when do I lecture you?"

The little boy eyed her speculatively. "You don't, very much, I thuppothe. But if I tell you, do you promithe to let me go without thcolding?"

"Very well, old fellow. Word of honor."

The boy grinned up at her, a dimple making a sudden appearance in his left cheek. "I'm going down to thee the gypthieth," he admitted in an excited whisper.

"The gypsies?" Ada's eyes lit up interestedly. "Are there gypsies down there? Wait till I change, and I'll go with you."

"No, no," the boy said firmly. "It'th no plathe for girlth."

His sister's eyebrows rose in amusement. "Isn't it? Why not?"

Stanley shrugged. "Too dangerouth for you. Gypthieth are very wicked, you know. They thteal girlth from their bedth and cook them in thtew." And with that dire pronouncement, he squirmed free of her hold, darted under her arm, scooted down the stone steps, ran through the garden and disappeared from her view.

"Cook them in stew indeed!" Ada laughed, shaking her

head and turning to the door. "Wherever does that child get such wild ideas?"

The laughter faded from her eyes as she stepped over the threshold and made her way across the hallway to the stairs. Ada had the most tender affection for her brother, and her concern for his welfare was never far from the surface of her mind. Seeing him go off all by himself as he'd just done gave her heart a little twinge. The boy was wonderfully independent for his age, she realized, but she couldn't help feeling sorry for him. He was such a lonely little tyke. But there was little she could do to improve things. The Farrington family situation was such that there was no possible way to change Stanley's life for the better.

It was the peculiar history of the Farrington family that was at fault, she realized. The family arrangement was not normal. And it was Stanley who paid the price for it.

She strode into her bedroom and shut the door behind her, her brow creased with worry. Forgetting that her purpose in coming upstairs was to get out of her riding dress, she went to the window and stared out upon the autumn landscape with unseeing eyes. *Poor Stanley,* she thought with a tightness in her throat. *Why did he have to be born into a family like ours?*

Ada did not know all the details of how the family came to their present situation, for no one had ever told her the entire story, but she'd pieced together enough of her background to know that the story was odd. Not that one needed to know the story to call her family odd, she thought ruefully. Anyone would know they were odd as soon as they learned that nine years separated the first-born from the second, and eleven years separated the second-born from the third.

But everything Ada had ever learned about the family history was odd, so odd that she often wished she'd been born into a more ordinary family. She knew that her mother, the former Lady Isabel Rolfe, had married Edward Farrington, the Earl of Wycoff, when she was only sixteen and that she'd had a son, Lionel, after only a year. There was nothing very odd in that, but the story turned strange immediately thereafter. The marriage must have soured shortly after Lionel's birth, for Ada managed to learn that her mother and father separated in their second year of married life. The couple lived apart for the next several years, Lord Farrington keeping himself in London and Lady Isabel residing here at Farrington Park in Suffolk.

The next strange thing Ada learned about her parents was that there was a reconciliation between them which occurred eight years later, resulting in the birth of a girl, Ada herself. The reconciliation must have been brief, for Ada remembered that her father did not live in the Suffolk manor house during her childhood. When she was ten, however, another reconciliation took place. This one was permanent; Lord Farrington returned to the country house to live, and soon Stanley was born.

The next few years were the happiest that Ada remembered. Even though Ada and her brothers were widely separate in age, they were fond of each other and often played together despite their age differences. In addition, they were happy to see their parents living contentedly together after so many years of separation. Their mother seemed to bloom, and their father, Lord Farrington, showered his children with such sincere affection that it made up for the years when he was missing from their lives.

When Lionel, the Earl's eldest son and his heir, turned twenty-five, he betrothed himself to a Miss Lydia March-banks, whom the Earl and the rest of the family did not like very much. Lydia, a perfectly proper choice, was from a perfectly respectable family and had a perfectly suitable education, perfectly admirable manners and a perfectly satisfactory appearance. But her lips were always pursed, and her remarks were always prefaced by a little sigh, which seemed to suggest that it took too much effort for her to bother to communicate her very deep thoughts to the superficial people who were listening. Stanley and Ada, when they spoke of her in private, called her Miss Prunes. Lionel, however, convinced the Earl that he was sincerely attached to Lydia and wanted her for his bride. Lord Farrington then swallowed his disappointment and made the best of Lionel's choice by arranging a magnificent wedding-fête for his heir. He ordered that the west wing of the house (which contained an enormous ballroom) be opened for the first time in thirty years, and he and his lady hosted what was judged the most elegant and fashionable affair of the season. Three hundred guests came from far and wide, their number including two dukes, the Prime Minister Lord Liverpool, and the Prince Regent himself. The ball was so grand that it was spoken of for months afterward, even in London.

Unfortunately, however, the Earl contracted an inflammation of the lungs that same winter, and after a lingering illness he died. And then, as if the fates wanted to underline this already peculiar history with a final irony, they arranged that the Earl's burial should take place on Stanley's seventh birthday.

That, as Ada managed to piece it together, was the family's recent history. It was not a commonplace story, she realized, nor could it—except for those first six years of Stanley's life —be considered a happy one.

She sank down on the window seat, pulled off her pert little riding cap and tossed it aside with a sigh. Papa's passing had been tragic for everyone, she knew, but it seemed to her that her mother and Stanley suffered the most. Poor Stanley seemed to draw into himself, and Ada, try as she might, couldn't pull him out of the doldrums. There were no boys his age anywhere in the vicinity that he might play with, and she, the sibling nearest his age, was really too old for him. Though she spent a good part of each day with him, she knew she was not an adequate companion. She could read him stories and engage him in fierce games of skittles, but the running, tagging, active games that little boys loved were no longer for her. He might think of her as a tomboy (as did the rest of the family), but she knew she was growing out of that tendency. Romping with him in the underbrush was beginning to seem to her to be inappropriate behavior for a nineteen-year-old. After all, if Papa hadn't died last year, she would have already come out. The hoydenish ways that used to amuse her now made her feel uncomfortable. She was growing up . . . becoming a woman. She liked this new, womanly feeling very much, but she knew that Stanley would miss the girl she used to be.

She was Stanley's only chum. What would happen to Stanley when she no longer could indulge in their outdoor games? Poor Stanley would then have even fewer outlets for his boyish energy.

What made matters worse was the change in her mother since Papa's death. Papa had passed to his reward more than a year ago, but though Mama was no longer wearing black, her heart was still in mourning for him. Mama seemed to have lost interest in family activities and in all society. Now reduced to being only the Dowager Lady Isabel, Mama sat all day at the window staring out in morose contemplation of who-knew-what. She still smiled sweetly at anyone who interrupted her thoughts, and she responded to their questions with her usual good sense, but there was no enthusiasm or liveliness in her anymore. And it was Stanley who was most hurt by the change in his mother. Her pensive demeanor confused him, and her abstracted replies to his questions troubled him. He didn't know how to speak to her anymore.

Ada rose from the window seat and began to pace about the room. The family situation was bleak, and she saw no promise of improvement. The only members of the family who had benefited from her father's passing were Lionel and Lydia. Lionel was now the Earl, and Lydia positively oozed smugness when the servants addressed her as Lady Farrington. Each day she was becoming more obnoxiously overbearing in her new role as Mistress of the Manor. And Lionel, who'd been a decent enough sort before the acquisition of his title, was becoming more pompous every day. He was merely twenty-eight years old, but his new sense of importance made him behave like forty-eight. *It's all so sad,* Ada thought with a heavy sigh. *My once-happy family is no more.*

She returned to the window and discovered, to her surprise, that it had turned dark. She must have been brooding for hours! She shook off her lethargy at once and quickly went into action, throwing off her riding dress with unseemly haste. She didn't want to be late for dinner, for Lydia set great store by her time schedule and would pout all evening if anyone was late.

By the time she'd thrown on an evening dress it was almost six, and she still had to dress her hair. *Dash it all,* she muttered under her breath. *I'm going to be late again!* Lydia would put on her frozen face, and everyone at the table would be uncomfortable all through the meal. And, worst of all, Ada had no time now to run up to the nursery to keep Stanley company while he ate his lonely dinner. (She wondered how old the boy would have to be before Lydia would permit him to join the adults in the dining room for his meals.) *Blast!* she muttered under her breath. *If I could think of a way to do it, I'd take Stanley and run away!*

The family had all gathered in the library by the time Ada came down to join them. It was customary for the Farringtons to dine early. Country hours were particularly congenial to Lydia at this time, for she was breeding. This being her first pregnancy, Lydia was taking extraordinary care of her health. Going early to bed, rising late and completely avoiding any physical effort were the three principles that guided her life during these significant months. And no one in the family saw fit to object. Ada did not particularly relish the early dinners and the resultant extension of the dull evening hours, but she never gave voice to a word of disapproval. She realized that Lydia was now the mistress of the household and that she, her mother and Stanley were living in the house on Lionel's and Lydia's sufferance.

Ada found the family in their usual places, just as she expected they would be. Lionel was leaning on the fireplace mantel, Lydia was seated nearby on the armchair with her feet resting on a hassock, and Mama sat at the window, staring out into the dark and looking morose. "Ah, there you are, Ada," her sister-in-law said at once. "I was about to send Pinkney to seek you."

"Why? Am I late?" Ada asked with cheerfully dishonest innocence as she crossed the room to her mother and kissed her cheek.

"A bit," Lionel answered, exchanging a look of patient resignation with his wife. "You are always a bit late, you know, my dear. When Lydia says six, she means six on the dot."

"I thought it *was* six on the dot," Ada retorted cavalierly, throwing herself on a chair near her mother. "In fact, I just heard the hall clock chime."

"The hall clock has been several minutes slow this week," Lydia said. "Remind Pinkney to fix it tomorrow, will you, Lionel, my love? I've been meaning to tell him so for days."

"Yes, my dear, I'll see to it. Meanwhile, Ada, do take your

sherry without further procrastination. Dinner has already been announced."

"If it's been announced, then let's go in," Ada said, rising. "I can do without the sherry."

"There's no need to do without it, Ada dear. We can wait a few minutes more," Lydia said with pompous graciousness.

"Yes, do have your sherry, love," Lady Isabel said suddenly, rousing herself from her contemplation of the darkening landscape. "I haven't finished mine yet, either."

"Very well, Mama," Ada replied, helping herself to the last glass on the tray and reseating herself, "if you wish me to."

She had just taken her first sip when Pinkney, the butler, appeared in the doorway. "Mrs. Jolliffe wishes a word with you, my lord," he said.

"Now?" Lionel's eyebrows lifted in surprise. "Didn't you tell her that we're about to go in to dine?"

"Yes, my lord. But she says it's very important. She seems quite distressed."

"Distressed?" The dowager's head came up abruptly, and she seemed to shudder to attention. "Good heavens! Something must be wrong with Stanley!" she cried, starting from her chair.

"Nonsense, Mama," Ada said, jumping up and gently pressing her mother back in her seat, at the same time trying to ignore a feeling of foreboding which seemed to leap up from the pit of her stomach to her chest. "I saw him just this afternoon. He was fine."

"I suppose, however, that we'd better hear what Mrs. Jolliffe has to say," Lionel said with an impatient sigh. "Send her in, Pinkney. And then go down and tell Cook to delay the first course for ten minutes."

The butler stood aside, and Mrs. Jolliffe hurried in, her step dangerously unsteady. The governess's face was white, and her hands were clasped nervously at her bosom. "Oh, Lady Isabel!" she cried in a high tremolo. "I don't know how to tell you! I'm half out of my mind. He's *disappeared*!"

"Disappeared?" Lionel echoed in annoyance. "*Stanley*?"

"Oh, my God!" The wineglass Lady Isabel had been holding slipped from her hand.

"What is this about?" Lionel demanded of the governess,

ignoring his mother's agitation. "How can the child have dis-appeared?"

Mrs. Jolliffe began to cry. "I shouldn't have let him go. But he'd been cooped up all morning, and I thought—"

Lionel gritted his teeth. "For God's sake, woman, don't babble. You shouldn't have let him go *where*?"

"To see the gypsies."

"*Gypsies*? Oh, no!" the dowager moaned.

"Good God, woman," Lionel shouted at the governess in disgust, "are you saying that you let the child go to a gypsy encampment all by himself?"

"Well, ye see, he promised to go only as far as the hedge on the north field. He was only going to peep at 'em."

"But why didn't you go with him?" Lydia asked, placing her hands on her extended stomach as if to protect the life within from a similar fate.

"He doesn't like me leading him by the hand everywhere he goes, ye see. He says I baby him too much. It seemed a harmless little outing to go down to the north field. I didn't dream—"

Ada, after listening to this exchange with a kind of be-numbed alarm, suddenly leaped to her feet. As far as she was concerned, there had been much too much talking. She couldn't bear to hear any more. *What good is talking?* she asked herself impatiently. Why didn't someone *do* something? "If he hasn't come back yet," she said in her gruff, boyish way, moving toward the door, "then I'll run right down there and fetch him."

"I've already been there," the governess said, her tears flowing unchecked down her plump cheeks. "The gypsies say they never saw him at all."

"Well, he's there somewhere," Ada insisted firmly. "I'll go at once—"

"Stop where you are, Ada," her brother ordered. "Go in with Mama and Lydia and have your dinner. This is man's work. If Stanley's to be found, I'll find him. Leave the matter to me. I'll take care of this."

Chapter Two

Man's work indeed! Ada thought resentfully as she followed her mother and Lydia obediently into the dining room. But she didn't wish to be obedient. She wished she had the courage to disregard her brother's orders and go out to look for Stanley herself. Despite her annoyance with herself and her brother, however, she took her place at the table. It proved to be a very silent meal. No one said a word as the butler, assisted by two footmen, served each of them a bowl of pearled barley soup. No one even lifted a spoon. Ada kept her hands clenched in her lap, feeling helpless and inadequate. She ached to be out there at the gypsy encampment herself, doing her own searching for her brother. She felt imprisoned here at the table. It was *she* who knew Stanley's secret habits and hiding places, not Lionel. Lionel should have permitted her to go. What good did it do for her to sit here listening to her mother make those moaning sounds in her throat? She should be down in the north field, searching under the hedges, where Stanley was probably lying fast asleep. *Blast Lionel!* her mind cursed furiously. *How dare he put me under virtual house arrest!*

At a sign from Lydia, Pinkney and the footmen removed the untouched soup, but before they could serve the next course, Lionel burst in. "They're *gone!*" he announced hollowly. "The deuced gypsies have broken camp and gone off."

Ada winced, Lydia gasped and Lady Isabel shuddered in horror. "My *baby!*" she cried. "They've run off with my baby!"

"Now, Mama, there's no need to become discomposed," Lionel said in annoyance. "We don't know for a *fact* that—"

"But, my love, what else can explain the boy's disappearance?" his wife asked tremulously.

12

"He might be asleep under a hedge," Ada suggested. "Let me go out and look. I know where he likes to hide."

"I've already thought of that," Lionel responded. "I searched the hedges myself. And I have all the stablehands out beating the bushes right now. So there's no need, Ada, for you to—"

"No *need*?" Ada said in an exasperated croak. "Are you saying that you expect us all to sit here and do *nothing*? At the very *least* we should track down that gypsy caravan and give it a thorough search!"

"That's exactly what I intend to do, my girl. They're bringing round my horse at this very moment. Pinkney, please go and fetch my riding boots. I intend to leave at once."

"I want to go with you," Ada insisted.

"No, my dear, your place is here with Mama. You can sit with her and keep her calm. Besides, I'll travel faster on my own. I've learned that the caravan's headed south. I expect to catch up with those miscreants within an hour. They can't move as quickly with their rickety wagons as I can on horseback."

"Gypsies move with remarkable swiftness when they have to," Lady Isabel said fearfully.

"I'll catch them, don't worry," Lionel declared, striding out the door. "They won't get away from Lionel Farrington."

The ladies, left alone again, agreed without words to leave the table. They moved silently back to the library, where they took places near the fire and sank into their own thoughts. Ada, perched on a hassock at her mother's feet, let her head sink down on her mother's knee and tried not to think of what Stanley might be suffering at this moment. In the far corner of the room, still huddled in the corner where they'd left her when they went in to dinner, sat the disconsolate Mrs. Jolliffe. The only sounds in the room were the crackling of the fire and Mrs. Jolliffe's sobs.

Thus they remained for many hours. The clock struck midnight and then one. Ada periodically tried to convince her mother and the pregnant Lydia to seek their beds, but they steadfastly refused. At two, Mrs. Jolliffe stopped her weeping long enough to bring in a pair of lap robes to cover Lydia's legs and to wrap round the shoulders of the now-trembling

Lady Isabel. By three, Lydia had fallen asleep, Lady Isabel was ashen-faced with terror and Ada was ready to scream in impatience.

She got to her feet and went over to the despairing governess. "Do stop crying, Jollie," she whispered, putting a fond arm about the woman's shoulders. "Let's just talk. Perhaps you'll think of something that will help us find Stanley."

"I don't know what to s-say," the governess blubbered. "I've t-told everything I kn-know."

"Yes, but one never knows what may come out in talking. Tell me, what did Stanley say when he left you? Did he say exactly where he was going?"

"Yes, Miss Ada, he did. Just as I told his lordship, he said he was going to the end of the north field and watch the gypsies by peeping through the hedge. He wasn't going into their camp. He promised he wouldn't."

"How did he know the gypsies were there? *I* didn't know it."

"Well, y' see, you could see their flags and wagons from the nursery window. They'd made camp there yesterday, and Stanley went out right away to look them over."

Ada was surprised. "He'd gone there *before*? I didn't know that."

"But he did. He went yesterday, right after they'd made camp. That's why I didn't think anything would happen. Nothing went wrong yesterday. He went out for an hour or so and came back full of tales." And she began to cry again.

"Don't, Jollie. It does no good to cry. Tell me what sort of tales he brought back with him."

"Th-There was a giant there, he said, and g-girls dancing with tambourines." She smiled in tremulous recollection and blew her nose into an already sopping handkerchief. "He was so full of them, so excited. You know how he goes on when he's excited . . ."

"Yes, indeed. You say he said he saw a *giant*?"

"Oh, well, it's only a little tyke's exaggeration. He said the man was as big as a giant, with dark hair and a red and yellow bandana."

"Did he say anything else about him?"

"Well, let me think. Yes, I seem to remember that Stanley

remarked about a chain about his neck with silver coins on it. And golden rings in his ears."

"I see. That is interesting. No wonder he wanted to go back. Tell me, Jollie, did he say anything else?"

But the governess couldn't think of anything, and after another few moments Ada returned to her place at her mother's knee. It was almost four when the door opened and a weary Lionel entered the room. Ada knew at once, from the set of his lips, that the news would not be good. The sound of his footsteps brought Lydia instantly awake. Lady Isabel started from her chair, took a close look at her eldest son's face and sank back with a despairing moan. Mrs. Jolliffe, red-eyed and quite beside herself, lumbered across the room. "Oh, my lord, haven't you found 'im?" she cried in agony.

Lionel turned away from the four pairs of beseeching eyes. He went to the fire and held his hands out toward its warmth. "He wasn't there," he said quietly, unable to face them. "I found the gypsies camped at Barton Mills. We searched the camp from top to bottom."

"We?" Ada asked.

"The parish constable and I. I roused the fellow as soon as I found the caravan, and we searched together. We went over every inch of every cart and wagon. Stanley wasn't there."

Mrs. Jolliffe gave a heartbroken cry and fell to her knees, dropping her head in her hands. Lydia, too, covered her face with trembling fingers. Lady Isabel, white as a sheet, tottered toward her son. "Oh, my God!" she wailed, lifting her arms up in appeal as the robe slipped off her shoulders unheeded. "Lionel, what are we to *do*?"

Lionel turned and took the trembling woman in his arms. "I don't know," he said brokenly, tears appearing in his eyes. "I don't know, Mama. I'm at a loss. There doesn't seem to be anything else we *can* do. We'll give the whole area a thorough search in the daylight, of course, but . . ."

Lady Isabel looked up into his face. "But . . . ?"

He lowered his eyes and drew her head down on his shoulder. "But I'm very much afraid, Mama, that . . . that you'll have to accustom yourself to the thought that, unless a miracle happens, the boy is . . . well, he's gone for good."

Ada rose slowly from the hassock and stared at her brother

for a frozen moment. *Gone for good!* The words reverberated in her brain with the tremor of plucked harpstrings. *You'll have to accustom yourself...that the boy is...gone for good...*

A feeling, not of sorrow or despair but of violent fury, exploded in her breast. *No,* something cried within her, *I'll never accustom myself to that! Never!* And without quite knowing what she was doing, she turned on her heel and ran from the room. She heard her brother call her name, but she paid no heed. She raced up the stairs and down the hall to her bedroom, shut the door behind her and leaned against it, panting. "I'll never accustom myself to it," she said aloud. Stanley was alive somewhere, she was certain of that. Even gypsies didn't kill innocent children. While she had a breath in her body, she would search for him. And if he were alive, she would find him. She would find him if it were the last thing she ever did.

Chapter Three

Lionel hammered at her door. "Ada! Ada, for heaven's sake, answer me! Open this door!"

"Go away, Lionel," Ada muttered from within.

"Isn't Mama disturbed enough by these events without your causing her further anxiety by flying out of the room in that histrionic fashion?"

"I didn't mean to be histrionic. Tell Mama I'm sorry."

"You'll have to tell her yourself in the morning. Lydia has put her to bed."

"Very well, then, I will. Tomorrow. But for now, Lionel, if there's nothing else of importance that you want to say to me, will you please go away?"

There was a moment of silence. "There is something else, Ada," he pleaded more quietly. "Please open the door."

She opened it a crack. "What is it?" she asked, showing only one eye in the space.

"I know you're upset," he said. "We all are. But you mustn't behave as if this were my fault."

"I never said it was your fault."

"No, but you think it."

"I *don't* think it."

Lionel threw up his hands. "All right, you don't. But you think I haven't done enough, isn't that so?"

The one eye glared at him. "Do *you* think you've done enough?"

"I don't know what else to do, Ada," the troubled brother admitted. "Tell me what you think I ought to do!"

"I don't know, exactly. But I know that, in your place, I wouldn't rest until I'd covered every inch of ground for miles around."

"I *will* cover every inch, I promise. As soon as it's light, I'll gather all the men on the estate and we'll scour the entire area."

"Good, then. I shall pray that you'll find him."

Lionel nodded and made as if to turn away. But before she closed the door he turned back. "Ada?"

"Yes?"

"I love him, too, you know."

Ada sighed. "I know. But if you truly love him, don't give up hope so easily. As long as you keep hoping, you'll keep searching. Good night, Lionel."

"Goodnight, Ada," he said morosely.

Ada watched him walk away. His step was slow, and his shoulders sagged. It was clear from his very posture that her brother had given up hope already.

As she closed the door, the thought came to her that she was the only one in the household with any hope. She, herself. Therefore, if Stanley was to be found, *she* would have to be the one to find him. She would have to steal out of the house this very night and look for him herself.

She had no doubt that Lionel would institute a thorough search of the grounds as soon as the sun came up, in less than two hours. But Ada no longer believed that they'd find Stanley on the grounds. She'd thought, at first, that her little brother must have fallen asleep under the hedge, but she could no longer believe it. If he had, the cold night air would have awakened him by this time and he would have made his own way home. Since he'd not done so, Ada couldn't believe he was anywhere on the grounds. The only logical possibility was that the gypsies had taken him.

But what had they done with him? Why hadn't Lionel and the constable found him hidden in the gypsy caravan? She didn't know, but she *did* know that her search for her brother had to start with the gypsies. She had to go at once to Barton Mills, before they broke camp again and disappeared forever.

And she had to take action at once. There was no other choice. She had to take what money she had in her possession, steal out of the house and go to find the gypsies. She had four or five guineas in her reticule. That would certainly be enough for a couple of days' travel.

But now that her course was clear, the prospect seemed suddenly frightening. She'd never travelled more than ten miles from home, and even that ten miles had been in the company of her family. Could she find the gypsy caravan by herself? And if she managed that, would she be able to confront a giant of a gypsy with a red and yellow bandana and rings in his ears? The prospect was terrifying.

Coward! she accused herself aloud. *If you're going to find Stanley, you can't permit yourself to be craven!* For Stanley's sake she would have to face her task with courage and determination. Taking a deep breath and squaring her shoulders, she marched to her wardrobe. What should she wear for her journey, she wondered? Perhaps she should ring for her abigail, Tilly, to assist her. Tilly was a sensible girl who, though only seventeen, had seen more of the world than Ada herself. Her advice would be useful at a time like this. But it was so late; it would be cruel to waken her now. This entire enterprise was something Ada would have to do all by herself.

She opened the wardrobe and took from it the warmest, plainest cloak she owned. With this cloak and her stoutest riding boots, she would be protected against any vagaries of weather. But when she sat down to pull on the boots, it occurred to her that, although a warm cloak and a sturdy pair of boots might provide sufficient protection from the weather, they would certainly not offer sufficient protection from any other dangers an unescorted young female might encounter on her way. The only protection a young female could rely on when travelling on deserted roads or crowded city streets was a male escort, and she couldn't pull one of *those* from her wardrobe.

While struggling to pull on the high-topped boots, she heard a scratch at her door. "Miss Ada?" came a voice from the hallway. "Might ye be needin' some 'elp t' undress?"

"Is that you, Tilly?" Ada asked in astonishment.

The door opened and a youthful housemaid (whose neatly starched white mobcap contrasted amusingly with the dishevelled hair, twinkling eyes and pointed, impish chin beneath) poked her head in the door. "Yes, Miss, it's me. I tho't ye might be needin' me."

"As a matter of fact, I *do* need you," Ada murmured,

glancing ruefully at her resistant boot. "But what on earth are you doing up at this hour? It must be half after four!"

The girl shrugged and stepped into the room, closing the door quietly behind her. "I couldn' sleep. None of us below stairs cin. We're all too worried 'bout poor little Stanl—" It was then she noticed that her mistress was struggling with a pair of boots. "Good 'eavens, Miss Ada, you ain't tryin' to put those *on*, are ye?"

"Yes, I am. But I'm having a terrible time of it. I don't know why; I usually manage them perfectly well by myself. Help me with them, will you please, Tilly?"

The maid knelt down before her, and they both tugged at the boot. "You surely ain't thinkin' of goin' ridin' *now*, are ye, Miss Ada?"

"No, of course not. All I can think of now is Stanley." The boot slipped into place in an abrupt surrender, and she picked up the second. "I'm going to find him."

The maid sat back on her heels and gaped. "Now? By *yersel'*?"

Ada frowned at the maid worriedly. "Yes, but you mustn't breathe a word of this, Tilly. Don't tell anyone you even saw me tonight. Do you promise?"

"'Course I promise! I'm real glad yer goin' t' seek 'im. If anyone cin find 'im, it's you. I'm always sayin' t' Cook that Miss Ada's the real clever one o' the family."

"Thank you, Tilly," she muttered, staring absently at the still-resistant second boot, "but I don't know if I'm clever enough for this. Or brave enough, either."

"Y're brave enough, Miss, I cin assure you of that. I seen ye take jumps with yer 'orse that would make anyone else empty 'is breadbasket."

Ada eyed the maid with amusement. "Empty his breadbasket? I don't think I've ever heard that expression before."

"Ain't ye? It means—"

"I can guess what it means, you goose. But as for being brave on a horse, I don't think it signifies. I've been jumping horses all my life, while this will be the first time I've ever ventured off the grounds alone."

"Whyn't ye take me with ye, Miss Ada? A young lady like yersel' shouldna be traipsin' about without a chaperone."

"Yes, I know." Ada bit her lip as she considered the offer, but after a moment she shook her head. "No, taking you is not the answer. We'd be *two* helpless females instead of one."

Tilly nodded in reluctant agreement. "That's true. What ye need, Miss Ada, is a *man*."

The force with which she emphasized the last word tugged the second boot into place. Ada got up and began to pace. "Where on earth am I to find a male escort?" she muttered, more to herself than to the abigail. "My brother's the only man in the household except for the servants, but he's out of the question. He's already told me that searching for Stanley is a man's job. Perhaps I should ask a footman . . . or one of the stableboys—"

"Oh, no, Miss; I wouldn' do that!" Tilly exclaimed. "It wouldn' be proper at *all*."

"No, I suppose it wouldn't. Lydia would say it was shocking. And Lionel would probably sack the poor fellow as soon as he learned of it. Besides, a footman or a stableboy wouldn't be likely to have any money, so my expenses would be doubled. I don't have enough of the ready for that."

"I might be able to scrape up a few shillings, Miss Ada," the maid offered earnestly.

"No, thank you, Tilly. That was kind of you, but I shall manage."

"But ye know, Miss Ada, the outside world's full of dangers ye'd never dream of. Per'aps ye should change yer mind. I don' think you should run off without an escort."

Ada eyed her worriedly. "But there *isn't* anyone to escort me. And I must go to search for Stanley, that much is clear. So there's no choice. I'll *have* to go alone."

She squared her shoulders decisively. She could face whatever dangers lay in her path, she assured herself. She only hoped that she would not encounter some well-meaning stranger who would notice an unescorted female and take it upon himself to deliver her back to her family. "Dash it all," she said aloud, "it's too bad I'm not a boy! No one takes notice of a boy travelling alone."

"That's true, they don't," Tilly agreed.

Ada stopped her pacing abruptly, and her eyes lit up like

stars. "Wait a moment!" she croaked excitedly. "Why *can't* I be a boy?"

Tilly blinked. "What'd ye say, Miss?"

"If I dressed myself in breeches and hid my hair in a cap, I could very possibly pass for a boy. Then I could make my way south without attracting anyone's notice. I certainly have the *voice* for it. All I'd have to do is find some suitable clothing. Then, if I walk about with a peacocky stride and say things like 'Rubbish!' and 'Stubble it, old fellow!' and 'Hang it all!' I'm sure to seem like a boy to any passing stranger."

"Oh, Miss, I dunno," Tilly demurred, alarmed. "It'd be mightly chancey. What if someone guessed?"

But Ada was not listening. She was noticing that the dawn was already beginning to light the sky. In a few minutes, Lionel would be readying himself to begin the search of the grounds. Once he was up and about, she would not be able to make her escape. There was no time now to disguise herself. If she was to leave this house, it had to be now.

"Tilly, if I give you a few hours' time," she said speculatively, her mind racing, "can you manage to collect some boy's clothing without anyone seeing?"

"Boy's clothing, Miss Ada? What—?"

"A pair of breeches, a shirt and a coat, that's all. These boots are just like a boy's, and the cloak I'm taking is short enough to be a man's, so they're no problem."

"Yes, Miss, I unnerstan' what ye need. But where—?"

"One of the stableboy's, perhaps. Jemmy, for instance. He's about the right size. I'll give you some money to pay him for the items, but you mustn't tell him the reason why you want to buy them. Oh, dear . . . we shall have to give him *some* reason for such a strange request. Can you think of something?"

"I cin deal wi' Jemmy right enough," Tilly said, a grin appearing in the corner of her mouth despite her misgivings about the wisdom of the disguise. "Sweet on me, 'e is."

"Is he, indeed?" Ada laughed, throwing on her cloak. "So that's what goes on belowstairs, eh?"

"On'y a bit o' flirtin'," Tilly said with a blush. "But I don't know 'ow I cin explain to 'im why—wait! I *'ave* it! I'll tell 'im Cook needs t' dress a scarecrow fer the kitchen garden."

"Tilly, that's perfect!" Ada exclaimed, hugging the maid enthusiastically. "It's *you* who's the clever one. Here, take this guinea. Do you think it will be enough to pay Jemmy with?"

"Oh, much too much, Miss Ada. You keep it. You may 'ave need of it. I'll pay Jemmy, don' ye fret. Leave it to me."

"Very well, Tilly. Thank you. Now, listen to the rest of the plan very carefully. Later, when your morning chores are over, I want you to take the clothes, wrap them up in brown paper and slip out of the house. Be sure no one sees you, mind! Then you're to walk to town and bring the clothes to the inn. You know the one I mean—"

Tilly nodded. "The Green Gander's what y're speakin' of."

"That's right. The Green Gander. I'll be there waiting. I'll use the name . . . er . . . Smith. Ask for Miss Smith."

Tilly leered at her. "Smith? That's real uncommon, now, ain't it?"

Ada glared back. "Smythe, then. Miss Smythe. Is that uncommon enough for you?"

Tilly grinned. "It's better n' Smith. But, Miss Ada, why do ye want t' bother stayin' at the inn? Why can't you just stay here until mornin'? I cin get the clothes from Jemmy first thing, and bring them right up to ye an' help ye dress."

"No, if I wait till daylight, I'll never be able to make my escape. I've got to go at once, before Lionel starts prowling about." She put her hands on the maid's shoulders and propelled her toward the door. "Oh, one thing more, Tilly. Be sure to ask Jemmy for a cap. And bring some hairpins with you as well. Then when you get to the inn, you can help me pin up my hair and get me into my disguise. Well, Tilly, do you think you can manage all that?"

"Yes, Miss, I think so." At the door, the abigail turned and studied her mistress with appraising eyes. "Ye'll make a proper lad, so nice and slim ye are. A fine, proper lad. There's on'y one thing . . ." Here she paused, and her brow knit worriedly. "One thing . . ."

"Go on, Tilly. What is it?"

"Ye said ye want me t' pin up yer hair?"

"Yes." Ada cocked her head at her maid thoughtfully. "Is there something wrong with that?"

"I think so, Miss. Y'see, when a lad meets a lady—which 'e's bound t' do several times a day, passin' one on the road, say, or when 'e goes to an inn fer a bite o' supper—'e's gotta lift 'is cap politely, don't 'e?"

"Yes, I suppose he does. You mean that when I lift my cap—?"

"Yer 'air. Yer *beautiful* 'air. It'll give you away fer certain."

"Oh, dear!" Ada ran to her dressing table and stared at herself in the mirror. "Are you saying I'll have to *cut* it?"

Tilly gasped in horror. "Oh, *no*, Miss Ada! Ye can't do *that*! Not yer lovely 'air!"

Ada's hands flew to her tresses of their own accord, as if to protect them. "I suppose I must . . . unless we can think of some other way . . ."

Tilly scratched her head. "Per'aps I cin find some sort of wig . . ."

"Where on earth could you find a proper wig? We'd have to send to a London wigmaker for that, and there's no time." She forced her hands away from her hair and shrugged. "We'll have to cut it, that's all."

"No, it ain't right!" Tilly went up to the mirror and smoothed back Ada's hair with dramatic intensity. "Per'aps ye'd best give up the 'ole idea. Lord Farrington'll find Stanley soon 'r late."

" 'Soon or late' is not soon enough for me," Ada muttered. "I *won't* give up the whole idea! If getting Stanley back means the hair will have to go, then it will have to go."

The words were spoken bravely, but Ada felt very much like crying. Her lovely hair! It would never look this way again. She lifted up a lock and let the long, silky strand sift through her fingers. Then, with a sigh, she turned away from the mirror with a decisive swing of her head. The motion made the hair lift like an ocean wave. It caught the light, glinted for a moment and then settled down again on her back. The maid, appreciating the beauty of the tresses she'd so often brushed and combed, groaned. "Oh, Miss *Ada*," she murmured sadly.

Ada fixed a stern eye on her. "Hair is only hair, Tilly. Let's not make a tragedy of it. Losing Stanley is the tragedy."

Once again she propelled the maid to the door. Then, while Tilly stood watch in the hallway, Ada took her few guineas from her reticule, tied them into a handkerchief and thrust them into the bosom of her gown. That done, she wrapped her cloak closely about her and prepared to follow the abigail. But before leaving, she looked back at her lovely, comfortable room—the warm nest she'd never left before. She was departing, with very little preparation, for the first real adventure of her life, and she was going to do it disguised as a boy. Was it a terribly foolhardy decision? She couldn't even imagine herself as a boy. Could she pull it off? Would she fail? Was she going to sacrifice her hair for nothing? But she was making too much of the hair. She forcefully banished all thought of it from her mind. She had more important things to worry her.

But as she silently closed the door behind her, she realized that the problems she faced did not dismay her. She felt exhilarated. For the first time in her life she was going to be free of all constraints. She was setting out on a most important mission that she'd sworn she would not fail to execute. *Stanley, love,* she whispered to herself, *don't despair. I'll find you somehow.* She lifted her head and, swinging her arms energetically at her side, she strode down the hall in what she hoped was a boyish stride. For better or worse, she was on her way.

She and Tilly walked together down the hallway to the top of the stairway, where they had to part. Without a word, they hugged each other fondly. Then Ada started down the stairs, with Tilly tearfully watching from the top. "Oh, Miss Ada," the maid couldn't help whispering, "are ye *sure*—?"

Ada turned and fixed a firm eye on her. "Yes, I'm sure. Stubble it, my girl! Let's have no more shilly-shallying." She descended two more stairs and turned back again. "And remember, Tilly," she added in a hissing whisper, "when you come to the inn with the clothes tomorrow, *bring a pair of scissors!*"

Chapter Four

Derek Rutledge, Viscount Esterbrook, descended the rickety stairs of the Green Gander Inn, glancing round the hallway and into the taproom in disgust. Never had he spent a night in a more ramshackle, ill-kempt hostelry. It had been dark when he'd arrived and he'd been too weary to take note of his surroundings, but he'd known, as soon as his head touched the pillow, that he'd made a mistake. Not only was the bed lumpy, but it smelled of damp neglect. Moreover, the fireplace smoked so badly that he'd had to open a window despite the cold. He could hardly wait for morning so that he could depart the premises, but this morning had dawned so rainy that the prospect of departure was as unappealing as the prospect of remaining. His feelings were further complicated by the fact that he'd awakened feeling absolutely ravenous. If he was to assuage the hunger pangs in his belly, he'd have to take his breakfast in these grimy, unappetizing surroundings. But what made the whole situation utterly ludicrous was that it was his mother—his own supposedly fond, devoted, loving and *fastidious* mother!—who was the cause of his being here.

He reached the bottom of the stairs, pulled a handkerchief from the breastpocket of his coat and wiped the banister's dust from his hand. He was standing in a tiny hallway, on an uneven, unswept stone floor. The outer door was in front of him and to his left was an open doorway which led to the taproom. That room was large and square, with a scarred wooden floor on which two long tables and several small ones were arranged. It was probably, on good days, a cheerful-enough place, for the four wide windows undoubtedly provided a good deal of light, but today the light was depressingly dim.

A leaden sky was preventing the slightest ray of sunshine from getting through. The room was made even darker by the heavy raindrops that ran down the windows in streams.

His lordship went into the taproom, approached the nearest window and gazed out on the gloomy day. It was most likely the weather that was keeping the many tables of the taproom unoccupied. He was glad of that, at least. He would not have enjoyed being ogled by the locals, and ogled he would have been if there had been any customers hanging about. His London coat alone would have been cause for interested observation.

Derek Rutledge, the well-known Viscount Esterbrook, was indeed out of place in this tiny country inn. A prime specimen of the *haute ton* (and positively gleaming with what the matrons like to call "town bronze"), Derek Rutledge was from top to toe a Londoner: His dark hair was expertly cut to fall over his forehead in careless curls; his expressive mouth, strong chin and knowing eyes revealed both sophistication and breeding; his shoulders—broad and muscular and in perfect proportion to his six-feet-one-inch of height—were admirably emphasized by the superb cut of his grey tweed coat; his neckcloth could only have been tied by a valet of the first rank; his breeches were of the finest chamois cloth; and his magnificently polished topboots could only have been made by Hoby, bootmaker to kings. Anyone seeing him here would know at once that he could have found himself in such a place as the Green Gander only by the most ridiculous mischance.

Lord Esterbrook turned away from the window abruptly. He was about to call out for some service when the innkeeper appeared, having bustled out from a room at the rear. "Ah, your lordship," he said obsequiously, bowing while wiping his hands on an apron that seemed not to have been laundered in weeks. "Good mornin' t' ye. I trust ye slept well."

"I've slept better," Lord Esterbrook responded bluntly. "I hope you can provide me with a better breakfast than you did a bed. I'll have a couple of eggs, some of your country ham, muffins if they're freshly baked and a pot of tea. And serve it in your private parlour, if you please."

"Well, y'see, yer lordship, I cin serve ye just the breakfast ye desire—me missus just baked a batch o' muffins as light an' airy as any ye ever tasted—but as to a private parlour..."

His lordship looked down at the innkeeper from his superior height with an I-might-have-expected-it expression and shook his head in despair. "You *have* no private parlour, is that it?"

"No, yer lordship, I don't. The Green Gander's on'y a small, simple place, y' see. Two bedrooms upstairs an' this room an' the kitchens down 'ere. But I cin fix you up real comf'table in the corner there, where I promise ye won't be disturbed by nobody. An' ye'll 'ave a better breakfast than ye'd ever get in London."

The prospect of a decent meal (despite the unlikelihood of its turning out to be half as good as the innkeeper promised) overrode his lordship's dislike of the public room. "Very well," he agreed, "show me to the table. And, then, if you will, tell my man to get the horses ready. I want to be on my way as soon as the rain lets up."

He followed the innkeeper across the room and seated himself at the corner table. In due course, the innkeeper's wife made an appearance. While she spread the table with a cloth that, to his relief, was so freshly laundered that it still held the warmth of her iron, she simpered, blushed, giggled and mumbled something to the effect that she was honored to have "so important an' elegant an' 'ansome a gennelman" in her dinning room. Then, placing a filled teapot and cup at his elbow and promising to return momentarily with "the bestest breakfast ye ever ate," she left him to his thoughts.

His thoughts were not cheerful. He had passed a dreadful weekend in Lincolnshire, and he'd made his escape only to find himself putting up at *this* unprepossessing place. To make matters worse, he had either to remain imprisoned here until the rain let up or make his way through the downpour to London in nothing more comfortable than the half-open curricle he'd brought with him. It was all his mother's fault. *How did I ever permit her to get me into this deuced fix?* he asked himself, propping his elbows on the table and dropping his chin on his hands.

It had all started six months ago, when he'd just turned thirty-two. He remembered the day vividly. His mother had

dropped by his town house without warning and had burst in
on him just as he was finishing a festive bachelor luncheon
with three of his cronies. Taking no notice of his hints that her
timing was inappropriate, she'd handed her cloak to his man,
McTeague, placed her flounced umbrella right on his table and
sat herself down in their very midst.

Lady Rutledge was a tall, well-built woman of sixty-four,
given to wearing black lace gloves and huge feathered hats,
neither of which eccentricities detracted one whit from the
dignity of her carriage and the charm of her manner. Derek
was both excessively proud and excessively fond of her. His
affection for her, however, did not prevent him from feeling
annoyed at her high-handed interruption of his bachelor gathering.

She, however, pretended not to notice his irritation. Without using the least subtlety, she let his friends know that she
wanted to speak to her son on a private matter, giving them no
choice but to take themselves off. Then she peremptorily
waved McTeague out of the room and leaned back in her chair
with the aplomb of a queen mother. "Happy birthday, my
love," she said coolly. "You're thirty-two today, are you not?"

"You, Mama, should know that better than I," he rejoined,
smiling at her pleasantly, having decided to make the best of
the situation.

"I do know. Thirty-two. That, my dear, is not young. Did
you know, Derek, that I've been hoping since you were
twenty-two that you'd take care of a certain matter very dear to
my heart? Ten long years!"

Derek knew perfectly well what she was hinting at, for
he'd heard about that "certain matter" more often than he
cared to remember. But he would not make this exchange easy
for her. "What matter, Mama?" he asked innocently.

"You know very well what matter! I've waited long enough
for you to take care of it yourself, you scapegrace, but here
you are at the advanced age of thirty-two, and you've made no
move. It appears that you've no intention of doing so."

"Doing *what*, Mama?" he stalled, filling his pipe and taking a deep puff in preparation for the worst.

"Getting yourself a wife, of course!"

"Oh, *that*!" he said in genuine disgust. "Is *that* what you spoiled my luncheon to tell me?"

"Yes, *that* is what I spoiled your luncheon to tell you! Derek Rutledge, you'll be the death of me! How long do you intend to wait before you get yourself leg-shackled? Do you want to send me to my grave without giving me even a *glimpse* of grandchildren?"

"It will be a long time before you go to your grave, Mama. I see no urgency—"

"Oh, you don't, don't you? Well, *I* do! The longer you postpone action—while you dawdle your time away with the lightskirts and doxies you seem to fancy—the harder it will be to find someone suitable."

He eyed his mother with indulgent amusement. "And what, ma'am, do you know about my fancy for doxies and lightskirts?" he mocked. "It seems a singularly inappropriate subject of discussion between a mother and her son."

"No subject is inappropriate between a mother and her son," she retorted. "I know a great deal about your doxies. I've heard of your Polly Stanhope, for one. I live in the world, do I not? And I have a great many sources of information."

He snorted loudly. "What a charming circumlocution for 'gossips.' 'Sources of information,' indeed!"

"You're not going to sit there and pretend that my information is untrue, are you?"

"I'm not going to pretend anything. Nor am I going to admit anything." He threw her a broad grin. "I'm quite willing to discuss almost any conceivable subject with you, my love, but I draw the line at discussing my relationships with doxies with my mother."

"I don't want to discuss doxies, anyway," she declared with a toss of her head, causing the feathers on her hat to tremble violently. "I want to talk about *wives*. *Prospective* wives. I've made a list of ten eligible, desirable, available females, all of them suitable."

"Good God! *Ten*?"

"Ten. All pretty, all well-reared, all charming."

He sneered. "All, eh? Very likely *that* is!"

"You'll see for yourself soon enough, for I intend to invite each one to tea, one every week until we discover one who pleases you. Surely out of ten presentable females there will be *one* whom you'll consider."

"Are you saying I must meet all *ten*?" he asked, wincing.

Not troubling to answer, she reached for her umbrella. "Thursdays, I think, will be most convenient for me." She fixed her eye on his threateningly. "It goes without saying that you will be present at these teas."

He knew that he was trapped, but he struggled for his freedom anyway. "I'm afraid, Mama, that Thursdays are not convenient for *me*," he countered, knowing full well what a weak strategy it was.

She rose slowly from her chair and brandished her umbrella at him. "I am not *requesting* your presence, my lord. I am *ordering* it!"

He looked up at her with his most forbidding scowl. "Ordering, ma'am?"

She merely stared him down. "I know there are not many in England who can give you orders, my boy," she said, not in the least perturbed by his glare, "but there are two people whose orders you *must* obey if you are not to be considered a complete cad—your Prince's and your mother's." She strolled to the door without acknowledging his choked groan. "I shall expect you on Thursday at four. And," she added before departing, "*be prompt!*"

And that was how, on the third Thursday of this hideous exercise, he'd met Cynthia Chadwick.

The first two Thursday teas had been disastrous. Miss Deering, the first candidate, had a bulbous nose and thick ankles. She made up for these defects by being intellectual, but since the books she chose to discuss were strange to him, Derek had little to say to her. The second of his mother's choices, a Lady Irene Moncrief, had evidently once been told that she was a "charming child," so she remained childish in the extreme. She giggled and tossed her curls and made little baby sounds until Derek wanted to run from the room. When the afternoon was over and Lady Irene had taken her leave, Derek turned to his mother and told her flatly that he intended to drink no more Thursday tea. "Why is it," he mused as he put on his hat and sauntered out of her drawing room, "that

you mothers show so little talent in choosing girls for your
sons?"

"Why is it," his mother retorted, following him to the door,
"that you sons can't see the quality in a female if she doesn't
look like a doxy? And as for drinking no more tea, I don't
care what you drink, Derek Rutledge. I'll give you port, if
you like. But *you will be here next Thursday at four on the
dot!*"

He tried to excuse himself from that third meeting by sending McTeague to his mother's place with a message that he
had a dreadful toothache, but McTeague returned with a note
which read, *Your toothache is quite welcome to accompany
you to my tea. But toothache or no, you are expected here at
four. Should you fail me, I shall see to it that a headache of
gigantic proportions be added to your list of ills. Your loving
mother, Felicia Rutledge.*

The candidate at the third tea party caused him to gape in
surprise. Cynthia was tall, slim and graceful as a willow. She
had shiny auburn hair that she wore drawn back in simple
elegance from an oval face and knotted in a bun at the nape of
her neck. Her eyes, a soft brown, had a tantalizing almond
shape, her nose was Grecian perfection and her mouth lu-
sciously pink and shapely. Derek could scarcely believe his
luck! If it occurred to him to wonder if his mother had shown
him two ugly ducklings first just to emphasize the comparison
between them and this . . . this *swan*, why, he banished the
idea from his mind.

Cynthia moved with regal dignity, spoke softly and not too
often and smiled up at him with sufficient frequency for him
to decide that she was not lacking in any quality he admired,
even humor. After only half a dozen meetings, he admitted to
his mother that he was seriously considering making her an
offer. He only waited for a meeting with Lord Chadwick, her
father.

That meeting was quickly arranged. An invitation, en-
graved in gold leaf, promptly arrived, requesting his presence
at their country estate in Lincolnshire for a fortnight of festivities. It was to Chadwick Manor that he'd gone a mere four
days ago.

From the moment he'd climbed from his curricle at their

door, the stay had been a shocking disappointment. He began
to suspect the worst as soon as the butler came to assist him
from his carriage. The butler was accompanied by two footmen, all three clad in livery of the most ornate style. Their
shoulders were so covered in gold braid and their demeanor
was so formal that Derek jokingly asked his host if he was
expecting the Regent for dinner. Lord Chadwick did not smile
at the sally. In fact, during the entire two days of his stay,
nobody smiled at any attempts Derek made to lighten the
deadly serious atmosphere of Chadwick Manor.

The problem was that the Chadwicks were rigidly formal.
Everything was done according to the strictest rules of propriety. Every meal, even breakfast, was presented like a formal
banquet, with the table loaded with gold plate, magnificent
china, crystal goblets and every sort of ostentation. Derek had
never seen so many silver serving pieces used to serve so few
people. ·

Dress had to be changed six times a day. Conversation was
carried on in such carefully phrased sentences that one would
have thought it was all being recorded for posterity. Both Lord
and Lady Chadwick were equally stiff and precise in their
manner, and in their company their daughter seemed to behave
in the very same way. That was how Derek came to realize
that he didn't want Cynthia for his bride. She no longer
seemed beautiful in his eyes. In only two days he found himself wondering what he'd ever seen in her. The dignified demeanor he'd first admired in her now seemed nothing but
stiffness; her restrained manner of speaking now seemed no
more than exaggerated propriety; and her smiles he now interpreted as utterly meaningless—nothing more than polite, superficial, automatic responses to everything that was said to
her.

After two days of this wearying, ostentatious, humorless
formality, Derek could no longer bear the company of *any* of
the Chadwicks. He and his resourceful valet, McTeague, arranged for an urgently worded message, ostensibly from
town, to be delivered to him. The message bore the information that his mother had been taken ill and wanted him home.
That very afternoon, with the message as his excuse, Derek
hurriedly took his leave of them. He and McTeague, driving

the curricle at top speed, put as many miles between them and Chadwick Manor as they could before darkness fell. By nightfall they'd reached Suffolk, and, coming upon the Green Gander, Derek decided to put up there for the night.

So anyone can see that this entire fiasco is Mama's fault, he told himself bitterly as he turned his eyes away from their unseeing examination of the sodden landscape outside the taproom window. To his surprise, he discovered that the innkeeper's wife had already placed his breakfast on the table before him. He picked up a fork and began to eat, immediately delighted to discover that the innkeeper had not exaggerated after all. The eggs were fresh and done just as he liked them, the ham was sweetly flavored with honey and the muffins were light and piping hot.

As his hunger pangs diminished, his mood improved, but not enough to soften his determination to give his mother a proper set-down as soon as he returned to town. Never again, he would tell her, would he submit to her "teas." Never again would he permit her to make a match for him. She had no talent for matchmaking, and he intended to tell her so in no uncertain terms. And furthermore, he would say, he intended to choose his own mate or die a bachelor!

At that moment he was distracted from his thoughts by a commotion at the door. A girl, sturdily booted and wrapped in a short cloak, had come stamping into the inn. She paused just where he could see her through the taproom door and was now brushing the raindrops from her shoulders. The innkeeper approached her, and Derek watched as they exchanged a few words. The exchange soon became a whispered but sharp argument. Derek couldn't hear them very well from where he sat in the far corner, but he gathered that the girl wanted a room for a couple of hours only and the innkeeper wanted her to pay for a full day's lodging. The girl was adamant, however, and the innkeeper—evidently realizing that he was unlikely to get many other offers on such a day—finally surrendered. Biting and then pocketing the coin she gave him, the innkeeper asked her to wait until he readied the room, and he lumbered off up the stairs.

The girl took off her cloak and shook it out, revealing herself to Derek's appreciative eye in her full young womanhood. *Now why,* he asked himself, *can Mama never find a creature like that one to introduce to me?* This girl was, of course, much too young for him (for the chit was obviously just out of the schoolroom), but an older version would have suited him very well. She was a delight to look upon, from the splendor of her long, carelessly dressed reddish hair to the unaffectedness of the boyish riding boots that could be seen beneath the hem of her simple muslin dress. Here was a girl who didn't put on airs. There was no rigid formality about *her,* he thought. She seemed to exude a charming nonchalance, an air of excitement, a *joie de vivre.* He watched with real pleasure as she followed the innkeeper up the stairs, admiring her tiny waist and the swing of her shapely hips, the outline of which could just be seen beneath her rather shapeless dress. As she disappeared from his view, he couldn't help sighing. *Oh, Mama,* he thought ruefully, *if only you could look at females through my eyes!*

He turned back to his breakfast, speculating idly about the girl who'd so pleased his eye. Was she a little country miss, the daughter of a farmer or the local blacksmith? He rather doubted it, for most of the country misses were wont to be diffident and shy, while this girl carried herself with the confidence of a duchess. Her gown was simple enough to be a country girl's, but the cloak she'd worn seemed to be of excellent quality and cut. *Perhaps,* he thought, taking a bite of muffin, *she's the daughter of the local squire.* He wondered briefly why any daughter of the local gentry would want a room at a shabby inn for a few hours, but the hearty breakfast soon recaptured his attention, and the girl was forgotten. To a man who finds the world full of lovely females to enjoy, no one particular female is terribly important. For him, out of sight was out of mind. Thus it was only to be expected that the rakish man-of-the-world, Derek Rutledge, Viscount Esterbrook, would permit the mysterious, intriguing young lady— who only a moment ago had captured his eye and his imagination—to pass completely out of his thoughts.

Chapter Five

More than an hour went by without any letup in the rain. His lordship, bored to teeth-gritting impatience, had twice ventured outside to see if it were possible to continue his journey, but each time he'd concluded that the downpour was too heavy to permit him to travel in his half-open curricle. He'd even, in his desperation to quit the place, considered leaving the curricle behind and hiring a coach, but the innkeeper informed him that no one within miles had a coach to rent. He was now seated at the window, his feet propped up on a nearby chair, trying to find something of interest to read in a week-old newspaper he'd found lying under the long table in the center of the room. He was trying to absorb himself in an exceedingly dull account of the purchase of Lord Elgin's Greek marbles by the British Museum when a sudden draught of damp air brought his attention to the taproom door and, after a moment, he saw another girl appear in the hallway near the stairs. She paused right in his line of vision and took off a soaking shawl from her head. It as immediately apparent to him that she was a maidservant; she wore the mobcap and black bombazine that were such common vestments of housemaids as to be universally recognizable. When the innkeeper came out to greet her, she gave him a bobbing curtsey and asked for a Miss Smythe. The innkeeper pointed upstairs and the girl, clutching a wet parcel in her arms, ran quickly up and out of view.

This minor incident was enough to bring the first girl back to Derek Rutledge's mind. *So,* he mused, throwing the newspaper aside, *the chit's name is Smythe*. The other lass was evidently her maid. He wondered what it was that the maid had carried in the mysterious bundle. Having nothing else of interest to occupy his mind, he let himself speculate idly on possible reasons why a young lady of quality and her maidservant would arrive separately at—and remain only briefly in —this country hostelry. He decided that Miss Smythe (an obviously fabricated name) had come here to meet and run off with a swain of whom her family disapproved. He had no doubt that, at any moment, a young, bandy-legged jackanapes would appear at the door, spirit the girl out to a waiting hired rig and make off for Gretna.

But another hour went by, and no young swain presented himself. By that time his impatient lordship, Viscount Esterbrook, had lost all interest in the eloping female, her maidservant, the innkeeper, his wife and all else connected with the Green Gander. He wanted only to see the rain stop so that he might proceed on his way to London. He shouted for the innkeeper and asked again if there was any place in the vicinity where he might procure a carriage. The innkeeper repeated that there were no rental hacks to be had anywhere nearby, but this time added an additional bit of information. "If yer lordship would consider ridin' the stage," he suggested, "there's one due t' make a stop in the courtyard in 'alf an 'our."

While Lord Esterbrook weighed in his mind the advantages of quitting this place over the disadvantages of riding to London on the public stage, the little maidservant came back down the stairs and, pausing near the taproom door to throw her shawl over her head, slipped out of the inn without a backward look. His lordship watched from the window as the girl, still keeping her parcel clutched in her arms, ran through the rain across the courtyard and disappeared down the road. He wondered briefly why the eloping girl upstairs would need the services of her housemaid and what on earth the maid could have been carrying in her parcel, but he soon dismissed the whole question from his mind and returned his attention to the question of whether or not to take the stage.

At last, his mind made up to take the stage, he requested the innkeeper to send for his man. While he waited for McTeague to present himself, he gazed idly out the window again. To his surprise, he saw that two fellows, both carrying baggage, were standing at the far side of the courtyard, huddled against the building under the second-storey overhang to protect themselves from the rain. They were obviously waiting for the stage. It occurred to him, with a stab of annoyance, that with two persons already waiting to board the stage at this quiet crossroad and he himself making a third, the stage might be very crowded indeed. Perhaps he should remain where he was after all.

A sound on the stairs drew his eyes away from the window. To his surprise, a young lad of about sixteen years of age came clumping down and passed quickly by the taproom door. Derek had only a momentary glimpse of the fellow, but the sight of him was puzzling. Where had the lad come from? The innkeeper had said there were but two bedrooms upstairs; Derek still possessed the first, and the girl—Miss Smythe— had booked the second. Where could this boy have been hiding? What on earth was going on here?

Derek heard the outer door bang shut. He turned quickly to the window and watched the young lad cross the courtyard. The fellow had a cap pulled down low on his forehead and was wearing a coat that looked too light to give the wearer the warmth required for this bone-chilling weather. The coat, so ill-fitting that the sleeves hung inches below the lad's wrists, had seen better days, for it was patched at the elbows and frayed at the edges. The boy's breeches, too, were patched and shabby, but his boots were shiny-new. Derek wondered if the fellow was the innkeeper's son, but how a stocky, brutish fellow like the innkeeper could sire a lad as slim and fine-boned as this one was a puzzle indeed.

The boy made a nervous tug at his cap, giving Derek a momentary glimpse of a little lock of red-gold hair. Didn't the girl—that Miss Smythe—have hair that color? Before he could find any significance in that observation, however, he noticed that the boy had crossed to the far side of the courtyard and taken a place with the little group waiting for the stage. *Good God,* he thought in disgust, *now there will be four of us boarding the stage!*

McTeague came in from the kitchen at that moment. He was a grizzled, sixty-year-old Irishman of less than average height, with a protuberant belly and chubby cheeks, but he had a pair of shrewd blue eyes that could see a person's character in his face and a pair of hands that could hold four raging horses back with as much ease and grace as they could tie a neckerchief in pristine folds. He had been his lordship's valet, butler and coachman for so long that neither of them remembered what life had been like without the other. He came up behind his lordship, who was staring out the window taking no notice of his valet's approach, and put his hands angrily on his hips. "That idiot innkeeper says y're takin' the stage, me lord," he declared in loud, accusing tones. "Y're not, are ye? It'll not be a journey to yer likin', I'll be bound."

"I know that," his lordship answered absently, his eyes fixed on the scene in the courtyard. "I'm going anyway."

"Without me?" McTeague asked in offense.

"You'll have to drive the curricle back. But never mind that now. What do you think of that lad out there, McTeague? The one standing by himself, with the cap. Do you see something strange about him?"

The valet leaned over his master's shoulder and peered out. "The boots, I'd say. Too well made t' fit in with the rest of him."

"Yes, that's what I thought, too. I also think I've seen those boots before. A young lady came in here a couple of hours ago wearing those same boots."

McTeague raised a quizzical eyebrow. "Since when, me lord, have ye begun t' take notice of a young lady's *boots*? A certain Miss Polly Stanhope, back in London, would be amused t' learn how yer taste has declined."

"Keep a civil tongue in your head, man, and answer the question. How do you suppose that fellow got hold of the young lady's boots?"

McTeague shrugged. "How should I know? Copped 'em, I suppose."

Derek shook his head. "How can he have done that? Pulled them from her feet? Besides, his hair's the same color as hers."

The valet looked at his master curiously. "What has that t' say to anything? Let me guess what it is yer gettin' at, me lord. Yer sayin' that a young lady—a pretty one, no doubt?—"

His lordship grinned. "Very pretty."

"A *very* pretty young lady with reddish hair came in to this inn wearin' those boots, right?"

"Right. She took a room upstairs. Since there are only two rooms, it must be the room next to mine. And two hours later, that young man—also with reddish hair—comes down wearing her boots. Don't you think there's a bit of a mystery here?"

McTeague snorted. "Not much of one. It's her brother, which explains the hair. He's borrowed her boots so he won't get his feet wet waiting out there for the stage. Sorry, me lord, but it don't seem like much of a mystery to me."

"Ah, but you see, I never saw the boy come in at all, and I've been sitting here all morning. All I saw was the young lady's maid, who came in with a parcel and departed with a parcel. If the boy is her brother, explain if you can how he got upstairs without my seeing him?"

"Easy! He was up there before you came down."

"No. It was she who bespoke the room. I saw her do it."

McTeague rubbed his chin, eyeing his lordship thoughtfully. "Are ye sayin', me lord, that, since it was a young lady that went up and a young fella that came down, the boy out there an' the young lady ye saw takin' the room are one and the same?"

His lordship nodded. "Good thinking, McTeague. I can't devise any other explanation, can you?"

"I can think of a way to test yer theory, though. We could go up and see if the young lady is still up there in her room."

His lordship got to his feet. "I don't know, McTeague. It's none of our business, after all."

McTeague's eyes began to twinkle. "No business of ours a-tall!" he agreed.

"If a girl wants to dress herself up as a boy and run off, it's not our place to interfere."

"No, me lord, it ain't."

"We're not a couple of prying old biddies, are we?"

McTeague grinned. "Och, begorra! Certainly not, me lord."

Derek grinned back at him. "Shall you lead the way, or shall I?"

"Oh, after you, me lord," McTeague insisted. "After you."

They started across the taproom, curiosity giving his lordship a feeling of animation for the first time that day. McTeague, however, remained skeptical. "I doubt if a young lady comes to an inn to dress herself up like a boy. Doesn't make sense, me lord. There must be another explanation we ain't thought of."

"Want to make a wager of it?" his lordship offered. "The usual guinea?"

McTeague hesitated. "I lost the last couple of times. I dunno . . ."

"I'll give you odds. Two to one if I'm wrong."

"Done!" the valet said promptly.

The two men went swiftly up the stairs. They walked past the door to his lordship's bedroom and stopped before a second door a few yards down the corridor. Derek tapped on it firmly. "Miss Smythe?" he called.

There was no answer. McTeague tried the doorknob, which turned easily, and they pushed the door open. The room was empty. Not only was the girl not there, but there were no signs that she'd ever occupied the room. The bed had not been disturbed; no article of clothing had been left littering the chair; no comb or brush marred the bare expanse of the dresser-top. "Seems ye were right, me lord," McTeague muttered disappointedly, crossing over the threshold. "Begorra, it looks like ye've taken me again."

He looked about him, hoping to find something to solve the mystery in a way that would be favorable to him. He peered behind the door first and then under the bed.

"There's no point in your searching about, old man," his lordship taunted. "She's not here. You may as well pay up."

"I shoulda known better," McTeague mumbled irritably, continuing to poke about the room. "You had the advantage, havin' seen the girl come in. I'll end me days in the poor house, makin' these idiotic wagers. Och, begorra! Look at *this*! Proves yer right fer certain."

"Oh? what have you found?"

"This," McTeague said, holding out a wastebasket for his lordship to see. Derek peered inside. There on the bottom of the basket was a pile of long strands of shorn-off red-gold hair.

"Good God!" His lordship lifted a handful of silky strands out of the basket and peered at it. "What beautiful hair! The girl must have been desperate to make a sacrifice like this."

"It ain't nothin' to the sacrifice I've got to make," McTeague grumbled, pulling a guinea from his pocket and handing it to his lordship. "Blasted female. If she'd kept her hair on her head, I'd be a richer man."

"Serves you right for gambling," his lordship laughed, pocketing the coin. "I've warned you for years that gambling is a fool's pastime. Well, I'm off to catch the stage. I don't think I'll mind it so much, now. Unraveling the mystery of the little chit's reason for disguising herself will make the journey more bearable."

"More bearable than mine," McTeague complained. "I've got t' drive yer blasted curricle through the rain."

His lordship stopped in his tracks. "You will *not* drive through the rain," he declared, wheeling about and glaring at his man. "You will wait until it clears. That's an order, McTeague. I don't want you returning to London with an inflammation of the lungs. Here. This should be sufficient for your expenses on the way." And tossing the fellow a small sackful of coins, his lordship strode out of the room.

McTeague was closing the door behind him when his lordship came back. "Oh, one thing more, McTeague," he said. "Take a lock of that hair out of the basket and save it for me in an envelope."

"If ye wish, me lord," the valet said with lifted eyebrows, "but whatever do ye want it *for*?"

"I have no idea," Derek answered, sauntering back toward the stairs. "Perhaps it will bring me luck. After all, it's won me a guinea already."

Chapter Six

Eight passengers were crowded into the stagecoach, and four others sat on top, exposed to the downpour. Although none of the inside passengers would have wished to change with the poor wretches who sat above, they had no love for their own situation either. They were crushed into a space that would have been inadequate for six, the smell of human sweat was overpowering and the rocking of the carriage was so violent that several of the riders found it nauseating. To Derek Rutledge, who had not experienced such discomfort since his days in the army (when he'd served under Wellington in the Peninsular Wars), the ride was uncomfortable enough, but to Ada Farrington, who'd never experienced anything like it in her life, it was unbearable. His lordship, observing her from beneath half-closed eyes, noted with alarm that she was turning quite green. He'd been vastly amused, when they'd first boarded the coach, by her attempt to sit boyishly, with one booted leg raised and bent so that the ankle rested on the other knee. But now she was making no attempt to be boyish. Both her feet were flat on the floor, her hands were clenched in her lap and her lips were pressed together as if she were in pain. "Are you not well, lad?" he asked, leaning across to where she sat opposite him, wedged between an overweight farmer (who with appalling rudeness was stuffing himself with a greasy sausage and pieces of a very smelly cheese) and a gentleman with a hooked nose on which a pince-nez was perched, who was so bookish that he'd not looked up from his reading for one moment since they'd boarded.

Ada lifted her eyes and blinked suspiciously at the questioner. "Are you speaking to *me*, sir?"

"Yes, boy, I am," he said, surprised at the boyish croak of

her voice. "You don't look very well. Is there something I can do for you?"

"I *am* feeling queasy, but I don't know what you can do—"

"I can give you my seat, here near the window. I'll open it a bit, and you can breathe some fresh air."

The girl showed an immediate and instinctive gratitude, but this impulse was soon overtaken by the look of wariness. "Fresh air might be the very thing," she said cautiously, in her charmingly croaking voice. "I do thank you, sir. You are very kind."

They both rose, and Derek, lurching awkwardly, lifted her up, turned them both round and managed to help her into his seat. But when he tried to seat himself in her place, the farmer loudly objected. "Not enough room," he said with his mouth full. "Y're too big."

"Quite right," the bookish man agreed, looking up from his book at last. "You're twice the width of that little fellow."

Derek, standing between the two rows of passengers and almost doubled over because of the low roof, had no intention of spending the rest of the trip in that awkward position. Choosing the thinnest man in the row in which he'd been sitting, he pressed him to take the vacated seat. Grumbling, the fellow did as he was asked. Then Derek made the others move over to make room for him next to the lad he'd helped. In this way, he managed to place himself just exactly where he wanted to be. He took his place and stretched his legs out as far as they could go, smiling inwardly in satisfaction. It bothered him not at all that the farmer made a few loud complaints about the draught from the open window and that the bookish man muttered something about London dandies who think their fine clothes give them the right to order everyone about. He merely ignored them and turned his attention to the girl-in-boy's-clothing, who had turned her face to the window and was breathing the outside air in huge gulps. "Feeling any better?" he asked her softly.

She turned to him with such a meltingly grateful look that he felt a clench in his chest. It had been her magnificent hair and the elfin shape of her face that had caught his eye at the inn, but he now realized that it was something about her eyes that made her beautiful. Their color—something between grey and sea-green—was quite bewitching, and the way they tilted up at the corners was an utter delight. But, he warned himself, it would not do to think of her as a girl. She was too young and naive for him to think of in a flirtatious way. And to think of her in a brotherly way would require him to offer her his protection, a troublesome situation to be in. The girl was very young and very vulnerable, but he did not want to be responsible for her in any way. He wanted only to return to London, where he'd always found an abundance of lovely females who offered him pleasure without difficulty. He was a rake, not a hero, and a rake he intended to remain. This girl had excited his curiosity, but he would not let her excite his chivalry. Once he found out what her game was, he would leave her alone to play it and go on his way.

Hardening his heart, he smiled down at her with avuncular interest. "You *are* feeling better, I see."

"Oh, *yes*," she said, addressing him with boyish bravado, "much, much better. Hang it all, I was afraid, for a while, that I would have to ... to ... empty my breadbasket, if you know what I mean. But I've quite recovered now. I don't know how to thank you!"

"No need to thank me at all. Glad to be of service, Mr ... er ..."

Her eyes became wary again. "Mr. Smythe," she offered after a moment's hesitation. "Ad ... Ad ... Addison Smythe."

"How do you do," Derek said, putting out his hand. "My name's Rutledge. Derek Rutledge."

She shook his hand with mannish firmness. "How do you do, Mr. Rutledge," she said with formal politeness.

"Are you going to London on business, Mr. Smythe?" Derek asked, prying shamelessly.

"I'm not going to London. Only as far as Barton Mills."

"Barton Mills, eh? That's less than an hour from here, I believe. Do you live there?"

"No. I live in East Harling, not far from where we boarded."

"Ah, I see. Barton Mills is a rather quiet little town, if my memory serves. Not much business a man can do there. You must be visiting someone there, I suspect." He smiled at her disarmingly. "A sweetheart, I'll be bound. Have I caught you out, Mr. Smythe? Are you on your way to pay court to a pretty little coquette?"

The girl's eyes fell. "Nothing as pleasant as that," she said quietly, turning away from him.

His lordship felt a twinge of guilt. In all his observation of the girl, he'd been making light of her situation, laughing at her in his mind. But if she'd disguised herself for some serious reason, it was unkind and tasteless of him to pry. "I'm sorry," he said with genuine embarrassment. "I shouldn't have asked—"

"Rubbish!" she exclaimed with a boyishly dismissive gesture. "I don't mind your asking. There's no reason for me to be secretive. You see, I'm searching for my brother."

"Oh? Run off, has he?"

Her eyes fell, and she twisted her fingers in her lap in a way that wasn't boyish at all. "He disappeared with a gypsy caravan."

Derek nodded understandingly. "Yes, boys are often tempted to run off with gypsies. There's something so adventurous and romantic about them."

"No, I'm certain he didn't run off with them. Not voluntarily. He's not the sort to run away."

"In any case, Mr. Smythe, I hope you won't take offense when I say that it seems to me you're a bit young to be doing this on your own."

She did take offense. "I'll have you know, Mr. Rutledge, that I'm not as young as you think," she snapped, turning away from him again, as if to indicate that the conversation was over.

"But I haven't *told* you what I think," Derek pointed out tauntingly.

She couldn't resist responding. "All right, confound it, tell me! Go on . . . how old *do* you think I am?" she asked over her shoulder.

"Sixteen," he said promptly.

"Ha!" she snorted. "What would you say, hang it all, if I told you I'm past *nineteen*?"

"I'd say you were bamming me. Nineteen? That's a bit hard to swallow, you know."

She turned back to him angrily. "Dash it all, I *am* past nineteen."

He had to struggle to keep from laughing aloud. Not only were her earnest protestations of her advanced age amusing, but her tenacious use of what she thought were boyish expressions was positively hilarious. "You look a great deal younger, Mr. Smythe," he said, managing to keep his expression serious. "I would have wagered seventeen at the most."

She cast him a quick, suspicious glance and then put up her chin. "I know I'm small for my age, Mr. Rutledge, but, dash it all, I make up in determination what I lack in stature."

He could barely contain a smile. "Well, good for you, Mr. Smythe. *Dash it all*, I daresay you'll accomplish your mission in short order."

"I hope so," she muttered, too preoccupied with the problem ahead of her to notice his teasing. "The time can't be too short for me. The thought of poor little Stanley out there alone . . . among strangers . . . is very disturbing to me, so the sooner I find him the better." Her eyes clouded, and her underlip trembled. "He's such a little boy, you see. Only eight."

Her distress was so sincere that he had to fight the urge to take her hand in his. "I shouldn't become unduly alarmed if I were you, Mr. Smythe," he said consolingly. "I know that gypsies are notorious for lying and cheating and performing all sorts of disagreeable tricks, but I have yet to hear of them murdering anyone. You'll find the boy, I'm sure of it. He'll undoubtedly be none the worse for the experience and a great deal wiser."

"Do you think so?" she asked, looking up at him with endearing hopefulness. "Thank you, Mr. Rutledge. You've made me feel a great deal better."

Derek patted her shoulder, feeling very satisfied with himself. He'd found out all he wanted to know. The girl, in order to go out and find her brother, had decided that the safest course was to face the world as a boy. She was quite right, too. The boy's garb would protect her from molestation. If the gypsies were camped at Barton Mills as she expected, she would undoubtedly have her brother in hand within an hour and be on her way home by late afternoon. He didn't have to worry about her.

He leaned back against the cushion and closed his eyes. Now that his curiosity was satisfied, he could put the girl and her problems out of his mind. With a long, unpleasant journey ahead of him, the way to make the best of it was to sleep through it, and that was exactly what he intended to do.

But the rocking of the carriage was anything but gentle, and his conscience kept prodding him with feelings of guilt. *What sort of gentleman are you,* his conscience asked, *to let an innocent female deal with gypsies by herself?* But he stilled that nagging voice by reminding his conscience that he was no blasted evangelist going about the world doing good works. If it weren't for his mother's machinations, he would never have been here in the first place and would never even have encountered this female calling herself Addison Smythe. And if the weather had been less contrary, he would be tooling toward London in his own curricle, completely unaware of the girl and her difficulties. Besides, her difficulties were no business of his. He was merely an innocent bystander. Just because he'd been observant enough to see through her disguise did not make him responsible for her, did it?

Feeling that he'd won this inner debate handily, he shut his eyes again and tried to sleep. But he was still wide awake when the coach rumbled to a halt before another country inn, this one called the Hart and Hare. He heard the coachman shout "Barton Mills," and an ostler from the inn let down the steps and threw open the door.

The girl put out her hand to him again. "Good-bye, Mr. Rutledge," she said briskly. "Hang it all, I hope you have a safe journey."

"And I hope you find your brother without difficulty," Derek replied, shaking her hand. "Good-bye, Mr. Smythe."

The girl stepped out of the coach, and the ostler slammed the door shut. Derek leaned back against the seat and shut his eyes again, telling his conscience angrily to "take a damper!" As the coach started off again, Derek became uncomfortably aware of the sound of the heavy rain on the roof. *That poor creature's going to be drenched,* he thought.

Impelled by some impulse over which he seemed to have no control, he lowered the window all the way down (ignoring the cries of protest from the other passengers) and stuck his head out. He could see her marching up the road in the opposite direction from the one the coach was taking. She was swinging her arms and lifting her feet in what she took to be a masculine stride, ignoring the rain. *Dash it all,* he muttered to his nagging conscience, *why hasn't she the sense to wait at the inn until the rain stops? Can I really let that little chit go on her quest alone?*

As he debated with himself, he noticed that the ostler, now joined by another shabby fellow, were making their way up the road behind the girl. From the stealthy way in which they moved, Derek had no doubt they were up to no good. Were they intending to rob her? The chit was undoubtedly plucky, and might hold her own against one of them, but certainly not against two!

That thought settled the matter for once and all. He leaned forward and pounded on the little panel located just over the plump farmer's head, the tiny panelled window that opened to the coachman's box. "Driver, stop!" he shouted. "I have to get off!"

The panel slid back, and the coachman's face appeared in the little window, angled sharply to the side, for the fellow had to bend down from the box to reach it. "Ain't stoppin' till Newmarket," he said in annoyance. "Why din't ye git off when—? Oh, it's yersel', sir. I tho't ye wuz goin' to Lunnon."

"Changed my mind," his lordship said shortly, pulling a gold sovereign from his pocket. "Here. Will *this* make it possible for you to stop long enough for me to jump down?"

The coachman's face disappeared from the opening and was promptly replaced by a hand. Derek put the coin into it, the little panel slid quickly closed and the coach jerked to an abrupt halt. While the other passengers muttered vituperations against the unauthorized stop, Derek threw open the door and leaped to the ground.

The coach set off immediately. As it trundled away down the road, Derek looked up in the other direction to see how far the girl had got. But he couldn't see her at all, for there was a rise in the road that cut off his view. He put up his coat collar, but the act did not a bit of good in warding off the rain.

Annoyed with himself for having yielded to what now seemed
a very foolish impulse, he set off at a trot up the rise. "Derek
Rutledge," he muttered aloud as he sloshed through the pud-
dles in the ruts of the road, "somewhere during this deuced
journey you've gone and lost your wits!"

Chapter Seven

The ostler had been very polite when Ada, just off the stage, had asked him where the gypsies were encamped. He'd pointed up the road, told her it was no more than a half-hour's walk, warned her that the gypsies were a "brummish bunch, always pokin' bogey" (which she took to mean that they were dishonest) and tipped his cap to her. Thus she was completely taken by surprise when, a few minutes later, he came up behind her on the road, pulled her arms behind her back and told her to give over her "brass" to his confederate, a monkeylike fellow with sloping shoulders and short legs who leered at her ominously as he asked, "Where is it, eh? In a coat pocket? In yer boot?"

Ada, despite the feeling of alarm that threatened to overwhelm her, reminded herself that she must pass as a boy and that she should therefore not react to this assault as a lady might. Therefore, she put up a desperate struggle to free her arms and, seeing the monkeylike fellow approach, kicked out at him wildly. One of her boots met its mark, for the fellow howled in pain and backed away.

The ostler pulled her arms tighter. "If y're gonna raise a dust, ye whopstraw," he hissed in her ear, "I'll make ye a lot sorrier than ye are now. Quit yer kickin', or ye'll feel me fives in yer puddin'!" With that he dragged her to the side of the road and through the hedge which bordered it, Ada wriggling frantically in his grasp. She proved a handful for him, and he shouted to his groaning confederate to "come 'ere an give me a 'and before this noddle 'as me bum-squabbled!"

The other fellow burst through the hedge in a vengeful rage. "Kick *me*, will 'e?" he shouted. "Let me at 'im!" And he raised a huge, menacing fist.

51

Ada's heart froze in terror. Never had anyone ever raised a hand to her before. She shut her eyes, bracing herself for the imminent onslaught. But instead of feeling the pain of a blow to her jaw, she heard a gasp. Her eyes flew open. There behind the startled assailant stood Mr. Rutledge, the gentleman from the stagecoach. He had grasped the miscreant's upraised arm in a painful, viselike grip and was slowly pulling it back in such a way that the fellow had to twist his shoulder around to keep the collarbone from breaking. "*Ow*! Y're breakin' me *arm*!" the fellow screamed. "Le'me *go*!"

"Perhaps I will," Derek said calmly, "after *your* friend releases *mine*."

The ostler dropped his hold on Ada and began fearfully to back away. But Derek, releasing the other fellow (who fell to his knees, groaning and rubbing his shoulder), caught up with the ostler in two strides and grasped him by his neckerchief. "This," he said, smashing his fist against one side of the ostler's chin, "is for betraying the trust that a traveller must place in those of you who handle coaching horses. And *this*," he added, landing a blow on the other side of the fellow's chin, "is for using a confederate and doubling the odds against a lone boy who's half your own weight to begin with!" Then he released his hold on the ostler's neckerchief and let him fall to the ground.

"*Mr. Rutledge*!" Ada breathed, as surprised as she was relieved. "It seems I must thank you again. I wish I knew what to say to express my gratitude."

"Don't say anything, Mr. Smythe. Just let's remove ourselves from this shrubbery."

Ada looked down uneasily at the prostrate ostler and his still-groaning confederate. "Do you mean that we should just . . . leave them here?"

"What we *should* do, I suppose, is drag them to the nearest magistrate. But that would take too much time and trouble. Let us merely leave them to lick their wounds. Here, come this way."

They pushed back through the hedge. "But what are you doing here, Mr. Rutledge?" she asked curiously. "I thought you were on your way to London."

Derek gave a rueful shrug. "So did I."

She blinked up at him, her eyes taking on their wary, suspicious look. "Good heavens, sir, do you mean to imply that you've postponed your journey for *my* sake?"

"I do not mean to imply anything. But, to tell the truth, I was not in any particular hurry to get to London. And when I noticed those fellows following you up the road, I suspected that they might be up to some mischief, so I got off the stage and came after you."

Ada felt an unexpected wave of anger. "In other words, you did not believe I could manage the situation on my own?"

Derek cocked a surprised eyebrow at her. "Have I offended you, Mr. Smythe? That certainly is not the reaction I expected."

"You expected my gratitude. And you have it, of course. If you hadn't gotten off the stage on my behalf, I might now be suffering a bloody nose and empty pockets. Naturally, I'm grateful. But I can't say I'm *flattered* by your action."

"What on earth has flattery to do with anything?" Derek asked sourly, having half-expected the chit to fall into his arms in thankful tears and annoyed at himself for feeling cheated of the satisfaction of that scene.

She put up her chin proudly. "I would have preferred it if you'd thought of me as capable of dealing with the matter myself."

"I do beg your pardon, Mr. Smythe," he retorted with exaggerated sarcasm. "Next time I see you being attacked by brutal thieves, I'll stand aside and let them bloody your nose and pick your pockets to their—and your—hearts' content."

She stared up at him for a moment and then lowered her eyes in shame. "I'm sorry, sir. I'm speaking very foolishly. I assure you that I really am extremely grateful to you. In fact, your concern for my welfare leaves me quite breathless. Getting off the stage was an act of extreme generosity. It was more generous than I had any right to expect, considering that we are mere chance acquaintances."

"All right, old fellow, that will be enough," Derek said, giving her a sudden grin. "No need to put it on so rare and thick. Too much gratitude is as bad as too little."

Ada grinned back at him. "But, hang it all, Mr. Rutledge, it *was* an amazingly kind act. Are you always so concerned for the welfare of strangers you meet on the stage?"

"Since this was the very first time I've ever travelled on the stage, I really can't say. I suspect that my so-called generosity was inspired more by the impression you made on me than my inborn nature, which, my own mother would be the first to tell you, is quite shockingly selfish."

She shook her head. "I don't believe that for a moment. But what, sir, was there about me that inspired such generosity? All you can possibly know about me is that I have a queasy stomach."

"I had many more interesting impressions of you than that, my boy. But among other things, I suspected that you've not been trained to use your fives. I came after you because I feared you were not particularly adept at fisticuffs and might need a bit of help."

Her expression hardened again. "There, you see?" she growled, glaring at him. "You're always very quick to belittle me, aren't you? What makes you think I haven't been trained in fisticuffs? As a matter of fact, I'm very handy with my fives!"

"Good God, boy, you needn't be so quick to take offense! But before we go any further with this discussion, may I suggest that standing here arguing in the rain is a foolish way to pass the time? Let's get back to the inn where we can continue to insult each other at a roaring fire with a couple of mugs of mulled wine in our hands."

Ada blushed to realize that she'd forgotten all about the rain. "I'm sorry, Mr. Rutledge," she mumbled in embarrassment, "but, hang it all, I'm afraid I can't join you. I'm on my way to the gypsy camp, you see."

"Not in this downpour, surely. Can't you wait until it clears?"

"I'd like very much to postpone that confrontation, sir. No one dreads it more than I. But when I think of Stanley, I realize that I mustn't put it off."

"An hour or two can't make much difference," Derek argued.

"It can, though. What if he's frightened and homesick? What if he's in danger? An hour or two to us might very well seem like a nightmarish *week* to him."

His lordship stared down at her for a moment, and then, with a hopeless shrug, he acquiesced. "Very well, then, if you insist, let's get on our way."

But Ada had no intention of accepting his reluctant companionship. *"Our* way?" she echoed with a negative shake of her head. "I thank you, Mr. Rutledge, but, dash it all, I won't accept any further generosity from you. I'll be on *my* way, and you, sir, must go on *your* way to the inn and your mulled wine."

He expelled a breath in vexation, telling himself that that was just what he ought to do, but he knew he would not. "A fine time I'd have with my conscience," he retorted, "sitting and drinking at a fire while you were out in this rain haggling with gypsies. Come on, boy, let's go and get this over with!" And giving her no opportunity to argue with him, he pulled her after him down the road.

They were drenched to the skin by the time they reached the gypsy camp. To Ada, the wagons looked much less colorful in the rain than they'd seemed from the windows at Farrington Park. The brilliant paint on the wagons, and their intricately carved posts and cornices, looked sodden and dim on this wet, grey day. There were no pennons flying, no dark-haired dancing girls and no cooking fires. All the gypsies had evidently decided to protect themselves from the elements by retreating into their wagons. Ada and Derek went from one wagon to another, knocking on the posts and calling through the fabric flaps that were tied over the doorways, "Stanley? Are you in there?"

There was no answer to any of their shouts, nor did a single flap open to reveal a gypsy face. Finally, Derek, his patience exhausted, pounded on the side of the largest wagon. "Come out, damn it, or I'll bring the law down on you! Where's your leader?"

The flap was pulled aside and a large-breasted woman, with a scarf tied over a head of dark, unkempt hair and a dirty shawl draped over her shoulders, appeared in the doorway. "What you want here?" she asked in a gruff voice, stepping out with bare feet upon the top of the rough wooden stairs, three steps high, that led to the wagon's doorway.

Derek approached the stairs and looked up at her. "We're

looking for a little boy named Stanley," he said in his most lordly manner. "We think he might be somewhere in this caravan."

"No. Not here," the woman said with finality. "No Stanley here."

"But he must be here," Ada said, coming up beside Derek. "The last time anyone saw him, he was heading toward your camp. It was yesterday, when you were still in East Harling."

"East Harling?" the woman echoed blankly. "I no remember East Harling."

"But you were there! You camped just outside of Farrington Park, don't you remember? You *must* have seen my brother. He's a little fellow, only this high, with reddish hair like mine, see?"

She pulled off her cap to show the woman her hair. Derek, remembering the long, silken strands in the wastebasket at the Green Gander, couldn't help staring at her. The contrast between her present coiffure and the way her hair had looked when he'd first seen her was painful. What was now left of her hair fell over her forehead in blunt, uneven clumps. She and her maid had cut it with pathetic ineptitude. Yet he had to admit that the mutilated hair detracted very little from the charm of her face.

The gypsy woman shook her head. "No. Saw no little boys yesterday."

"But you *must* have!" Ada insisted. "Please try to think! His hair is curly, not straight like mine. And his eyebrows and lashes are very light, almost invisible. He has a sprinkling of freckles, here and here. And his eyes crinkle up when he laughs, and a dimple shows up . . ." Her voice choked as her brother's face appeared, sharp and clear, in her mind. ". . . one l-little dimple only, in his left cheek . . ."

Derek, touched, wanted to put an arm round her shoulders, but the gypsy woman was unmoved. "No, not see," she repeated. "A man, he come last night looking for little boy Stanley. He looked top to bottom, no Stanley."

Derek, startled, raised a quizzical eyebrow at Ada. "A man came looking last night?" he asked her.

Her eyes fell. "My elder brother. I didn't tell you because . . . well, it doesn't matter."

"Doesn't it? If your elder brother has already been here searching—"

Ada frowned in disgust. "My elder brother's an idiot. He was already saying last night that we should get used to the idea that Stanley's gone! Well, hang it all, I *won't* get used to it! A little boy can't just disappear into thin air, can he?"

Derek hesitated before answering. This matter was more complicated than he'd bargained for. If she had an older brother and he'd already searched the caravan, then why had *she* come? It was plain that she adored her little brother and had felt impelled to do something about his disappearance. But although Derek felt considerable sympathy for her in her dilemma, he couldn't help believing that a second search of the caravan, after the first fruitless one, was pointless. "No, I don't suppose a little boy can just disappear, Mr. Smythe," he answered gently, "but perhaps you're searching in the wrong place."

Ada turned a pair of agonized eyes on him. "I don't know where else to *look*," she exclaimed in desperation.

For some inexplicable reason, Derek found himself unable to resist the appeal in those grey-green eyes. He turned to the gypsy woman again. "We want to search the caravan once more," he told her.

A man appeared in the doorway behind the gypsy woman. Ada gasped at the sight of him. He was very large, almost giantlike, and had a gold earring in one ear. In addition, a red and yellow kerchief was tied on his head, and a chain of coins hung round his neck. "What do these *gajos* want?" he asked the woman.

"To search the *vardo* again."

The man turned to Derek. "No," he said sharply.

But Derek had heard his companion gasp and was staring at her. "Do you know this man?" he asked her.

"It's the *giant*! Just like Stanley described him," she whispered, her eyes fixed on the tall gypsy.

"You will not search," the man said angrily. "Once is enough."

"We are not the ones who searched before," Derek explained. "We want to see for ourselves."

"No!" the gypsy said again.

Ada put up her chin. "I'll get the parish constable again, just as my brother did," she threatened.

The giant merely glared at her. Then, grasping the gypsy woman's arm, he pulled her with him back into the wagon and let the flap fall shut between them and the "gajos" still standing out in the rain.

"Damnation!" Derek muttered, clenching his fists. "I'd like to tip him a settler!"

"Yes, so would I," Ada said, disheartened.

Derek looked down at the dejected, rain-soaked young girl with a feeling of helplessness. "Don't look like that," he said, putting a supporting arm about her shoulders, convinced in his heart that her little brother would not be found in the gypsy camp but unable to tell her so. "Your idea about bringing the constable is a good one. We'll roust him out first thing in the morning. But for now, my lad, I don't see that there's anything to be gained by hanging about. Let's take ourselves back to the inn and dry off."

Ada, her hopes crushed, did not trust herself to speak. If she said a word, she knew she would cry, and she didn't see how she could convince anyone she was a nineteen-year-old male if she spilled tears down her cheeks. She merely nodded and let him lead her, heartsick and spiritless, back down the road.

Chapter Eight

Mr. Hewitt, the innkeeper of the Hart and Hare, looked over his two new guests (whom he'd just settled into the private parlour) with shrewd eyes. He was a man of long experience with travellers, and he knew at once that the older of the two was a gentleman of the first stare. The gentleman's coat, despite the fact that it was soaked through, was of the finest cut (a coat that only a Weston or a Stultz could have tailored), his boots must have cost a fortune and his hair, wet though it was, was unmistakably a Brutus, one of the latest of the London modes. It was a style favored by the Corinthians, and this detail was the final clue that proved to the innkeeper that this gentleman calling himself Mr. Rutledge was undoubtedly a nobleman travelling incognito.

The boy with him was quite another matter, Mr. Hewitt decided. The lad's clothes, except for his boots and the cape he'd draped over his shoulders, were suitable only for stableboys. But this was no stableboy. One look at his hands proved to the innkeeper that the lad hadn't done a real day's labor in his life. There was something havey-cavey about him, that much was certain. But he was certainly not a gentleman; Mr. Hewitt was willing to bet on that.

He turned to Mr. Rutledge and made a low bow. "I hope this room suits you, sir. You can have all the privacy you need in here. And now, if you're so inclined, I'll take your coat— and the young lad's, too—and have one of the maids dry them near the kitchen fire and press them for you."

"Yes, thank you," Derek said, removing the sodden coat at once and handing it over.

But Ada shook her head. "You may take my cape," she

59

said, giving it to the innkeeper and crossing to the fire, "but I'll wear my coat, if you please."

The innkeeper took the garments and started out. "As you wish, sir, as you wish. I'll have two hot toddies ready for you in a moment."

"Oh, by the way," Derek called after him, "we'll need a couple of bedrooms for the night. I trust you can accommodate us."

The innkeeper paused at the door and bit his lip. The rain had induced several travellers to postpone their departures, and all four of his bedrooms were already bespoken. But none of his guests was as important-looking as this gentleman, so he had to think of something. It would not do to turn away someone who might be a peer of the realm!

But Mr. Hewitt had been an innkeeper for too long to be thrown for a loss by the need for extra space. There were a good many tricks to his trade, and he knew them all. For one thing, he could persuade the fellow in the largest room to double up with one of the other guests, and if he proved resistant Mr. Hewitt could sweeten him by reducing his cost for the night's lodging by half. Then, by charging *this* gentleman twice the regular price (for London gentlemen were quite used to paying high prices for their lodgings), Mr. Hewitt could do very nicely for himself. He turned from the door and smiled at his new guest obsequiously. "It's a very busy night, Mr. Rutledge," he said with the confidence acquired by years of successful management, "but I think I *might* be able to provide you with one room. It's quite large, and we can make up a cot for the young lad—"

Derek was aware that the girl stiffened. The poor creature was finding herself in a worse than awkward situation. She could not allow herself to spend the night in a bedroom with him under any conditions. If it ever became known that she'd been in the same room with a man for a whole night, she would never be able to live it down, no matter how she explained it or how innocently she'd passed the time. She was undoubtedly wondering at this very moment just how she could manage to avoid it without giving away her disguise.

What the girl did not know, of course, was that she was perfectly safe under his care. He would not permit her to be compromised. It was clear to him that the chit was gently reared, and he was not the sort to besmirch the name of an innocent lady. He would find a way to protect her reputation without forcing her to give herself away. *But,* he said to himself with mischievous glee, *not before I take a full measure of entertainment from this humorous situation. Besides, she deserves a bit of a set-down.*

His lips twitched in amusement as he shook his head at the innkeeper. "No, no, Mr. Hewitt—you did say your name was Hewitt, didn't you?—that won't do at all. I'm afraid I don't like to share my sleeping quarters. Besides, I would not be at all surprised to learn that Mr. Smythe over there was a snorer. He looks like a snorer to me. Doesn't he seem so to you?"

"I do *not* snore!" Ada snapped, whirling about from her contemplation of the fire, taking instant umbrage instead of realizing that she might be talking herself out of a private bedroom. "*What* makes you think—?"

"No one thinks of himself as a snorer, old fellow," Derek said obnoxiously. "It's one of those things an unmarried man doesn't know about himself. Come, come, Mr. Hewitt, there must be other arrangements we can make."

"Other arrangements?" The innkeeper rubbed his chin thoughtfully. "That may not be easy. I don't wish to disoblige you, sir, but I have five guests now for the four bedrooms, not counting you and Mr. Smythe. If Mr. Smythe would consider doubling up with one of the other guests, I could probably work something out. Or, there's a room over the stable—"

Derek drew himself up in lordly indignation. "The *stable*! I'll have you know, Mr. Hewitt, that Smythe here is a friend of mine, and I do not permit my friends to sleep in stables. And as for his doubling up with a stranger, that is also out of the question." He turned to Ada and said with bland innocence, "I'm afraid the cot in the large room will have to do. Don't you agree?"

Ada felt her cheeks grow hot. "Really, Mr. Rutledge," she declared nastily in her attempt to mask her embarrassment, "I don't see why you take it upon yourself to make arrangements for me. Besides, perhaps I *do* snore. Hang it all, I'll take the room in the stable."

"Nonsense!" Derek exclaimed, taking wicked enjoyment in her confusion. "I won't hear of it."

"I don't see that you have anything to say to the matter,"

she said firmly. "I'll take the stable room, Mr. Hewitt."

"Very well, sir. But I must warn you that you may have to put up with some . . . er . . . rodents. Stables, you know, are not easy to keep free of rodents."

"Rodents?" Ada echoed with a shudder. "Do you mean *r-rats*?"

"Of course he means rats," Derek put in with evil satisfaction. "Come now, Smythe, let's hear no more about stable rooms. I'll put up with your snoring, if I must, rather than permit you to sleep in the stable." He turned to the innkeeper and waved him out. "Very well, Mr. Hewitt, go along and make the arrangements you suggested in your large bedroom. We'll make the best of them."

Ada tried, for the rest of the afternoon and evening, to concoct a scheme by which to extricate herself from this new difficulty, but she had little time to think. She was kept much too busy concentrating on being a manly companion to Mr. Rutledge. While they sat at the fire drinking their toddies, she had to watch him carefully so that she could copy his manner of downing his drink. And she had to position herself so that her booted legs were resting on the hearth with the same careless nonchalance as his. And all through the enormous dinner that Mr. Hewitt later served them, she had to ape Mr. Rutledge's way of eating. (He, for example, attacked his slice of mutton with an enthusiastic energy that was very different from the delicate way she would normally have cut into it). The most difficult feat was sipping the after-dinner port. She was already much too full of food, and the wine, being much stronger than any she'd ever been permitted to drink, made her dizzy and quite sick to her stomach. Therefore, by the time he suggested that they "turn in," the prospect of a bit of rest was so appealing that she didn't remember they were to share a bedroom until she was following him up the stairs.

She stopped her climb with a start. Her heart began to race in her chest, and a feeling of desperation threatened to overwhelm her. How was she to get out of this situation with her reputation intact? Before she could even attempt to uncloud her mind from the wine-induced fog that enveloped it, Mr. Rutledge turned round to see what was detaining her. "Come along, lad," he said cheerfully, holding his candle higher to help her see her way. "Don't dawdle."

He held the door of the bedroom open for her, and he watched her cross the threshold with so reluctant a step that he had all he could do to keep from laughing aloud. "What's the matter, lad?" he asked, placing the candle on the bedside table. "Don't you like the look of that cot?"

She frowned at the little bed that had been placed alongside the large four-poster that dominated the room. "Well, I . . . I . . ." she stammered.

"Yes, I see what you mean. This lumpy pallet does not look at all inviting," Derek said, testing the cot's flat mattress with his hand. "Oh, very well, my boy, there's no need to look so glum. You may share the big bed with me."

"I wish you'd stop calling me 'my boy'!" Ada mumbled irritably. "And I . . . I don't mind the cot, so you may stop putting words in my mouth. I have no desire at all to sleep in the big bed. I wouldn't wish my . . . my *snoring* to keep you awake."

"No, no, you needn't worry so much about your snoring. It won't be much more disturbing to me if we're a couple of feet closer." Pretending not to notice her look of horror, he sat down at the foot of the larger bed and lifted one leg. "Where is that blasted innkeeper?" he muttered. "I told him I'd need some help with my boots. Do you think you might give me a bit of assistance, Smythe?"

"*Assistance*, Mr. Rutledge?" Ada asked fearfully, frozen to the spot where she stood near the door.

"Since you've brought up the subject of how we should address each other, Smythe, I wish you'd stop calling me Mr. Rutledge. All my friends call me Derek. Here, now. If you'd only straddle my leg, you see, and grasp the boot by the heel . . ."

Ada, in a muddle made of embarrassment, fear, misery and wine, did as he asked. She straddled his leg and grasped the boot. Then she felt his other foot pushing against her back. Before she knew it, he'd propelled her forward with such force that the boot slid off and she was sent tottering halfway cross the room.

"Good lad!" Derek exclaimed, grinning at her as she regained her balance and gaped at him. "Now, let's get at the other one, and then I'll do the same for you."

She straddled his other leg with more assurance, and this

time she only tottered a few steps forward when the boot slid off in her hand. But when he straddled *her* leg, she found the position so embarrassing, somehow, that she did not have the courage to push her other foot against his buttocks as he had done to her. What would he think, she wondered miserably, if he knew it was a girl's leg he was straddling?

"You've got to push me harder than that, old fellow," he told her. "Don't you have any muscles at all? If you have, use them! You won't hurt me."

"I don't care if I hurt you or not!" Irked at his irritating male smugness, she pushed against his back with all her might. The boot flew off in his hands, and he shot forward so abruptly that he fell face down on the floor. He gave a pained grunt and lay there on his stomach for a long moment.

"D-Derek?" Ada asked in a flurry of remorse. "Are you all right?"

He took a deep breath, turned over and, lifting himself up on one elbow, eyed her with rueful amusement. "I suppose I deserved that," he muttered. "So, Smythe, my lad, you *do* have muscles after all."

"I wish you would not keep calling me 'Smythe' or 'my lad,' Derek," she said coldly. "I, too, have a given name, you know."

"Yes, I remember your telling it to me. Addison, wasn't it? Much too much of a mouthful, that is. Is that what your friends call you?"

"Some of them call me . . . er . . . Addie. You may call me Addie, if you like."

He got to his feet and looked down at her. "Addie, eh? Yes, I do like it, rather. Suits you, I think. Well, Addie, let's have your other boot. And I hope you'll not try to send me flying through the wall this time."

"There's no need for you to pull off my boot at all. I can do it myself. I've done it many times." And she reached down, lifted her foot and yanked the boot off without any difficulty.

Derek gave a snorting laugh. "Good God! If you're agile enough to wriggle out of your boots as easily as that, why didn't you tell me so at once?"

Ada shrugged. "I didn't wish to show you up," she said with a triumphant smile.

"Touché, my friend, touché. Your point." But his smile

widened wickedly as he told himself that her feeling of triumph would not be long-lasting. He strolled round to the head of the bed and pulled back the coverlet with evil deliberation. "Well, don't just sit there, Addie, my lad. Get ready for bed. By the way, where's your bag?"

"Hang it all, I didn't pack one," Ada said, desperately trying to pierce the fog in her brain for a way out of this muddle. "I didn't think I would have to stay away overnight, you see."

"Mine is on the stage, almost in London by this time. Too bad we have no nightclothes." Chuckling inwardly, he watched her expression from the corner of his eye as he pulled off his neckerchief and began to unbutton his shirt. "I suppose we have no choice but to sleep in our smalls."

Ada, reddening to the ears, dropped her eyes and turned away. She had to find a way to get out of the room, but she didn't know how. "I'm too cold to sleep in my . . . er . . . smalls," she muttered awkwardly. "I think I'll stay in my clothes."

Derek, seeing the back of her neck redden below the ill-cut locks of hair, felt a stab of pity for her. *Dash it, I've amused myself at her expense long enough,* he berated himself. The poor chit was in agony. He'd never intended to make her suffer. "I don't blame you, Addie," he said, padding to the fireplace in his stockinged feet and throwing another log on the flames. "This blasted room is too cold. Get under the covers, while I go down and find the innkeeper. We need another comforter or a couple of extra blankets."

"But . . . you're in your stockinged feet!"

Derek shrugged. "That doesn't matter." He opened the door and paused. "If you don't object, Addie, I think I may sit downstairs in the parlour and have a drink of home brew. I feel a sudden thirst. Don't wait up for me. I may be awhile."

Ada watched the door close behind him and breathed a sigh of relief. She was alone! Her solitude was only temporary, but she was grateful even for that brief respite. She lay down on the bed, blew out the candle on the bedside table, pulled the coverlet up to her neck and closed her eyes. Mr. Rutledge— Derek (*such a lovely name, Derek,* she murmured sleepily)— had inadvertently given her a wonderful idea! She would rest while he drank his ale and then, when he returned, *she* would be the one to be thirsty. She would say she wanted a drink of home brew, too, and would leave the room and simply not return. She would find someplace to hide until morning, at which time she would reappear with some excuse for her absence. She could not now think of any excuse, but perhaps by morning . . . by morning, she . . . by morning . . .

She sat up with a start, realizing with a clench of alarm that she'd fallen asleep. How long had she slept? she wondered in terror. It must have been *hours*, for the fire had dwindled down to mere embers. *Dear heaven*, she asked herself, *am I still alone?*

But she couldn't be alone. How long would it have taken a man to down a drink of ale? He must be lying there beside her! *Good God,* she thought, *I'm ruined!* What would Lionel say when he learned of this? And Mama! She would never be able to lift her head in society again.

She slid a shaking hand over the counterpane to the other side of the bed, trying timidly to determine just how far from her he was lying. Her hand crept farther and farther across the bed until it was fully extended, but she felt nothing under the flat counterpane. With a trembling intake of breath, she sat erect. Her eyes, becoming accustomed to the dim light thrown by the glowing embers, turned to the pillow beside hers. It was pristinely smooth. No one but she had been in this bed. Mr. Rutledge had not returned!

For a moment she felt nothing but a blessed relief. But after a while, it occurred to her to wonder what had become of Mr. Rutledge. Where on earth was he? Where could he be keeping himself for all these hours? Had something dreadful befallen him? She could not lie here in bed and tell herself that it was not her business, for the man *had* been her benefactor, no matter how hard she'd tried to deny it. And he would not be here but for her. She could not do less than go out and determine his whereabouts.

She slid out of bed. The room was so cold that even in her clothes she found herself shivering. She pulled her coat tightly around her. Then, lighting the candle, she crept in her stockinged feet from the room.

There was no sign of life in the upper hallway, so she started for the stairs. Below the candle's gleam the stairway looked forbiddingly dark. Nevertheless, she stole down. The taproom, too, was dark and empty, and there was no glimmer of light discernible in the back hallway where the kitchens were. The private parlour was the only other place to look. She pushed open the door and held the candle out before her. There, in an wing chair pushed up to the fire, was Mr. Rutledge. He was fast asleep, his feet propped up on the hearth, a lap robe over his knees and his head slumped down against the wing of the chair. Ada sighed in relief. The poor man must have decided to spend the night here in the chair rather than go up and endure her snoring!

Smiling broadly, she tiptoed to the chair and gently lifted the lap robe up over his shoulders. He sighed and snuggled cozily into its warmth, a small smile appearing at the corner of his mouth, as if he were having the most amusing of dreams. Suddenly his eyelids flickered, and he made a slight movement of his shoulders. She watched tensely, not breathing, until his dark lashes settled against his cheeks and he sank back into deep sleep again. Then he expelled a breath that was very like a snore. She wanted to laugh out loud. *Aha, Mr. Rutledge,* she said to herself, gazing down at his face that, in sleep, seemed suddenly very vulnerable and startlingly handsome, *it's you who's the snorer!*

He twisted his shoulders once more, turning his face into the wing of the chair so that she could not see anything more than his ear and a bit of lean cheek, and gave another snoring breath. *Derek, you dear,* she thought with a rush of gratitude and affection that she'd fought all day against feeling, *may you have the most wonderful of dreams!* Then she gave a gurgle of laughter as she added, *as long as you don't have them in my bed!*

And with that she tiptoed out, closed the door and returned to her deliciously solitary room.

Chapter Nine

By morning Ada had forcibly pushed the memory of the drama of the night before to the back of her mind, the fore-front of it being preoccupied with the real purpose for which she'd embarked on this escapade: the rescue of her brother. It was Stanley she had to think about, she reminded herself, not a handsome stranger with whom she'd almost but not quite spent the night.

It was a sunny morning, so bright that one might have thought the heavens were trying to atone for the dreariness of the day before. Ada, with her clothes dry and her face washed, faced the day with renewed optimism. She ran down the stairs with eager steps, said a cheerful, boyish good morn-ing to a housemaid and the innkeeper who were readying the taproom for the day and opened up the parlour door. To her surprise, she found Mr. Rutledge still asleep in his chair. She could not imagine how he managed to continue to sleep in that uncomfortable position while the noisy morning bustle was taking place outside the parlour door, but she did not have the heart to waken him.

She backed out the door stealthily and, crossing to the tap-room, asked Mr. Hewitt for some notepaper and a pen. As soon as these were provided, she sat down at one of the tap-room tables and scribbled a note (hoping that the scribbles were both masculine and legible) to the sleeping Mr. Rut-ledge. That done, she folded the sheet, gave it to the inn-keeper with instructions that it be delivered to Mr. Rutledge after he awakened and, after receiving from Mr. Hewitt the direction to the constable's abode, set off on her mission.

Derek woke not half an hour later, aching and stiff in every muscle of his body. His mood was foul. He wondered why he'd allowed himself to become involved in a situation that had nothing to do with him, that had thus far provided him with the most uncomfortable night of his life and that promised to come to no good end. The little chit dressed in boy's clothing would probably not find her brother in the gypsy camp after all, and he would have to try to console her—a hopeless task in itself, for the girl was certain to be inconsolable. Then, being a man of decency, he would have to deliver her back to her family before he could even *think* of continuing his journey home. *Good God!* he swore irritably as he plunged his face into the icy water of the lavabo that the innkeeper had provided for his morning ablutions, *how did I get myself into this stupid coil?*

He was about to go upstairs and roust the girl out of bed when Mr. Hewitt came in and gave him the note. *Now what?* Derek asked himself as he opened it.

Dear Mr. Rutledge, he read, *I write only to thank you for your kindness to me and to say good-bye. I know that it was tacitly understood yesterday that we would go to see the parish constable together this morning, but I hadn't the heart to wake you after having driven you from your bed last night because of my dreadful snoring. Besides, there is no reason for me to involve you any further in my affairs. I realize that you do not think me capable of managing matters on my own, but I assure you that you need feel no further responsibility for me, especially since I will have the constable at my side when I face the gypsies again. Therefore, tell your troublesome conscience to give me no further thought. Please accept my heartfelt gratitude for the efforts you have taken on my behalf, and accept my best wishes for your safe journey back to London. Yours most sincerely, Addison Smythe. Post Scriptum: I hope you will not take offense at my having paid Mr. Hewitt for the bedroom. Since you did not use it, it would not be fair of me to permit you to pay for it. A.S.*

Derek read the first sentence with a sense of annoyance. He snorted with amusement at her interpretation of his departure from the bedroom because of her "snoring," but by the time he finished he was much more irritated than amused. The blasted female was dismissing him! Had she no appreciation for him at all?

Second thought made him realize that he had no reason for irritation. The girl had generously given him a perfect opportunity to remove himself from this entanglement. She was offended by his offers of help, so the devil take her! Let her deal with the gypsies on her own, since she was so insistent that she wanted things that way!

But somehow he knew he wouldn't let himself be dismissed. He couldn't. Something inside him—something decidedly foolish!—was keeping him from turning his back on the girl. He was perfectly willing to admit that she was an intrepid chit, but she *was* a girl. He couldn't leave for London without first being certain she was safe at home; he would not be able to dismiss her from his mind if he didn't see this affair through to its conclusion.

Hating himself for this unwonted tendency toward benevolence, he hastily downed a cup of coffee (burning his throat in the process) and, with the same information from the innkeeper on the constable's location that the girl had been given, set out after her.

He found the place quite easily, for the constable, a Mr. Harry Walsh, lived in a small cottage (what Mr. Hewitt had described as bachelor's quarters) in the center of the town only a few steps from the Hart and Hare. The constable was still at breakfast when Derek was shown in by a dour, taciturn housekeeper. Mr. Walsh was a portly fellow, well past sixty, who greeted his new arrival with an indifferent nod and neither got up from the table nor invited him to sit down. He had evidently not even asked the girl to be seated, for she was standing at the table opposite him looking very chagrined.

The constable flicked a quick glance at Derek and then returned his attention to his eggs. But the girl's expression brightened at once. "Mr. Rutledge!" she exclaimed impulsively. "I'm so glad you've come."

"Are you indeed?" he retorted drily. "From the tone of your note, I would have surmised that you'd have preferred me in Timbuktu."

She dropped her eyes. "Well, that was before I discovered that this . . . this *mule* is unwilling to go with me. He will not be budged. He says he won't go to the gypsy camp again!"

"No, I won't," Mr Walsh muttered with his mouth full. A

blunt, independent fellow, the constable didn't believe in toadying. He was the sort who said and did as he liked. He'd held his position in the parish for so long that he no longer was impressed with its importance. Nor did he any longer believe in the formality of public office. Therefore, he continued to down his breakfast while Derek repeated the request, in very lordly tones, that he accompany them to the gypsy encampment.

Mr. Walsh made no response until his eggs had been devoured. Then he looked up at Derek and wiped his mouth with his sleeve. "Sorry, sir," he said, studying Derek carefully, "but there ain't nothin' in that camp t' find. Lord Farrington an' me, we did a thorough search. No point in upsettin' everything again."

"I'm Lord Farrington's . . . er . . . brother," Ada declared, throwing Derek a guilty glance, "and I want to look for myself."

Derek stared down at her with raised brows. "Farrington, eh?" he asked, more amused at this discovery of another deception than angry at it. "Not Smythe after all?"

She bit her lip. "I'll explain later. Meanwhile, can't you convince Mr. Walsh here to come with us? How can we search the camp without him?"

"Ye cin save yer breath, sir," the constable said, pouring himself a steaming cup of tea. "I ain't going to the camp, an' that's that. If ye don't mind showin' yersel's to the door, I'd like t' finish my breakfast in peace."

"I think you're the most unobliging rudesby, Mr. Walsh!" Ada exclaimed in irritation. "We're only requesting an hour or so of your time."

Derek frowned down at Mr. Walsh, equally irritated. The man was an independent sort who would not be budged without the prodding of someone in higher authority. Derek, as Viscount Esterbrook, had that authority, of course, but he was reluctant to reveal his identity in front of the girl. He wanted, for some reason not really clear to him, to keep his true identity secret until she revealed *her* true identity to him. So he remained silent while she argued fruitlessly with the constable, his mind racing about trying to find a way to talk to the fellow alone.

He soon hit on a plan. "I think, Addie," he said, taking her aside, "that you should leave this stubborn ox to me. Meanwhile, go and find the nearest livery stable and rent us some sort of equipage. A coach-and-four would be best, but a curricle and pair will do in a pinch."

"First of all, Mr. Rutledge—I mean, Derek—I don't see why you think you can deal better with Mr. Walsh than I can. And secondly, why on earth do we need a carriage? The camp is not more than two miles down the road."

"You, my lad, are the most provoking fellow I've ever encountered!" Derek said in disgust. "In the first place, you only a moment ago *asked* me to change Mr. Walsh's mind! Do you want me to try or don't you? And in the second place, I, for one, feel the need of a carriage. I see no reason to take the time to walk the two miles when it will be quicker to ride. Besides, when you've found your brother, I'll have to get on to London, and I've had quite enough of the stage. If you truly have objections to riding in it, you are quite free to walk. But do, like a good fellow, go and hire it. Dash it all, Addie, do as I suggest, this once!"

She opened her mouth to argue, met his eye and surrendered. "Oh, very well," she muttered and slammed out of the house. Derek, shaking his head, turned back to the constable. "*Now*, Mr. Walsh, we can speak freely." He leaned over the table and glared down into the constable's face. "Put down your cup, man, and pay attention! I am Viscount Esterbrook, and that young man is in my care. If he thinks it necessary to search the camp again, then we will search the camp again, do I make myself clear?"

The constable, startled, put down his cup. But he quickly recovered himself and looked up at his visitor suspiciously. He met the Viscount's eye for a long moment and then slowly rose to his feet. "Well, if ye truly *are* Viscount Esterbrook," he demanded querulously, "why didn't ye say so right off?"

"For reasons of my own, I don't want the young fellow to know my identity."

"An' how am I supposed to know y're tellin' *me* the truth, eh?" the constable asked bluntly.

"Will this do?" Derek put a hand to the inside pocket of his coat, removed a silver card case and pulled out a card.

The constable looked at it closely before handing it back. "Very well, yer lordship, that seems t' be proof enough. I'll put myself at yer disposal. I'll take ye to the camp, if ye insist, an' I'll try t' make those gypsy louts turn the place upside down fer ye. But it'll do no good. The missin' boy's not there. If he was, they wouldn'a let us search the other night."

"What do you mean, they wouldn't have let you search? You're the parish constable. Haven't you the right—?"

"Per'aps I 'ave, an' per'aps I 'aven't. Those gypsies, they 'ave papers, ye see. They *all* 'ave papers, every gypsy band I ever came on. Scrolls, sometimes, or old letters, with signatures of kings and nobles that they claim give 'em the right to camp an' to travel through the country. The papers 'ave seals, too. Don't know 'ow they come by 'em, or even if they're legal, but it's too much trouble to find out. Even the magistrates, they don' know if those papers mean anything. But unless we catch 'em committin' crimes, we let 'em be."

"But you searched them the other night, didn't you? With Lord Farrington?"

"Aye, we did. They didn't put up much of a fuss about it, either. Sometimes they fight us tooth an' nail, and sometimes they run off so fast you wonder 'ow they manage it. That's when they're guilty of somethin'. When they give in so easy, ye know ye won't find nothin'."

"And that's why you feel sure that this lad's little brother isn't among them?"

"That's right. I'm as sure about that as I'm sure there's tea in that pot."

Derek rubbed his chin thoughtfully. "If you're so sure they're innocent, then why do you suppose they refused to let the lad and me search the camp yesterday?"

"I didn't say they was innocent, yer lordship. I just said the boy's not there."

"Then why didn't they let us search?"

The constable shrugged. "It was rainin' yesterday, wasn't it? Per'aps they didn't like t' be disturbed in the rain."

Derek nodded and turned to the door. "Well, the gir—the lad won't be satisfied until he's searched the camp himself. I can't say I blame him. If it were *my* brother, I would wish to

see for myself. Come along, Mr. Walsh. I'll see to it that this
errand is worth your time. But remember, I'm Mr. Rutledge.
Don't call me your lordship."

They emerged from the cottage and found that Ada had
procured a carriage and a coachman. The equipage was rickety and shabby, but it was a covered coach and was drawn by
four decent horses. "Good lad!" Derek said, clapping the girl
on the shoulder. "Are you going to ride with us, or are you
still determined to walk?"

She gave him a withering look, and the three climbed
aboard. The constable occupied himself during the drive by
repeating in calm but irritating tones that this effort would be
an utter waste of time. Fortunately for Ada's nerves, they
arrived in short order at the gypsy camp.

The place was much livelier and cheerier than it had been
the day before. The gypsy pennons were flying in the breeze,
the wagon door-flaps were open, the women were sitting out-
doors in groups, and children romped about freely. There were
only three men to be seen, for, as Mr. Walsh explained drily,
most of them had gone to town to trade with or swindle the
townspeople. The three men who had stayed behind were sitting at a spindly table near one of the campfires, playing a
card game and betting on the outcome with stacks of unfamiliar silver coins. One of the three, Ada noted, was Stanley's
giant.

The constable noticed the giantlike gypsy, too. Telling
Derek and Ada to wait, he approached the giant and spoke to
him briefly. When he returned, he said to Derek, "That man's
their leader, y' see. He says we cin go on an' search, if we
want to. But it's all a bit too easy, if ye ask me. We won't find
nothin'."

They walked about the camp, completely ignored by the
gypsies. They looked in and under all the wagons, poked
through bundles of bedding, opened trunks and peered into
boxes. They found nothing. After they'd exhausted every possible hiding place, the constable drew them both behind a
garish yellow wagon out of sight of the seemingly indifferent
gypsies. "Y' see what I mean?" he asked. "It's just as I told
ye. If they 'ad somethin' t' hide, they'd 'ave given us more of
a fight before we started."

"I suppose you're right," Derek admitted, discouraged.

"If y're plannin' to stay any longer, they won't stop ye. But I 'ope ye'll excuse me. Ye've no need fer me, an' I ought to be gettin' back t' town."

"Go on," Derek agreed, surreptitiously slipping him some gold coins. "We can manage on our own. Thank you for your help, Mr. Walsh."

"Y're welcome, yer lor—sir." He turned to Ada and patted her shoulder with paternal sympathy. "I 'ope, Mr. Farrington, that ye find yer brother, but it's more'n likely the child's lost somewhere in the woods round 'is 'ome. That's what usually 'appens. Well . . . good luck to ye."

Derek watched the constable walk away. When he looked back at the girl, he couldn't miss the expression of desperation in her eyes. "The constable's right, Addie," he said gently. "There's nowhere left to search. Don't you think we'd better go, too?"

Ada nodded, too choked to trust herself to speak.

Derek put an arm about her shoulders. "Your elder brother might have found Stanley by this time, if Mr. Walsh is right that in most cases a lost child is found in the woods right near his home."

"No, n-not Stanley," Ada managed to answer, swallowing her tears in manly style. "He knows the woods too well."

"Since the boy's not here, you can't be *certain* he's not home and safe by this time," Derek insisted. "Let's go back to the carriage. I'll see you home."

"Home? To Farrington?" She flicked a surprised look up at him. "I can't let you do that. It's *miles* out of your way. Besides, I don't think I want to go just yet. I can't get over the conviction that Stanley was here."

"You're being foolish, you know. There's not a shred of evidence—"

A large red ball came rolling up to his feet at that moment, followed by a dirty little urchin in a pair of ragged knickers and a roughly woven shirt. The child stopped short at the sight of them and eyed his ball with frightened indecision. Derek bent down, picked up the ball and handed it to the child. When he stood up, he saw that the girl was staring at the child with widely distended eyes. "What *is* it?" he asked in sudden alarm.

"Look!" she gasped, pointing down.

Derek gaped at the child. "That can't be . . . it isn't *Stanley*, is it?"

"No, no!" Ada whispered hoarsely. "His *sash*—!"

Derek blinked at the wide sash of wine-red wool which was wound several times round the boy's waist. "His *sash*?" he asked bewilderedly.

But Ada was not paying any heed to him. She knelt down and grasped the child by the shoulders. "Where did you *come* by that?" she demanded breathlessly. "*Tell* me!"

The child kicked out at her, pulled out of her grasp and darted off. But Derek caught him by the collar at the back of his shirt and grasped him in a tight hold. "What about his sash?" he asked Ada over the wriggling child's head.

"It's not a sash. It's evidence! You said you wanted evidence and now you have it!

"But . . . what makes you think—?"

"It's a muffler! Don't you see? It's *Stanley's muffler*!"

Chapter Ten

Derek was truly startled. "Are you *sure*?" he asked dubiously, having been convinced by the constable that it was unlikely that Stanley had ever set foot in the gypsy camp.

Ada didn't answer. She merely got down on her knees beside the squirming child and, while Derek held him still, unwound the scarf from about his waist. "See for yourself," she said, holding the end of the muffler up to Derek's face. There, embroidered in white silk and standing out clearly against the wine-colored wool, were two intricately entwined initials, *S.F.*

"Good God!" Derek exclaimed.

"Make him tell us where he found it," Ada begged in a choked voice.

Derek, keeping a firm hold on the child's arms, set him on his feet. "All right, brat, *speak*! Where did you come by this?"

The child continued to squirm but would not open his mouth.

"Please, child," Ada pleaded, softened by the fear in the child's eyes, "it's terribly important! I promise you that no harm will come to you if you tell us the truth."

"On the other hand," Derek said with menacing coldness, "a great deal of harm will come to you if you don't!" He didn't feel so kindly to the child. As long as he'd believed that Stanley had never been with the gypsies, he'd felt little animosity toward them, but now his feelings underwent a marked change. Stanley Farrington *had* evidently been among them— the muffler was proof—and, if so, the situation was dire. If Stanley'd been here, where was he now? What had they done to him? For the first time since he'd crossed this girl's path, he considered the possibility that something truly evil might have

77

occurred. "If you *don't* tell us," he continued ominously, "we shall tie you hand and foot, and hand you over to the constable. What *he* might do to you, I can't say for certain, but I've heard he's quite adept at *skinning rabbits alive*."

"Derek!" Ada objected. "You needn't terrorize the child."

"I needn't coddle him, either. You do want to get to the bottom of this, don't you? Come on, brat! Speak to us!"

"Let the boy go," came a deep voice behind them. They looked up to find the gypsy giant looming over them.

Ada gasped, but Derek merely tucked the child under one arm and stood up. "Where is Stanley Farrington?" he asked the tall man in the same menacing tone he'd used to the child.

"Let the boy go, I say," the gypsy demanded, advancing on Derek menacingly.

"Not on your life," Derek said flatly. "Do you see the muffler my friend is holding? It belongs to his missing brother. This imp was wearing it. What have you to say to *that?*"

The tall gypsy stared at the muffler for a moment and then threw an angry, questioning look at the child. The child, who'd been peeping up at the gypsy man from under Derek's arm, made a crying sound and dropped his eyes. The gypsy, eyes blazing in fury at the child, uttered a curse under his breath.

"Well?" Derek prodded.

The gypsy hesitated for a moment, as if pondering alternatives. Then he threw up his hands in defeat and sank down on a ledge that ran along the back of the wagon. "Let the boy go, and I tell you," he muttered.

Derek shook his head. "First tell us. Then I'll let him go."

The gypsy giant shook his head, making the gold rings in his ears tremble. "It was mistake," he said apologetically. "Could not be helped."

"Then you *have* seen Stanley," Ada said tightly.

The man nodded. "He is little boy, freckles, hair like yours, yes?"

Ada nodded, holding her breath.

"Two days past he comes to watch dancing," the gypsy went on, crossing his arms over his chest and fixing his eyes on the ground. "Then he begins to play with children. We pay no mind to children playing. Village children—*gajo* children —they play much with our children, we take no notice. Sometimes they move on with us, no one cares."

"For some that may be true," Derek said darkly, "but it is not so for my friend. Go on, please. What happened when Stanley played with your children?"

"Then supper comes," the gypsy giant continued, "and he —this Stanley of yours—stays with one of our boys, Nanosh by name, and eats with him. Then Nanosh comes to me and says *gajo* boy is sick from our food. This is first I hear of him."

"Sick?" Ada cried in alarm.

"Sick in stomach. Not sickness to be frightened of. Goes away quick. A day or so sick, is all. But just at this time, nurse woman comes seeking little boy. From big mansion on hill. I see trouble coming. From this nurse woman, with boy sick, I think can come trouble. We Rom people, we no wish trouble with people from big mansion. I think to myself that it is wise to say nothing to nurse woman about boy. I plan later, when boy is better, to send him back. So we say nothing to nurse woman. Meanwhile, we put boy in *dunha*—how you say . . . featherbed?—and move south. Later that night, we make camp here. But then, lordship—little boy's other brother, the one older than you—he comes with riders and constable. Boy asleep but still sick. Now, I think will be *real* trouble, with lordship so angry and riders with him, and the constable. So we say 'No Stanley here. Never see Stanley.' We put Rom clothes on him, dirty his face, hide him in *dunha* with other children."

"I should have come," Ada moaned. "I would have recognized him. I told Lionel I should have come."

Derek patted her shoulder with his free hand but didn't take his eyes from the gypsy's face. "Very well, you hid him," he said to the gypsy impatiently. "But where is the boy *now*?"

"I not know."

"What do you *mean*, you 'not know'?" Derek demanded. "What did you do with him after Lord Farrington left?"

"Nothing. Nothing. Boy wakes up next day, feels better, runs off. Is not our business to care for *gajo* children."

"You lie!" Derek sneered. "You know where he is! You wouldn't have let him run off, knowing that when he was found he'd tell how you'd kidnapped him."

"I say all I know. Give me this boy now."

"I will, when you've told me the truth. *All* the truth. What did you do with Stanley after Lord Farrington left?"

"I say no more."

"Yes, you will, or there will be a great deal more trouble than you've ever known. We'll bring all of English law down on you. We now have the evidence—this muffler—to prove that you kidnapped a British child. Do you have any idea what can happen to you when English justice is meted out for the kidnapping of an English child of noble birth? Ah, I see you do. Then tell me the truth now, or I shall go to the nearest magistrate with my evidence of your crimes."

The giant peered up at him for a long moment. Then he rose slowly from his perch, turned on his heel and walked away. Ada made a movement to go after him, but Derek held her back. "He'll be back," he muttered. "Give him a moment to think."

As he expected, the gypsy promptly returned. "Give me child," he said, holding out his arms.

"Oh, remembered him, did you?" Derek asked drily. "I'll give him to you after you've told me what I want to know."

"I have no more to say. If you wish to keep child, keep him. Exchange for the one you lost."

"*Exchange!*" Ada gasped in horror. "Don't you care for this boy at all? What sort of man *are* you?"

The gypsy snorted. "I'm Rom. Rom do not set great value on children. Have plenty children. Too many."

"Well, we set value on ours," Derek said flatly. "We want our own. There will be no exchange. And I'm rapidly losing my patience. Tell us the truth, or we're off to see the magistrate . . . we and the muffler and this dirty little urchin here."

The giant glared at him. "You are only two, you and the Stanley child's brother there. And he not much bigger than a boy. I have *twenty-two strong men*. You no make threats to me or you vanish, too, like Stanley, from the face of the earth."

Derek was unmoved. "You are not so stupid as that. You know perfectly well that our disappearance would bring trouble upon you such as you've never experienced in your life. Not only does the constable know we're here, but also—"

"I make bargain," the gypsy cut in, suddenly taking on a more conciliatory air. "I tell you what I know, you let *vardo* —caravan—go away with no more questions, no more constables."

"I make no bargains with kidnappers and thieves," Derek answered promptly.

"Say you agree, Derek," Ada pleaded. "I want to know where Stanley is."

"I don't like such bargains," Derek muttered. "You can never make a good bargain with liars."

"Derek, *please*! Stanley may be sick. He may need help. We're wasting precious time standing about exchanging words with this man!"

Derek drew in a surrendering breath and fixed a narrowed eye on the gypsy's face. "Very well, I'll agree. But if we find that what you tell us is not true, then the bargain's off. I won't rest until I find you and put you and all your twenty-two men behind bars!"

"I will tell truth, but you will be angry. I sold the child."

"What?" Derek gasped.

"*Sold* him?" Ada cried.

"Too much danger to keep him. Everyone coming and looking for him. Lordship, constable, then you. Much trouble. Better for us to be rid of him."

Derek shuddered in fury. "You damnable bastard!" he muttered. Setting the gypsy child down and releasing his hold on the girl, he stepped forward with clenched fists.

The child darted away unheeded, while Ada caught Derek's arm. "Don't, Derek! Striking him won't help. Just find out who took Stanley."

"Well?" Derek asked the gypsy, feeling furious yet utterly helpless.

The gypsy shrugged. "I don't know name. Man from London. Says he needs little boys to work for him. Skinny fellow, half bald. Thing here—wart, you call it—on side of nose. Is all I have to tell you. Man from London."

"Oh, my God," Ada groaned in despair, dropping her head in her hands. "*London*! I'll *never* find him now!"

Chapter Eleven

Ada pulled her cap down so that the peak shielded her eyes and strode with sturdy courage back to where the coachman waited with the rented carriage, but Derek could see that she was completely unnerved. When they came up to it, she paused with her head lowered. Derek felt helpless to comfort her. "I can go back to Constable Walsh and tell him what we learned," he suggested quietly. "Or I can go directly to the nearest magistrate—"

"No. We gave our word."

"The devil with our word! Bargains made with kidnappers don't signify."

"It wouldn't help Stanley if the gypsies were tried and punished. Besides, by the time you brought the authorities back here, they'd have broken camp and gone. I have a distinct feeling that they're readying themselves right now to slip away."

"You're probably right. By the time we're a mile down the road they'll have disappeared."

She lifted her head. "I must thank you again, Mr. Rutledge," she said, putting out a hand bravely. "You've been more than kind to a chance acquaintance."

"Am I back to being Mr. Rutledge again?" he teased. "You may save your thanks, my lad, until we say good-bye. I'm going to take you back to your family. And speaking of your family, I suddenly remember that it is called Farrington, not Smythe." He looked down at her with taunting disapproval. "The gypsies, it seems, are not the only ones guilty of prevarication."

"I'm sorry, Derek. I didn't mean to prevaricate. It's just that when you asked me my name on the stage, I didn't think

83

it wise to reveal it to a stranger. It was a foolish precaution, I suppose. I just gave you the first name I could think of."

"Given name, too?" he asked, watching her face closely. "Is that a fabrication also?"

"Oh, no!" she said hurriedly, dropping her eyes. "Ad-Addie is what everyone calls me."

"Very well, then, Addie Farrington, I'm glad we've cleared up that matter. Now, shall we start out for—what was it I heard you call it? Farrington Park?"

She shook her head. "I'm not going back to Farrington Park."

His eyebrows lifted. "You're not?" Then, as the realization of her intention burst on him, his expression darkened and he glared at her in disgust. "I might have known! You're considering going to London, aren't you?"

"I'm not considering it. I'm going."

"Don't be a clunch! That's a ridiculous plan. You'll never find your Stanley in London. It's a bit larger than a gypsy camp, you know. You won't even know where to begin."

She glared back at him. "You needn't be so obnoxiously sure. I'll begin by looking for a man with a wart on the side of his nose."

"Oh, you will, will you? I wish you luck. There are only one million two hundred thousand people in London. I have no figures for you on what percentage of those have warts, but I'm willing to wager that the number is not inconsiderable."

She kicked glumly at the ground with the toe of her boot. "I didn't think it would be easy," she mumbled.

"But how do you propose to go about it, eh? Stand in the center of Piccadilly Circus and watch the world pass by?"

She flicked up an enigmatic glance. "Piccadilly Circus?"

"Good God!" he exclaimed, putting a hand to his forehead. "You've never heard of it, have you. You've never even *been* to London!"

"I'll learn my way about quickly enough," she said sullenly.

"You don't know what you're talking about! London stretches *ten miles* along the Thames. And it's probably three miles across from Southwark to Moorfields. It's the largest city in the world! I've lived there all my life, and I wouldn't claim to know my way about all of it."

"If you're trying to discourage me, Derek Rutledge, you're succeeding very well. But if you're trying to convince me to return to Farrington Park, you may save your breath. I may never find Stanley, but I shall die trying."

Derek expelled a hopeless breath and shook his head. "You are an intrepid little ch—lad, I'll grant you that," he said in reluctant admiration.

"You were about to say 'child,' weren't you?" she said furiously. "I've told you more than once that I'm nineteen. I wish you would stop treating me like an infant."

"I would, if you'd stop behaving like one. Any sensible nineteen-year-old would let me take him home."

"Is that so?" She looked up at him, suddenly earnest. "Would *you*?"

"What?'

"Answer me honestly, Derek. Would you, if *your* little eight-year-old brother had been abducted, give up and go home?"

"I?" He frowned over the question, the earnestness of her tone causing him to give his answer serious thought. "I suppose I wouldn't. But that argument doesn't hold for you, you know. I am, after all, a m—" He stopped himself just in time.

"Well, go on. You, after all, are a what?"

"A native Londoner," he said, recovering quickly. "And thirty-two years old."

"Oh?" She cocked her head and studied him with interest. "Thirty-two? As old as that?"

"Yes, you imp, as old as that."

She smiled. "I wouldn't have guessed it. You haven't even a grey hair."

"I suppose, you repulsive whelp, that you mean that as a compliment. But I would like to point out to you that *some* men of thirty-two—a very few, no doubt—have not yet reached decrepitude."

She giggled. "Obviously you are one of the fortunate ones. No one would ever call you decrepit."

"Thank you. Then, my lad, by virtue of the wisdom in this

not-quite-grey head, have I convinced you to return to Farrington Park?"

Her smile died at once. "No, Derek. I won't be deterred. I
can't, you see. Somewhere, my little brother is living in terrifying loneliness and bewilderment, and the only thing he can
cling to is the certainty—and I know it is a certainty for him
—that I am looking for him."

"Little Stanley knows you that well, does he?" Derek asked
softly. "Very well, then, climb aboard and let's get started for
London. If our driver knows his business, we can be in town
by bedtime."

She shook her head. "No, Derek. Thank you for the offer,
but I'll walk back to the inn and catch the stage."

"Confound it, Addie, must you quarrel about *everything*?"
he burst out in exasperation. "Get in without giving me another argument!"

"I don't mean to be quarrelsome, but there are all sorts of
reasons for me not to take further advantage of you. We are
strangers, after all. You are not beholden to me or responsible
for my welfare. You've already given me more kindness and
assistance than I can ever repay, and—"

"Are those your reasons?" he cut in. "They are not very
impressive, you know. See here, Addie, suppose I *admit* that
your concerns have cost me more time and effort than I'd
intended to spend. And suppose I further admit that I would
rather return to my own concerns than to continue to trouble
my head about yours. And suppose I leave you here with my
best wishes and take myself off. Do you know what the results
would be? I would sit huddled in a corner of this draughty
carriage and begin to wonder if you have enough of the soft to
pay for the stage. Then I would wonder if you knew enough
about London to look for lodgings in an acceptable neighborhood. And *then* I would wonder how you would go about your
search. And how you would manage to earn a living when
your blunt—which, no matter how plentiful, is bound to run
out before you've accomplished your aim—is gone. With
questions like these on my mind, I'd come home in a state of
nervous collapse! And what would be worse, this hair which
you say is so youthfully free of grey would have turned completely white!"

She had to smile. "Your conscience, again?"

"I'm afraid so."

She stared at him for a moment and then looked down at her boots. "What if I told you that I had plenty of blunt? And an aunt who lives in a perfectly respectable neighborhood who would be delighted to take me in?"

"I would not believe you. Let's be honest, lad. You haven't the foggiest idea of what's ahead of you. You don't even know what anything costs. Why, the innkeeper told me you didn't leave him half enough to pay for the bedroom."

"*What*?" Her head came up, her eyes flashing fire. "That blasted *thief*! I left him three-and-six!"

"A good bedroom goes for almost a guinea in London," Derek pointed out gently.

She gasped in innocent disbelief. "For *one night*?"

He shrugged. "How much blunt *have* you in your pockets? The truth, now."

She put her hand into the pocket of her breeches and pulled out some coins. "Two guineas, four shillings and thrupence," she admitted.

After a brief, meaningful glance at the coins in her palm, he threw open the door of the carriage. "Get in."

She put up her chin. "I won't take your charity. You admitted that I'm a nuisance to you, so please go without me. You can tell your conscience that I shall manage. I always have."

Derek had had enough. Without another word, he lifted her bodily and tossed her up into the coach. Then, with a signal to the coachman (who'd been sitting on the box listening to their every word), he climbed in after her, pulled the door closed and, climbing over her prostrate body, settled himself upon the seat.

The coach began to move. The girl-in-boy's-clothing lifted herself up from the floor and brushed herself off. "You realize, Derek Rutledge, that you're abducting me," she said, seating herself opposite him.

"Quite," Derek agreed coldly, crossing his arms over his chest and turning away from her to stare out the window.

There was a long pause. "I don't want you to think I'm not grateful," she said at last in a very small voice.

He snorted. "How could I possibly think that?"

"I don't know why you felt it necessary to do this," she went on. "You've already done more for me than anyone could possibly expect. I'm nothing but a stranger you encountered on the stage. Even the most benevolent of consciences could not be expected to go so far for a graceless lout like me."

"You *are* a graceless lout," Derek said, his unexpected agreement causing her to start in surprise, "so my conscience is no longer troubling itself about you."

"Isn't it? Then why is it prodding you to take me with you?"

"Not for your sake, my lad. You may take my word on that."

"Then for whom—?"

"For Stanley. My conscience has heard you describe him so often and so lovingly, he's become almost real. My conscience is making me do this for *him*."

Ada felt her throat sting with tears. "Do you know what I think, Derek?" she asked softly. "I think you have a lovely conscience. Hang it all, your conscience must be one of the most beautiful consciences in the world."

Chapter Twelve

Derek, lulled by the rocking of the carriage and the serenity of his beautiful conscience, soon fell asleep, but Ada had too much on her mind to doze. She had no idea what sort of adventure she was heading toward. Derek had kindly provided her with this transport, but when they arrived she would be on her own. Even if he offered her the hospitality of his home, she could not accept it. It seemed obvious that he was a bachelor, and she could not take residence, even for one night, in a bachelor's abode.

But where *could* she lodge? Was it true, she wondered, that a decent night's lodging would cost a whole guinea? How could she continue to search for Stanley without sufficient funds? And how was she to institute the search when she had no connections in London at all?

Well, that wasn't quite true. She had *one* connection. She couldn't ask Derek Rutledge to support her, but she could ask him to *advise* her. "Where *should* I start, Derek?" she asked aloud.

"What?" Derek grunted, startled awake.

"Oh! Were you asleep? I'm sorry. I didn't realize . . ."

"Then I'm evidently not a snorer," he laughed, sitting erect. "Did you ask me something?"

"Yes, I did. I was wondering where you might start if it were *you* doing the searching for Stanley."

He stretched and rubbed his eyes. "Bow Street, I think. I am acquainted with a magistrate or two. I'm certain we can persuade one of them to recommend a runner."

"Runner?"

"You *are* a country bumpkin. Haven't you heard of the Bow Street runners? They're a group of men working under the Bow Street magistrates. They investigate crimes and bring criminals to justice. A very knowing group of men, the runners, acquainted with all sorts of London felons."

"Really, Derek?" she asked, brightening. "That's very promising! Why, one of them might know the man with the wart!"

"I wouldn't raise my hopes as high as *that,* if I were you."

"I can't help it. If I can talk to a runner right away, and if he can lead me to the man with the wart, then I might find Stanley almost at once, and I won't have to worry about all the things you've made me worry about."

"Such as—?"

"Such as proper lodging and earning blunt and standing in Piccadilly Circus to watch the world go by."

"You needn't worry about those things in any case. I have worked out a solution for all those problems."

"Have you indeed?" She drew herself up proudly. "I may have permitted you to provide me with transport, Derek Rutledge, but that doesn't mean I've turned over the control of my *life* to you!"

He eyed her warily. "You're not going to get on your high ropes again, are you? Because if that is your intention, then *I* intend to go back to sleep."

"I don't intend to get on my high ropes. But that doesn't mean I will permit you to order me about as if I were a . . . a . . . helpless *girl*!"

"Now, really, Addie," Derek objected, "is that quite fair? Have I ever, in any of our encounters, treated you like a helpless girl? I have followed you about from pillar to post, doing your bidding for two whole days, obeying your orders and taking your suggestions and obliging you in every possible—"

"Oh, rubbish!" she cut in impatiently. "You fought my battle with the ostler, didn't you? Isn't *that* something you would do for a helpless girl?"

"It's something I would do even for a helpless *cat*! Come now, Addie, let's cease this silly conversation."

"Do you know that you have an irritating habit of cutting off conversation whenever you're the one losing points? I'm beginning to think, Mr. Derek Rutledge, that your nature—

with the exception of your conscience, of course—is very devious."

"Devious? Because I have a solution for your problems?"

"Yes. Devious and manipulative. I can solve my own problems, thank you."

"Can you indeed? Then tell me where, for example, you intend to stay tonight."

She tossed her head proudly. "I'll find some decent lodgings, don't you fret! I can pay the required guinea."

"Would it be devious and manipulative of me to propose a better solution? I thought you could save your much-needed blunt and still be quite comfortable if you put up at my—"

"*No*! You may stop *right there*!" She'd suspected all along that he would sooner or later offer to let her stay with him in London, and she'd been bracing herself for the suggestion throughout this conversation. She knew she'd have to refuse the offer, generous though it was. But he was certain to point out that she hadn't sufficient funds to remain in decent lodgings for more than one night. How was she to respond to that? She'd have to answer him somehow. She could not, under any circumstances, take up lodgings with a bachelor! "I *knew* you would offer to put me up in your quarters," she burst out nervously. "I knew it! Well, I'll tell you right now that I *won't*! You've manipulated me into agreeing with every suggestion you've made since the first moment we met, but *this* time I am firm! I will *not* stay with you, and *that* is *final*!"

"But, Addie," he said with bland innocence, "I had no intention of asking you to stay with me."

"What?" she asked, taken aback.

"None at all. It's your snoring," he said apologetically. "The walls of my bedrooms are thin, and I'm afraid I'd hear you snoring even if I put you in the farthest room down the hall."

She blinked at him. "You were *not* going to invite me to stay with you tonight? Then what—?"

"You interrupted me before I'd finished. I was about to suggest that you put up at my *mother's* house."

"Your *mother's*—?" she gasped.

"It's a house full of females, of course—abigails and hairdressers and housemaids and such—and I know how repugnant that is to a mettlesome young buck like you, but the butler can be counted on to assist you in dressing when you need him, and the house is so large that Mama can put you on the third floor where there is no one near enough to hear you snore."

"Your *mother's* house!" she breathed yearningly. "What a lovely idea!"

"Is it *really*!" he muttered drily. "Not devious and manipulative?"

"Well, I . . . I . . ." She looked across at him hesitantly. "But you haven't even asked her. Perhaps she will not wish to take in a stranger . . . especially a shabby-looking fellow like me."

"My mother is an easygoing sort. She's often housed friends of mine when they've come in to town. Of course, you may have to permit my man McTeague to provide you with a couple of more suitable coats. And Mama will, I'm certain, order you to have a more stylish haircut, but otherwise I think she'll find you perfectly unobjectionable."

Ada's brows knit, and she peered intently at the man seated opposite. "I say, Derek," she asked abruptly, "are you and your family very rich?"

He was startled into a loud guffaw. "Rich enough to be able to put up a friend from time to time, if that's what's worrying you. In fact, we can easily afford to let you stay in my mother's house for however long you need lodgings."

"That, Derek, is the kindest thing you've yet offered me," she murmured, abashed and completely overwhelmed.

"Do I take it, then, that you'll accept the invitation?"

"Yes, if your mother is indeed willing. Th-Thank you!"

"Well! Did I really hear a 'yes'? Wonders will never cease! I hope, Addie Farrington, that, having made one concession, you are now ready to make another."

"What concession is that?" she asked suspiciously.

"Concede that you were exaggerating when you called me devious and manipulative."

"I'm not sure I can," she said with a little smile.

"What?" He drew himself up in mock offense. "After I've solved all your London problems for you?"

"Yes, you've been very, very generous. But, Mr. Derek

Rutledge, isn't it possible for a man to be generous and devious, too?"

He rubbed his chin ruefully. "It may be possible. Perhaps I am devious. There's one thing, at least, about which I've been devious. Your calling me *Mr.* Derek Rutledge reminds me that it is a matter on which I'd best be forthcoming before the truth is revealed to you by someone at my mother's house."

"Oh? Are you saying you've been dishonest with me? You are not Mr. Rutledge?"

"Not entirely. I omitted the rest of the name. There's a title added to it, that's all. Viscount Esterbrook. Like you, I didn't think it appropriate to reveal it to strangers on the stage. And later there was no opportunity. I hope you'll forgive me for any implied pretense."

"Of course, my lord. As you must forgive me for any implied disrespect by not calling you your lordship all this time."

He raised a reproving eyebrow. "You're not going to start 'my lord'ing me now, are you? Derek *is* my name to my friends."

"Thank you, my lord. I shall remember that when I'm feeling friendly toward you."

"Then I take it you aren't feeling friendly toward me now?"

"Not very. It's embarrassing to think that your little 'omission' caused me to treat a viscount in so informal a style."

"Good God, Addie, what balderdash! One would think you a little urchin from the streets. Your brother is Lord Farrington. What would you say if I began 'my lord'ing you?"

"You can't. I'm only an 'honorable.'"

He threw her a scathing look. "You do have an answer for everything, don't you! By the way, now that I think of it, for the brother of a peer of the realm, you wear the shabbiest clothes. Is that how you dress at home?"

She glanced down at her wrinkled, worn breeches and colored. "No, not as badly as this. I ran off, remember? I thought it better to hide my identity. Dressing like a stableboy seemed the best solution."

"I see. I'm glad you told me, for I was beginning to fear that your brother was a miser."

"No. My brother has faults, but that's not one of them."

"I'm glad to hear it. That, by the way, brings to mind another—"

But at that moment Ada's attention was distracted by something outside the carriage window. The day was rapidly darkening, and her eye was caught by an amazing number of glimmering lights. "Good heavens, what's *that*?" she cried, pressing her nose against the pane.

"What?" Derek asked, looking out on the darkened landscape.

"All those lights!"

He laughed. "Those, my country bumpkin, are houses. They mark the outskirts of London."

"Outskirts? But there are *hundreds* of them! When I look out of the windows at Farrington Park, I scarcely see a light!"

"You'll soon be seeing thousands of lights. Hundreds of thousands. I did try to warn you, you know."

"Oh, *my*!" she gasped, awed.

"I know you find the prospect fascinating, my lad, but take my word that you will soon see much more awesome sights. Meanwhile, may I have your attention for a moment more? I was about to introduce a subject of importance." He paused as she turned away from the window with a quizzical expression. "I know you'll say it's none of my business, Addie, but I think you should write a note to your mother at Farrington Park and tell her that you're safe. It's bad enough that your family has had to suffer the loss of Stanley, but to add to that the worry about *your* whereabouts is the outside of enough."

"They're not suffering over me," Ada muttered bitterly. "Mama has made a career of suffering since Papa died, so one more bit of suffering will hardly matter. And as for Lionel, he and his wife are expecting a baby, and *that*, I assure you, is of much greater concern than my disappearance."

"Nevertheless, I think you should write to them," Derek urged, struck with sympathy for the poor girl's life in such an unloving household as she described. He could see now why she and her little brother had formed so close an attachment. He had to admit, for the first time since the chit had come his way, that he was glad he'd tried to help her find him. It would give him enormous satisfaction to be able to assist in bringing brother and sister back together again. "You needn't give your family your direction, you know—or even tell them you're in London, if that is what you wish—but you can reassure them that you're safe."

Ada sighed. "I admit you're right in that. Very well, I suppose there's no harm in telling them I'm safe. As for giving them my direction, however, that's the *last* thing I want them to know."

"Suit yourself on that score, my g—lad. I promise that your secret is safe with me." He paused for a moment, studying her speculatively. This would be an appropriate time, he thought, for her to reveal her true identity. Now that she was to be ensconced safely in his mother's house, there was no real reason for her masquerade. There was no need for it now. She had him to act as protector, after all. They could as easily search for Stanley if she were in female garb. And he would be relieved of the effort of pretense. Guarding his tongue and keeping himself from calling her "my girl" was becoming a chore. Besides, she was such an adorable innocent that, if she admitted to being a female, he might very well give in to temptation and indulge in a little flirtation. Pretending that he took her for a boy was becoming more difficult by the minute. "I'm glad we've been able to have this honest exchange," he said with what he hoped was an encouraging smile. "I don't like secrets between friends, do you?"

She bit her lip. "No. Of course not."

"You don't have any other secrets to reveal, do you, Addie?" he prodded.

She tried to meet his eye but couldn't. "No, Derek," she said, stuffing her hands in her pockets as she'd seen boys do and fixing her eyes on the toes of her boots. "Hang it all, I haven't a secret in the world."

Derek, swallowing his disappointment, turned to the window. "In that case," he said with all the cheerfulness he could muster, "you may as well look at the sights again. We've just passed through Waltham. London, in all its nighttime splendor, lies just beyond the horizon."

Chapter Thirteen

Lady Rutledge's head bobbed under her beribboned nightcap as she blinked in astonishment at the shabby, unkempt lad that her son had brought to her drawing room at such an ungodly hour. *Where on earth,* she asked herself, *did Derek manage to pick up so scruffy, immature and unfitting a companion?* But aloud she merely uttered a pleasant how-de-do and, after pulling her ruffled dressing gown more tightly over her night-dress, permitted the boy to bow over her hand. Her head was in a muddle because Derek had ordered Lymber, her butler, to wake her from the soundest of sleeps just to introduce her to this seedy lad, so she was not at all sure she'd heard correctly. Had Derek really asked her to put the boy up?

"I knew you would have no objections, Mama," Derek was saying, looking at her pointedly. "It's his first time in town, you see, and I was certain you wouldn't wish to have him lodge with strangers."

"No, of course not," Lady Rutledge murmured, acceding to the unspoken plea in her son's eyes. "Delighted to have you, Mr . . . er . . ."

"Farrington," Derek said quickly. "Addison Farrington."

"Farrington?" Lady Rutledge echoed in surprise. "Not one of the Suffolk Farringtons?"

"Well, y-yes, ma'am," Ada said hesitantly.

"Heavens!" she exclaimed, eyeing Ada's stableboy coat in amazement. "You can't be . . . you're much too young to be *Lord* Farrington? The one who wed Lydia Marchbanks?"

"Of course he isn't Lord Farrington, Mama," Derek said with a grin. "Addie tells me he's only an 'honorable.'"

"Lord Farrington is my elder brother, your ladyship," Ada explained, throwing Derek a withering glance.

"I see," Lady Rutledge said, but she didn't see at all. What was her son doing with a boy who looked to be no more than sixteen? And why was a son of the Farrington family of Suffolk (who were wealthy enough to have thrown the season's most elaborate wedding a few years ago) wearing a shamefully shabby coat and the most ragged pair of breeches she'd ever laid eyes on? Besides, her son had a perfectly good town house of his own, not ten minutes walk from this place. Why hadn't he put his friend up there? Derek's living quarters were as uncluttered and masculine as hers were baroquely feminine. Wouldn't the boy feel more comfortable in those more manly surroundings? There was something peculiar about this business, but she knew that her son must have his reasons for behaving so strangely. And sensing that this might not be the proper time to discuss these matters, she decided merely to do as Derek asked. She gave the intruders a strained smile. "There seems to be a great deal we can chat about, Mr. Farrington, but I suspect that you both are exhausted after your long ride. We'll continue our conversation tomorrow, when you are rested. Right now, I give you leave to retire. I'll have Lymber show you up to your bedroom. The blue room, I think, would be most comfortable for you."

"No, no, Mama," Derek laughed. "The blue room is just across from your bedroom. If I were you, I'd put him on the third floor. He snores, you know."

"*Really,* Derek," his mother said reprovingly, "you can be the most dreadful rudesby! Third floor indeed! Only the servants sleep up there."

"I don't mind, my lady," Ada said earnestly. "I'm sure I'd be perfectly content in the servants' quarters."

"Nonsense, Mr. Farrington. You mustn't mind Derek. He says the most shocking things sometimes. As if a lad of sixteen snores!"

"But I'm nineteen, ma'am," Ada corrected.

"*Nineteen*? Heavens, fancy that! I would never have guessed—!" She rubbed her eyes and blinked at the smooth-skinned face of the boy before her. Was Derek playing some sort of trick on her, she wondered? Nineteen, indeed! If that boy was nineteen, she was sadly in need of spectacles. But this was not the time to dwell on the matter. There would be plenty of time to sort things out on the morrow. In the meantime, all she wanted to do was to get the fellow off to bed. "Well, even at nineteen a young man isn't likely to snore," she remarked, waving her hand as if to sweep the whole matter out of the way. "Besides, how would Derek know a thing like that? He hasn't slept beside you, has he?"

Ada, conscious that Derek was attending her response with an air of decided curiosity, felt her neck grow hot. "Well . . . er . . . no, my lady, not . . . exactly. But—"

"You mustn't let my son twit you, Mr. Farrington. He can be the most dreadful tease. I'm sure you don't snore. And even if you did, I wouldn't hear you. I sleep like a baby." She gave her son an icy glare. "When I'm given the chance, of course."

The butler presented himself at that moment, and her ladyship instructed him to ready the blue bedroom. When Lymber learned that their guest had no baggage, he revealed not a sign of dismay. "Don't worry, your ladyship," he assured his mistress, "we'll find a nightshirt for the lad." His voice revealed only the slightest touch of irony when he added, "Somewhere."

After an exchange of polite goodnights, Ada followed Lymber to the door. "Don't forget, Addie," Derek called after her, "you have a letter to write."

"Yes, I'll take care of it," Ada said, waving her hand at him reassuringly. She would write home that very night, she decided, and thus relieve her mother's mind of any worry on her behalf, but she would be careful to give the family at home no clue to her whereabouts. She did not want anyone to come to London seeking her and thus prevent her from accomplishing the one goal in her life that she was determined to achieve.

As soon as Lymber and the new houseguest left the room, Derek turned to his mother and kissed her cheek. "Mama, you're a great gun! Thank you!"

She pushed him away in annoyance. "Never mind the butter sauce, you jackanapes," she said querulously. "Where have you *been*? McTeague and I have been at our wits' end since he came home yesterday and learned you hadn't yet arrived. He said you should have been home before him."

"I was deflected *en route*, but it was nothing to cause you concern, I assure you."

"Easy for you to say, you heartless cad! You care nothing at all for the worry you cause me!"

"If you were worried, I'm truly sorry, ma'am. The delay was unavoidable."

"A delay caused by that peculiar young fellow you've foisted on me, I suppose."

"If you're fishing for information, Mama, you may as well cut line. I've no desire to go into details about Addie at this late hour. With your permission, my love, I'll take myself off to my place and relieve McTeague's mind."

"You will do no such thing!" his mother snapped. "I have a few words to say to you first."

"If they concern Addie Farrington, you needn't bother. I promise you the ch—fellow will be not the least trouble to you. As long as you've provided him with a place to sleep, I'll provide all the rest—clothes, meals, companionship, etcetera, I promise."

His mother narrowed her eyes suspiciously. "What sort of deep game are you playing, Derek? You're not the sort who'd spend his time squiring a young boy of nineteen about town."

"No? Well, perhaps you don't know me as well as you think you do," he said flippantly as he made his way to the door. "Goodnight, ma'am."

"Goodnight me no goodnights!" Lady Rutledge ordered. "Come back here and sit down! The words I have to say to you have nothing to do with the Farrington boy. They have to do with Cynthia Chadwick."

Derek stopped in his tracks. "Good God! Cynthia! I'd forgotten all about her." He turned back to his mother with a wary look. "Perhaps I'd *better* sit down."

His mother glared at him while he sank down on her striped-satin sofa. "I would appreciate an explanation, Derek," she said icily when he'd settled himself. "How *could* you have told the Chadwicks that you had to return to town because I was ill?"

He dropped his eyes like a schoolboy caught cheating. "Did McTeague tell you that?"

"No. Cynthia did."

"Cynthia? I thought she and her parents were fixed at Chadwick Manor for a fortnight?"

"So they would have been, if you hadn't lied to them. She and her parents hurried back from Lincolnshire as soon as you'd gone. They wanted to assist you in *taking care of me!*"

"Oh, no!" Derek groaned, wincing.

"You needn't look so stricken. I didn't fail you. I told them I'd made a miraculous recovery. Chest pains, I said, that frightened me enough to send for you but that left as quickly as they came."

He took a deep breath in relief. "I say, Mama, you *are* a great gun!"

"That's more than I can say for you, you make-bait! Why did you *do* such a thing?"

"Tell the Chadwicks that rapper, you mean? Mama, if you'd been there, you'd understand. They are *insufferable*. Formal to a fault. After two days I found I couldn't bear it."

"Really Derek, I don't understand you! I know the Chadwicks are a little stiff, but that's no excuse for—"

"A *little* stiff! You don't know what you're saying, Mama. You'd not have believed it if you'd seen it for yourself. Why, they dine in full regalia every night, they set their *breakfast* table with gold plate, they dress for riding as if the bridle path at Chadwick Manor were Hyde Park, and they're as stiff in their conversation as diplomats in negotiation. For all the ostentation they displayed, one would have thought Prinny himself were in residence! If that's how they conduct themselves in the *country*, I shudder to think how life with them might be in town."

"As bad as that, eh?" Lady Rutledge's brow knit worriedly as she sank down upon an armchair opposite him. "That will be a bit hard on you in the future, I'm afraid. I suppose the best way to deal with the problem is to tell Cynthia, after you're wed of course, to keep them out of your way as much as possible."

"After I'm *wed*?" He gaped at his mother in disbelief. "No, no, Mama, you don't understand," he said, rising slowly from the sofa and looking down at her. "Under no circumstances will I wed Cynthia Chadwick."

She blinked up at him. "What do you mean? You *must* wed her!"

"Indeed? And *why* must I, pray?"

"Because . . . because the girl *expects* it, that's why! You liked her well enough when I introduced you, didn't you? And when you took her driving and to the opera and to the ball at Holland House, I didn't hear you say a word in criticism of her. Come now, Derek, don't set yourself against the girl because of how her parents behaved in Lincolnshire. You won't be marrying her parents."

"When I took her driving and to Holland House, I didn't realize that she is *exactly like* her parents! Good God, Mama, what have I done to raise her expectations? I never did offer for her, you know. The trip to Lincolnshire had one thing to recommend it—it saved me from *that*, at least!"

Lady Rutledge began to wring her hands. "But you *almost* offered, don't you see? You were invited to Chadwick Manor for that purpose. And when you departed so abruptly, it was supposedly to care for *me*, not to break with *her*. So she still expects you to offer."

"The devil take her expectations!" Derek burst out angrily. "Damnation, ma'am, you're my *mother*! You don't wish to see me shackled to a rigid pomposity like that, do you?"

"No, of course not, if you feel like that about her," Lady Rutledge said unhappily. "But you can't cry off, my love! It isn't done! If you do, everyone will say that my son is a cad, a heartless rake and *no gentleman*!"

Derek ran a hand through his dishevelled hair. "But, dash it all, Mama, I don't have to cry off! I didn't make an *offer*!"

"Technically, I suppose that's true. But I'm afraid that expectations were raised too high before you left for Lincolnshire." She dropped her head in her hands. "It's all my fault, dearest," she moaned. "I'm the one who suggested to Lady Chadwick that they invite you."

"What difference does that make? Since when does an invitation to a country house presuppose a betrothal?"

She looked up at her son with brimming eyes. "Don't you see, dearest? Once you accepted the invitation, everyone expected you to make her an offer. The Chadwicks expected it, I expected it and every gossip in town expected it." Her face seemed to collapse as two tears rolled down her cheeks. "I never dreamed I w-was trapping you into a l-life of m-misery!"

"Don't cry, Mama," he said, her tears softening his temper. "You didn't trap me. I won't be trapped There must be a way to escape while remaining within the bounds of propriety." He bent down, kissed her cheek again and strode to the door. "Don't trouble yourself about this, my love. I'll deal with it. And I won't do anything that will cause your friends to say I'm not a gentleman. But if I *do* manage to extricate myself from this coil, I want this experience to be a lesson to you. Unless you can find me a girl like Addie, *don't ever make any more matches for me*!"

Lady Rutledge, in the midst of dabbing her cheeks with the lace ruffle of her sleeve, paused and stared at the door closing behind him. "What did he say?" she muttered. "A *girl* like *Addie*? Whatever did she mean by *that*?"

Chapter Fourteen

McTeague was full of questions as he helped Derek off with his coat. "Where've ye been, me lord? Why didn't ye return yesterday on the stage? Did I or did I not see ye take the stage at the Green Gander with me own eyes? Why did ye get off? An' what happened to the little chit in boy's clothing that boarded the stage with ye? Is she the reason y're so late? An'—Och, begorra! What happened to this coat? It looks as if ye slept in it!"

"Enough, McTeague. I'll tell you all in due course. First, get me a drink of brandy, will you? I'll have it in the sitting room before the fire. You've no idea how I've longed to sit in my own sitting room in my own easy chair before my own fire!"

McTeague brought him the drink and perched on the hearth. "It's the girl delayed ye, didn't she, me lord? I'd wager a monkey on it."

"And you'd win, too," Derek grinned. "She's a most amazing female, McTeague. She never once asked for my help. She had to face all sorts of difficult situations, but she never once let on that she's a girl. Bluffed her way through like a Trojan." Derek took a sip of his brandy and eyed his valet over the top of his glass. "I've deposited her at my mother's."

"*What*? Och, begorra! Are ye sayin' y're still involved with her?"

"Involved? I wouldn't call it involved. I'm just giving her a bit of assistance. She's trying to locate her little brother who's been abducted and is somewhere in London. She doesn't have an inkling of how to go about it, so she has need of some help.

103

I'll simply get the runners involved. It won't amount to much effort on my part."

"Won't amount to much effort? Have ye lost yer wits? Findin' a little tyke in this city might take months!"

"Oh, I wouldn't say that. We have a lead or two."

"Have ye now? A lead or two, ye say? Well, good luck, me lord. We'll see how much effort it all amounts to, won't we?"

Derek frowned at him in annoyance. "I can do without your sarcasm, McTeague. I'll admit it may be a nuisance, but what could I do? Leave her to search through a strange city all alone? I am a man of conscience, after all."

"Y' don't say! A man of conscience, are ye? Well, let's see how yer conscience assists ye when a certain ladybird, Miss Polly Stanhope, finds out yer squirin' another young female round town. She was in enough of a rage when she thought ye was gettin' yerself betrothed to Miss Chadwick. It took all me powers o' persuasion t' convince her it was all gossip."

"So Polly's been here already, has she? That's another female I'll have to deal with," Derek muttered.

"Ye've still another, I'm sorry t' tell ye. Miss Chadwick an' her mother stopped in. Twice! I'm t' tell ye they're expectin' ye t' call on 'em at yer earliest convenience. Begorra, fer a gent who thinks of himself as uninvolved, me lord, ye do have an abundance o' females hangin' about."

"So it seems. I'll have to think of what to do with each one of them, and soon," Derek said, forcibly dismissing them from his mind. The more immediate problem was Addie, who by morning would have to face his mother and the London world and who was not yet properly prepared for it. "In the meantime McTeague," he said, sipping his brandy absently, "we've got to do something about Addie's wardrobe."

"We, I take it, means *me*, me lord? An' Addie is the name o' the girl from the Green Gander?"

Derek nodded. "Right as usual, McTeague. You are a quick one! Her clothes will be a real problem, you see, because we certainly can't take her round to Weston's to be measured and fitted. If she takes off her coat, they'd be bound to notice her . . . er . . . figure, wouldn't they?"

"I expect so. If she *has* a figure."

"Oh, she has one. I noticed it quite particularly when she

came into the inn." He rubbed his chin thoughtfully. "I wonder how she manages to hide it, for one would think, even under a coat, that—"

"She does it by strappin' herself round her chest with bands of cloth, I expect," McTeague offered. "To flatten herself out, y'see."

Derek eyed him with real admiration. "How on earth did you know that, McTeague?"

The valet shrugged. "I once was what you might call close friends with an actress. Saw her play a boy on stage an' couldn't believe it was her. After the performance she . . . well, she showed me how it was done."

"McTeague," Derek grinned, "you are a constant source of pleasure and amazement to me. It occurs to me that, ingenious as you are, you might find a way to clothe Addie without taking measurements. Do you think you can do it?"

"I think I cin manage without measurements," McTeague murmured, already turning over in his mind various possible solutions to the problem. His annoyance with his master's involvement with yet another female was quickly being dissipated by the pleasure he took in accepting the challenge of solving the knotty problem his lordship had tossed at him. "I'll guess at the measures an' make the necessary adjustments meself once I've seen the clothes on her. Leave it to me, me lord."

"I knew I could count on you, McTeague," Derek said contentedly. "I've never known you not to come through." He finished his drink, rose from his chair and yawned. "If there's anything more inviting than my own chair at my own fireside, it's my own bed. I'm off, old fellow. Don't bother to come up. I'll manage on my own."

"Will ye indeed?" McTeague sneered. "Boots, too?"

"Boots, too. If Addie can remove hers by herself, I don't see why I can't."

"Addie, again?" McTeague muttered, peering at his lordship closely. "Takes off her own boots, does she? An' how do ye come to know *that,* me lord?"

Derek laughed. "Never mind how I know. You don't have to be privy to everything. By the way, old man, you'll have to trim her hair, too."

"I know that, me lord," McTeague muttered, picking up the brandy glass and heading toward the kitchen. "I *saw* her hair."

"That's right, you did. Speaking of the hair, did you take a lock of it from the basket, as I asked you to?"

"Aye, I did that. Have it right here." He glanced over his shoulder with a curious glint in his eye. "Want it, do ye?"

"Yes, Please."

"Will ye say it's impertinent if I ask ye what for?"

"Yes, you gamecock, very impertinent. But if you must know, I want to put it in my watch-lid."

"In yer watch-lid, eh?" the valet asked mockingly, handing him the envelope in which he'd stored the hair.

Derek's eyebrows rose. "I don't see why you're taking that tone. It's for good luck, that's all."

McTeague laughed. "Begorra, what else could it be fer?"

Derek threw him a glare and started up the stairs. "I sometimes wonder what it would be like to have a man who kept a civil tongue in his head," he murmured with ironic longing. "Goodnight, McTeague."

"Goodnight, me lord. I suppose we'll *both* be dreamin' o' reddish hair."

"What?" Derek looked over his shoulder at his valet curiously. "What do you mean by *that*?"

"I mean, me lord, that *I'll* be dreamin' of it because ye've given me the impossible task of makin' it presentable. An' *ye'll* be dreamin' of it because y're smitten."

"*Smitten*? Good God, McTeague, whatever gave you so ridiculous an idea! Just because I'm using her hair as a lucky charm? The chit's barely nineteen. Don't be an idiot! Goodnight."

McTeague looked after him as he disappeared up the stairs. "I ain't the idiot," he shouted up the stairs. "I know a man who's smitten when I see one." And shaking his head over the peculiar blindness of mankind in general and Derek Rutledge in particular, he made his way to the kitchen.

Chapter Fifteen

Ada was standing in the rain, watching a group of gypsy children dance in a circle. In the center of the circle stood the tall gypsy, snapping a whip at the ground. Suddenly his whip lashed out with a cracking sound and encircled one of the children. It was a child with a very dirty face. Slowly the gypsy reined the child into the center of the ring. "Dance!" he ordered.

"I c-can't d-dance," the child whimpered, beginning to cry. He pulled off the yellow bandana in order to use it to wipe his tears. Under the bandana was a head of red-gold curls.

"Stanley!" Ada cried, trying to get through the crowd that surrounded the dancers. "Let me through! It's Stanley!"

"Ada!" Stanley whimpered, reaching out his arms.

But she couldn't get through to him. The crowd kept getting in the way, and she stood completely surrounded, watching helplessly as his tears made two tracks of white through the dirt on his face.

"Mr. Farrington," the gypsy-giant shouted, snapping his whip with a peculiar knocking sound, "dance! Do you hear me, Mr. Farrington? Do you hear me—?"

"Do you hear me, Mr. Farrington?"

Ada sat up in bed with a gasp. She'd been dreaming!

The knocking on the door that had wakened her continued. "Do you hear me, Mr. Farrington?" said a deep voice outside her door. "It's McTeague, Lord Esterbrook's man. Are ye awake?"

Ada slipped out of bed and, shivering, ran barefoot to the door. "*Who* is it?"

"McTeague, Mi—Sir. Lord Esterbrook's man. He sent me t' assist ye this mornin'."

107

Ada, still groggy from sleep, looked down at herself nervously. The nightshirt Lady Rutledge's butler had provided hung so loosely on her that nothing of her figure was revealed, and last night, even though she'd dismissed the butler and undressed herself in private, she'd not unbound her chest. Therefore, she decided, she was probably fit to be seen. She opened the door. A portly man with an upturned nose, chubby cheeks and shrewd blue eyes, wearing the striped vest of a valet and carrying a large number of garments over his arm, stood before her in the hallway peering at her intently. "Did you say your name is McTeague and that his lordship sent you?" she asked him bewilderedly. "Whatever did he send you *for*?"

McTeague was immediately charmed by her croaky voice. He wondered if it was a natural phenomenon or an affectation for her role. "May I come in, Mr. Farrington? We don't want t' wake her ladyship, now, do we?"

"No, I . . . I suppose not," Ada said, standing aside to let him in. "But what are you doing here, Mr. McTeague?"

"Call me McTeague, sir. Just McTeague." He closed the door, bustled in and began busily to lay out the clothes on her bed. It was a large four-poster hung with blue chintz curtains and spread over with a ruffled coverlet and dozens of pillows. It was the most feminine bed he'd ever seen (as was the rest of the room, with its rose-covered wallpaper, its ornate decorations and its huge pier mirror). As he pushed the pillows aside, he couldn't help thinking that this was probably the first time that men's clothing would be tried on in this room.

"What is this all about, McTeague?" Ada asked, watching him curiously.

"Lord Esterbrook sent me t' see that y're properly fitted out. He says ye can't be traipsin' about town in what ye brought with ye. I've brought ye two coats t' try on, an' some breeches, as well as shirts, neckcloths and waistcoats. Och, begorra, I was forgettin' his message. His lordship says he'll be meetin' with his friend the magistrate this afternoon, an' he'll be callin' on ye this evenin' with his news."

Ada nodded, eyeing the garments worriedly. She realized that she needed a proper wardrobe, but she didn't see how she could permit this fellow, kindly and fatherly though he was, to try them on her. "It was very good of his lordship to send me all this," she murmured, trying to concoct an excuse for getting rid of the valet.

The voice is natural, McTeague decided, looking the girl over through narrowed eyes. She was slimmer and a bit shorter than he remembered, but her face was a surprise. He had no recollection of the "boy" at the inn having so charming an appearance. He was struck at once by the bewitching tilt of her eyes and the elfin shape of her chin. *No wonder his lordship is smitten*, he thought. *If I were twenty years younger, I might be smitten, too.*

But he had to concentrate on his task. She really was too slim to be entirely convincing as a nineteen-year-old boy, but he'd fix her up somehow. It seemed to him that the smallest of the coats he'd brought might do. The breeches would all be too large, but one pair would have to be made to serve for the time being. "I think this light brown superfine will fit ye very well," he said, holding the coat up.

"It is . . . very handsome," she said, taking it from him and looking it over. "Have you breakfasted, McTeague?" she said suddenly, fixing her eyes on the silk lining.

"Yes, sir. Why do ye ask?"

"Well, it isn't necessary for you to assist me to dress, you know. I've always preferred to dress myself. So I was going to suggest that you go down to the kitchen and get something to eat while I try these things on."

Clever minx, the valet said to himself. "I'd not take it amiss to have a cup of coffee, thank ye, Mr. Farrington, if ye're certain ye don't need me," he told her helpfully. "I can come back in a quarter of an hour t' tie ye neckerchief an' make the finishin' touches."

"Very good, McTeague, that will be fine," she said, expelling a breath of relief.

A quarter of an hour later, he found her standing before the mirror in stockinged feet, looking at herself dubiously. She was wearing the light brown coat and a pair of York tan chamois breeches which hung down almost to her ankles. "What do you think, McTeague?" she asked, discouraged. "I can't be seen in public like this, can I? The coat is passable, I think, but the breeches are impossible."

"If I move a button at the waist, the coat will be quite presentable," the valet said, pulling a threaded needle from the underside of his lapel and starting on the task at once. "As for the breeches, if we can stuff 'em into yer boots, we can make do until I alter the others. Just leave everything to me, Mr. Farrington. Ye've nothing at all to worry about. All ye have t' do now is decide whether ye wish yer hair cut into a Bedford Level or a Brutus."

"Goodness, are you going to cut my hair, too?" Ada asked, aghast.

"His lordship's orders, sir. Ye needn't come unstrung, y' know. I'm as handy a fellow with the scissors as ye'll ever find."

"I have no doubt of it," Ada said, unable to keep from smiling at his unabashed self-confidence, "but I haven't the slightest notion of what a 'Bedford Level' is, or a 'Brutus' either."

"Sure an' I'll be happy t' explain. The Bedford Level is short and cut flat on top—level, y' see—as worn by the Duke o' Bedford. An' the Brutus is cut longer an' more windblown, if ye take me meanin'. Like his lordship's cut, y' know. Ye might have preferred the Van Dyke Natural fer yerself, which is long and falls in waves t' the shoulder, but I didn't bother t' suggest it because ye don't have enough length fer it."

"Then it must be the Brutus, I suppose," Ada said, running her fingers through her hair uneasily. "I certainly don't want my hair cut level and flat on top."

"Aye, that's a wise choice. I would've chosen the same meself, if I were you."

A mere forty minutes later, Ada stood before the mirror and gasped. A very presentable young London gentleman stared back at her from the glass, his hair tossed across his forehead in artful dishevellment, his coat of superb superfine giving his shoulders a broad, manly width, his pristine neck-cloth folded below his high, starched collar in stylish elegance, his satin waistcoat sporting a gold fob (which McTeague told her Derek had sent with his compliments) and his breeches, cleverly tucked into his boots by the remarkable valet, seeming to stretch over a pair of shapely legs in an almost embarrassingly close fit. "Oh, McTeague," Ada breathed, looking at the youth in the mirror in disbelief, "you're a genius! I hardly know myself!"

McTeague chuckled. "Begorra, I *am* a genius, I admit. Ye're as handsomely turned-out a lad as ever was dressed by a Stultz or Nugee. Now, go on down t' breakfast an' let her ladyship have a peep at ye."

Lady Rutledge was still in her dressing gown, brooding over her morning coffee, when Ada appeared in the doorway of the cheerful little nook off the sitting room where her ladyship always took her breakfast. Felicia Rutledge's troubled face was the only cloud in the otherwise sunny room. She'd spent most of the night lying awake, wondering how she could help her son extricate himself from his entanglement with Cynthia Chadwick. The first light of dawn had already shown itself behind the draperies when she'd finally fallen into a troubled sleep from which she'd roused herself only half an hour ago, and she'd come down to breakfast feeling tired and cross. But when she looked up and saw the young man whom Derek had foisted on her looking so remarkably transformed, her spirits lifted at once. "Mr. *Farrington*!" she gasped, almost starting from her chair. "You are looking so fine this morning that I almost didn't *know* you!"

"Good morning, your ladyship," Ada said, entering with a jaunty swagger. "I have you, your son and his valet to thank for my improved appearance. Because of your generous hospitality, this has been the first restful night I've enjoyed in ages. And thanks to your son and his valet, I'm dressed and coiffed to the nines."

"The transformation is quite remarkable," Lady Rutledge said, smiling broadly as her eyes roamed over the good-looking young lad from head to toe. "*Now* I can see something of the Farrington lineage in you, which, I'm ashamed to say, I did not see last night. I may not have mentioned it last night, but I was somewhat acquainted with your father, you know, many years ago when he lived in town. You are not unlike him, though it seems to me that your features are more delicate. But, heavens, you can't really be nineteen, can you? I wouldn't guess you to be a day over fifteen!"

Ada's eyes dropped uneasily from Lady Rutledge's face.

"I'm . . . I've always been sm-small for my age," she mumbled.

"Well, you mustn't be ashamed of that, you know. Size is not everything. Do sit down, dear boy, and take some breakfast!"

As Ada took a place at the table, Lady Rutledge cocked her head and studied the "young man" with the eyes of a born matchmaker. Here was a young fellow whose matrimonial future she could really enjoy planning. What fun it would be! He was very young and green, but that would undoubtedly be an advantage, for in his naiveté he would be unlikely to make difficulties for her in the way that Derek did. In fact, his youth and innocence made it almost *necessary* for her to take him in hand. The fellow needed her, and she would find it delightful to put her influence to work in his behalf. Of course, since he was only nineteen (and looked even younger), it would be years before any matrimonial plans would come to fruition, but it was never too soon to make a start.

What a joy it would be to guide him into the social swim! He was quite handsome (although still a bit immaturishly small and smooth-skinned), he had a charming smile and he was from a good family. With her to guide him, these advantages would stand him in good stead. In a few years, he would be a true eligible. If she set to work on him now—when he was still so agreeably naive—she could direct him to make a spectacular match. He was a perfect subject for her talents.

Her delight in this new specimen was so great that it drove from her mind all recollection of the fiasco of her last matchmaking effort. She beamed across the table at him, her expression not unlike that of a plump cat about to devour a trapped mouse. "And while we're drinking our coffees, Mr. Farrington," she purred, "you must tell me *all about yourself*! You are not betrothed or in any way entangled, are you, dear boy? Because if you are not, I think you'll be happy to learn that there are a number of remarkably charming young ladies I would *very much* like to make known to you!"

Chapter Sixteen

Derek presented himself at his mother's house promptly at six, having (by dint of a charmingly worded note) extorted from her an invitation to dinner. He knew perfectly well that she never dined before seven, but he wanted an hour to speak to Addie while his mother was certain to be locked away in her bedroom dressing for the evening meal. As luck would have it, however, it was his mother he found waiting in the drawing room and Addie who was up in her room. "Well, Mama," he said cheerfully, hiding his disappointment and kissing her cheek, "what are you doing down so early?"

"I was hoping for an opportunity of seeing you alone," she said, taking his arm and drawing him across the room to the sofa. "I am simply bursting with news!"

"May I not have a sherry first," her irritating son suggested. "I'll ring for Lymber."

"Your sherry can wait until Addison comes down to join us," Lady Rutledge said uncharitably, pulling him down beside her.

"Addison?" Derek echoed, suddenly interested.

"I must tell you, Derek, love, that your friend is going to set the girls *agog*! He is utterly charming. I'm delighted that you brought him to me."

Derek's brows rose in surprise. "Addie? Are you speaking of *my Addie*?"

"Of course! Who else? Wait till I tell you the whole. I asked Irene Moncrief and her younger sister Charlotte to tea today—"

"Irene Moncrief? The giggly one?" He gaped at his mother in disbelief. "You asked her to tea . . . with *Addie*?"

"Why are you behaving so stupidly?" his mother asked

113

disgustedly. "I always have people in to tea on Thursdays."

"You asked Addie Farrington . . . to one of your *Thursday teas*?"

"I don't see why you're acting so strangely. He had nothing better to do, after all. And just because *you* did not care for Irene does not mean that some *other* gentleman might not find her attractive."

"Some . . . other . . . gentleman . . . ?" Derek asked, sputtering.

"Yes," his mother said, frowning in annoyance at his peculiar reaction to her tale. "Yes, certainly, some other gentleman! Addison Farrington, for instance!"

Derek bit his lip. "And *did* this other gentleman . . . the honorable Addison Farrington . . . find Irene Moncrief attractive?"

"As to that, I'm not certain. He seemed to observe her quite closely—and her sister, too—but I don't know what he really *thought* of them. But *they* were certainly taken with *him*! There is no doubt whatever on that score. I've never seen Irene more animated . . . laughing at every quip he made, and tossing her curls at him and patting his hand with her fan! And Charlotte, who is only seventeen, but quite mature for her age, was positively *lovestruck*! She stammered and blushed and followed Addison's every movement with the tenderest glances! I think Irene, at twenty-two, is probably too old for him, but Charlotte is just right. If I didn't wish to expose the boy to a few more such experiences before letting him tie himself down, I could make the match *right now*!"

"Make a *match*?" This was too much for Derek. He threw his head back and laughed until the tears came. "A *match!*" he managed between guffaws. "My incorrigible Mama . . . is making . . . another *match*!"

Poor Lady Rutledge gawked at her son as if he'd lost his mind. "I fail to see what has cast you into such transports, Derek Rutledge," she said with offended dignity when he at last stopped laughing. "What is so amusing about my endeavors to bring happiness to two young people?"

"Nothing, Mama," he said, struggling to keep his urge to laugh under tight control. "You are truly wonderful, my dear. If I'm not vigilant, I shouldn't be surprised to wake up one morning and discover that you'd actually *done* it! That you'd gone and . . ." Here he burst into guffaws again. ". . . gone and *married Addie off!*"

His mother jumped to her feet. "I don't know what has got into you, Derek! Your words aren't making an iota of sense. What did you mean when you said, 'if I'm not vigilant'?"

"I meant, Mama," her irrepressible son said when he'd regained his breath, "that I would not be a friend to Addie if I permitted you to endanger *his* future as you endangered mine."

Poor Lady Rutledge's face fell. "That, Derek, was not kind. I never meant to endanger your future but to enhance it. It is cruel of you to throw my error in my face. Besides, you told me not to worry about Miss Cynthia Chadwick. You said you would deal with it and that I was not—"

"Good evening," came a voice from the doorway. "I hope I haven't kept you waiting."

Mother and son turned at once to the door. Addie stood in the doorway resplendent in a black evening coat and satin breeches that McTeague had spent the entire afternoon making ready.

"Good evening, dear boy," Lady Rutledge said, the sight of her delightful guest restoring her good humor. "You haven't kept us waiting at all."

But Derek was rendered utterly speechless. Since he could no longer remember the face of the long-haired girl he'd noticed briefly in the hallway of the Green Gander Inn, and since the girl-in-boy's-clothing whom he'd been squiring about for the last few days had been unkempt, damp and scruffy, the well-dressed, elegantly coiffed Addie who stood in the doorway was someone quite new to him. He'd always been aware that she was a pretty little thing—in fact, he'd found her elfin face quite adorable—but now, at this instant, he suddenly realized that she was a beauty. With her hair transformed from the flat, blunt-cut locks that had framed her face before to the soft, wind-blown waves that were now brushed over her forehead, the oval shape of her face was delightfully emphasized, and her eyes looked larger and more green than grey. And her gleaming white shirtfront and black coat accentuated a graceful neck and the most breathtakingly golden complexion he'd ever seen. "Good god!" he whispered under his breath, won-dering how on earth his mother could have been fooled into believing that this glorious creature was a boy.

Ada, on her part, was rendered speechless, too. In the brief time she'd known Derek, she'd been for the most part preoc-cupied with performing her own false role, a playacting task for which she felt ill-rehearsed and ill-costumed. Therefore, her mind hadn't been free to study her benefactor's appearance with any real attention. She'd been aware that he was very handsome for a man of his age, but since he was older even than Lionel—who was already stodgy and middle-aged in his deportment, habits and outlook—she'd thought of Derek, too, as a member of an older generation than she. Only on the night when she'd found him asleep in the wing chair had she looked closely at his face, and then it had been in the dim light of the fire and only for a brief moment. Now, in the light of Lady Rutledge's crystal chandelier, she saw the urbane Derek clearly for the first time, in the full glory of his town bronze. She could see now that his tall frame, perfectly balanced by broad shoulders, was admirably proportioned from top to toe; that his black eyes gleamed with intelligence and humor; that his square-jawed face (whose strength she'd admired from the first) was topped with a full head of thick, dark, tousled curls (that hadn't quite shown to such advantage during their rain-soaked travels as they did now); and that all these admirable gifts of nature were set off to advantage by the finest, most impeccable evening clothes that wealth, sophistication and good taste could provide. The little country girl was dazzled.

They stood staring at each other, frozen in a timeless, breathless cosmos of their own, until Lady Rutledge (who had been watching Derek's face with amusement) laughed aloud. "So, Derek, even *you* are impressed at this improvement in your friend's appearance!"

"Oh, more than impressed, ma'am," Derek said, recover-ing himself with a blink of his eyes. "Astonished would be a better word. Addie, you look . . . top of the trees!"

Ada, slower to recover her equilibrium, continued to stare at him. "Top of the trees?" she repeated abstractedly.

He crossed the room to her and, taking her by the shoulders, grinned down at her. "Unquestionably top of the trees. You look a pink of the ton, at home to a peg, complete to a shade. In short, a nonpareil."

A slow flush crept up into her face. "Thank you, my lord," she said softly. "So do you."

"I flatter myself that my son is always top of the trees," Lady Rutledge remarked complacently as she rang the bellpull for Lymber to bring their sherries, "but even *he* did not make so favorable an impression on Lady Irene Moncrief as you did today, Addison."

"Ah, yes," Derek said, letting her go. "Mama has been telling me that you spent the afternoon flirting with two ladies."

"I didn't flirt! I wouldn't even know how."

"Nonsense, my boy," Lady Rutledge declared. "One doesn't have to *know* how to flirt. It's something one does quite naturally."

"I don't," Ada insisted. "I'm sure I don't."

"But the Moncrief girls flirted with you, I'm told," Derek said as Lymber entered with the drinks. "Were you taken with them, Addie?"

"*Taken* with them?" She was finding this conversation very awkward. Dropping her eyes from his face, she accepted the glass Lymber held out to her and sank down on the sofa. "Thank you, Lymber." She took a sip before facing Derek again. "I don't know what you mean, Derek."

"He wants to know if you found either of them attractive," Lady Rutledge pursued, taking her drink from Lymber and then dismissing him with a wave. "You did like Charlotte, at least, did you not?"

"They are both . . . er . . . very pleasant young ladies," Ada murmured, tossing a nervous, sidelong glance at Derek.

"But weren't you more taken with one than the other?" Derek pressed wickedly.

"No, not especially. I suppose I am not accustomed to the ways of London ladies. Are they always so . . . so . . ."

"Silly?" Derek offered.

Ada's lips twitched. "I was going to say animated."

"Yes, the Moncrief girls *are* animated," Lady Rutledge said, trying to derive from the adjective a little encouragement for her matchmaking scheme. "There aren't many girls in London who can be described so."

"For which, Mama, I give nightly thanks to the gods," Derek teased.

Ada gurgled appreciatively, but Lady Rutledge glared at her son. "We don't care to hear *your* feelings, you gamecock! *I* shall give thanks to the gods that Addison has not been corrupted by association with ladybirds and lightskirts and doxies as you have been."

"Not yet, perhaps, but time will soon take care of that. For what purpose do you think I've brought the boy to town if not to make him acquainted with ladybirds and doxies?"

"*Derek!*" his mother cried, shocked. She rose from her chair with a stately, matronly fury. "*You* may live a life of dissipation if you must—I certainly seem helpless to prevent you!—but don't you *dare* corrupt that boy!"

Ada, recognizing the amused gleam in Derek's eye and instinctively understanding it, crossed to her ladyship's side and put a comforting hand on her shoulder. "You know he's teasing you, ma'am," she said quietly. "You told me yourself last night not to pay him any mind when he speaks so. He brought me to town for one reason only—to help me find my lost brother."

She then proceeded to relate the events of the past few days, her story causing Lady Rutledge's anger at her son to change to admiration. "Well, Derek, if what Addison says of you is not exaggerated, you've been a good friend to him. I'm proud of you."

"There's nothing to be proud of as yet, Mama. We haven't found the child. But Addie, there *is* news. My friend the magistrate is sending over his best runner to see us. We'll meet tomorrow morning at my place so that you can give him as complete a description of Stanley as possible and I can give him as much information as we've managed to obtain about the man who bought him."

Ada threw Derek such a speaking look of gratitude that he felt the muscles of his chest contract. For a moment he didn't comprehend what he was feeling, for it was a peculiar sensation that could only be described as a painful sort of elation. At that moment Lymber announced dinner, so his mind couldn't dwell on the subject. But as Lady Rutledge offered each of them an arm, and they strolled into the dining room, Derek, still aware of the contraction of his chest, began to understand it. *Damnation,* he said to himself, *McTeague was right! I am smitten!*

Chapter Seventeen

Promptly at eleven the next morning, Ada came striding down Berkeley Street, where Lady Rutledge's impressive abode was located, and headed for Derek's modest town house in Portman Square. She was admirably turned out in her brown coat and chamois breeches (now shortened, tightened and dashingly buckled at the knee, thanks to McTeague's handiwork), with the added stylishness of a high-crowned beaver sitting jauntily on her head and an ivory-headed walking stick swinging from her hand. The cane was a delight to her. The ivory top, carved in the shape of a wolf's head, was surprisingly heavy and, as McTeague had pointed out, a useful weapon in times of emergency, but when she walked along swinging it jauntily, she felt very much the man-about-town.

When she arrived at Derek's door and was about to lift the cane and tap the ivory wolf head on the brass lion-head knocker, the door swung suddenly open, and an eye-catching female wearing a deeply décolletéd, flounced gown and a huge, plumed hat came storming out, crying in tight-lipped fury, "—not even if you came *crawling* to me on *bended knee!*"

Bent on slamming the door with appropriate vehemence, the immodestly dressed female failed to see Ada standing just a step behind her and blundered right into her. "Oh!" she exclaimed, startled. She took a step back, her eyes sweeping over Ada boldly from head to toe. Then, to Ada's intense embarrassment, her angry frown faded, her eyebrows rose and a small smile appeared at the corner of a very voluptuous mouth. "*Oh!*" she said again, this time with an interested lilt.

"I beg your pardon," Ada said, lifting the beaver politely.

"I beg *yours*," the female said flirtatiously, cocking her

head to one side and causing the plumes to wave. "Are you a
friend of his lordship?" She looked over her shoulder toward
the doorway, where Derek was now standing. "Who is *this*
charming boy, may I ask? I thought I was acquainted with all
your circle."

"Miss Stanhope, may I present the honorable Addison Farrington," Derek said, his tone ranging somewhere between
amusement and dismay. "Mr. Farrington, Miss Polly Stanhope."

"How do you do?" Ada said, bowing stiffly.

"Better than I did a moment ago," Miss Stanhope murmured. She smiled at her new acquaintance provocatively as
she opened her parasol. Then, keeping her eyes on Ada, she
twirled it over her shoulder while she said to Derek, "*You* may
not use my direction in future, you skirter-jilt, but you may
pass it on to this new friend of yours."

"May I indeed?" Derek asked drily. "Isn't he a bit young
for you, Polly?"

Miss Stanhope's smile broadened. "I always enjoy helping
young men to mature. Especially such attractive specimens as
this one. Good morning, Mr. Farrington." And with that, she
turned on her heel and walked with a taunting swing of her
hips down the steps and away down the street.

Ada looked after her in horrified fascination. "Good
heavens, Derek, is that—? Is she one of your . . . ?" Then,
realizing what she'd been about to ask, she colored to the
ears. "Oh, I beg your pardon!"

"Don't be foolish, Addie," Derek said, stepping aside and
admitting her. "You needn't be squeamish when we're talking
man-to-man. You were going to ask something about Miss
Stanhope, were you not?"

"Is she one of your . . . er . . ."

"Ladybirds?" He smiled grimly as he took her hat and cane
and led her down the hall to his sitting room. "She was, but
we have not been very—how shall I say?—*close* of late. She,
unfortunately, was unwilling to face that fact."

"Until today?"

"Until today."

"How very interesting," Ada murmured, mulling over the
incident as Derek led her to a sofa in his sitting room. "Good

heavens, then when she said that you may pass her direction on to me, did she mean that she was inviting *me* to . . . to . . ."

"To take my place? Yes, indeed she was." He leered at her wickedly as he slid down beside her on the sofa. "*Shall* I give you her direction, my lad?"

Addie lifted her chin. "No, thank you," she said boldly. "Miss Stanhope is not my sort."

"Isn't she? With all her very obvious charms? Why not?"

"That's just it. Her charms are a bit *too* obvious."

"That's a strange thing to say," Derek twitted her. "Most men would say that a woman's charms can't be too obvious. That's why Miss Stanhope dresses the way she does—to emphasize the obvious. And she succeeds admirably. She catches the eye of every man who passes by."

"Does she indeed?" Ada muttered drily. "I'm surprised she doesn't catch other things as well—like influenza."

Derek's appreciative laugh was cut short by the appearance of McTeague in the doorway. "The runner's here, me lord. Name of Willigill. *Willy* Willigill, if ye can believe it."

The fellow who entered Derek's sitting room looked not at all as Ada had expected. She had imagined that a man whose profession was the protection of the innocent against the criminal classes would be large, strong and impressively frightening. But Mr. Willigill was small—almost as small as she—and, except for a remarkably protruding stomach, as thin as a rail. The hat on his head was like none she'd ever seen before—low-crowned and rounded on top, with a narrow brim curled on the sides. Thin strands of brown, greying hair hung down below it, framing a narrow, ferretlike face. His clothes were rumpled but not dirty, and they were of such dull colors that no one would be likely to take any special notice of them. Even his waistcoat, which was pushed high up on his chest because it could not be buttoned over his bloated waist, was of an insipid grey. Ada would have wondered how Derek's magistrate friend had recommended such a specimen if she hadn't been struck by the fellow's eyes. There was something shrewd and knowing in those pale eyes. She had the distinct impression he could see right through her.

"Good mornin', m' lord,' the runner said briskly, nodding affably to Derek as his eyes quickly scanned the entire room.

Then he made a little bow. "Willy Willigill, Bow Street. An' *you,* sir, you mus' be Mr. Farrington, the cove what is lookin' for 'is brother?"

"Yes, Mr. Willigill. His name is Stanley."

"I know," the runner said, whipping a small notebook and a pair of spectacles from a deep pocket in his coat. He perched the glasses on his nose and flipped through the scribbled pages quickly. "Stanley Algernon Farrington, aged eight years three months; father, Edward Farrington, Earl of Wycoff, deceased; mother, born Isabel Rolfe; two siblings; all residin' at Farrington Park, Suffolk," he read aloud.

"How did you know all that?" Ada asked, amazed.

He flicked a glance at Ada over the top of his spectacles. "Research, Mr. Farrington, sir, research."

Derek peered at the fellow in fascination. "That's very good, Mr. Willigill," he said admiringly, "but just how *did* you—?"

"Just part o' the job, m' lord, just part o' the job. If ye don' mind, your lordship, since time's o' the essence, as they say, we should come t' the point wi'out roundaboutation." He removed the stub of a pencil from another pocket and licked the point. "The boy's description first, if ye please."

Derek and Ada exchanged quizzical looks. The fellow was methodical to the point of rudeness. "Certainly, Mr. Willigill," Derek said, "but won't you make yourself comfortable first? You can at least sit down."

"I thank ye, m' lord, but it ain't necessary. The boy's 'air, now . . . red, would y' say?"

In a very few minutes, Willy Willigill, Bow Street runner, had taken down all the information they had to give. Without further ado, the fellow pocketed his notes, his spectacles and his pencil stub and turned to the door. "If you've no objection, m' lord, cin ye show me the way out? I seem to disremember the way."

"But it's merely straight down the—" Derek began, but catching a significant look the fellow threw at him he stopped himself. "Of course, Mr. Willigill," he said, crossing the room quickly.

"But Mr. Willigill," Ada objected, "is that *all?*"

"That's all I cin do *'ere, sir*. Unless you 'ave anythin' else to tell me."

"No, but—"

"Then you'll be 'earin' from me. No need t' fret, Mr. Farrington. I'll go bail it won't take long till I 'ave news."

As soon as the door closed behind them, Derek caught the fellow by the arm. "So you 'disremembered' your way out, did you?" he asked accusingly. "Come now, Willy Willigill, you wouldn't 'disremember' your way out of *Windsor Castle*. Why did you want to see me alone? What do you want to tell me? Do you think the little boy's dead?"

"No, no, m' lord, nothin' like that. It's your Mr. Farrington that 'as me puzzled."

"Mr. Farrington? The fellow we just left in the sitting room?"

The runner nodded. "The old Earl, Edward Farrington that was, left on'y three children, y'see." He took out his notebook and spectacles again and read aloud, "Lionel, the present Earl, aged twenty-eight; Ada, the only daughter, aged nineteen; and the boy Stanley. So where does this Mr. Farrington come in, I ax you?"

Derek looked at him closely. "Where did you find out all that?"

Willy Willigill shrugged. "It ain't no mystery. I just looked 'em up in Burke's *Peerage*."

"The *Peerage*, of course!" Derek shook his head admiringly. "Now, why didn't I think of that?"

"Howsomever, yer lordship," the runner remarked, studying Derek's face with his shrewd eyes, "ye don' seem *surprised* that yer Mr. Farrington's pokin' bogey."

"Poking bogey?"

"Tippin' ye a rise, diddlin' ye . . . ye know, *shammin'* it."

"Lying, you mean." Derek sighed. "You've guessed it, haven't you?"

"That *he*'s a *she*? It don't take a genius. I put two an' two together, that's all. Addison Farrington is Ada Farrington. Ye cin *see* it if ye look close enough." He strolled off down the hall for a few steps. "What I *ain't* totted up is *why*," he said, turning back to Derek with a wrinkled brow. "It queers me what 'er lay is."

"She has no 'lay,' Mr. Willigill. She ran away from home to find her brother, and she felt she'd be safer dressed as a boy. There's nothing very underhanded in that, is there?"

The runner rubbed his chin thoughtfully. "No, I s'pose there ain't. But then, there's *you*, yer lordship."

"Me? What do you mean?"

"What's *yer* lay, m' lord? Ye've knowd 'er identity fer awhile now, ain't ye? But from whut I observe, ye ain't told nobody, not even the girl herself. Seems t' me a man wouldn't keep so interestin' a secret to 'isself unless 'e 'ad some bobbery in mind."

Derek stared down at the little fellow, startled. "I say, Willigill, what sort of 'bobbery' do you suspect me of? Do you think I mean some *harm* to the girl?"

"I admit, m' lord, that the possibility 'as occurred to me."

"Good God, man, what are you saying?" Offended, he drew himself up to his full height. "Didn't your magistrate tell you who I am?"

The runner seemed unimpressed with this display of lordly indignation. "I know y're the Viscount Esterbrook, m' lord. Ye needn't climb on yer 'igh ropes. But I been in Bow Street long enough t' know that a *title*'s never stopped a man from crime if 'is mind's set on committin' it."

"You're barking up the wrong tree, Willigill. There's nothing on my mind but the desire to help the girl find her brother. Why, I'm the one who asked for you to become involved in the first place! Would I have asked for the assistance of a Bow Street runner if I were planning some 'bobbery'?"

"That's a point, I'll grant ye," the runner said, writing something quickly in his little notebook. Then he squinted up at the taller man. "But if yer motives are so pure, why don't ye tell the girl ye know?"

"I have my reasons," Derek said, feeling himself flush. "I don't see that it's any business of yours. And it certainly has nothing to do with solving the problem at hand. Whether or not I tell Addie what I know will have no bearing on your finding Stanley."

"Mmm," the runner said, jotting down some additional notes in his little book before pocketing it. "Per'aps it will, an' per'aps it won't. But ye'd better remember one thing, yer lordship . . ."

"And what is that?" Derek muttered, glowering down at the feisty little fellow.

"A runner's got eyes in the back of 'is 'ead, m' lord. In the back of 'is 'ead. So even though I'll be lookin' fer this Stanley, I'll still be lookin' back, ye see. That's why you'd best be sure ye ain't plottin' any bobbery, 'cause I'll be watching every move ye make!" He glared up at the man who stood towering over him and shook a stern finger up at him. "So ye'd best not disremember, m' lord. As sure as me name's Willy Willigill, I'll be watchin' ye."

Chapter Eighteen

Ada wandered through the streets for several hours before returning to Rutledge House on Berkeley Street. She had left Derek with her head full of confusion and disquietude, and she needed time to think. For one thing, the handling of the problem concerning Stanley did not satisfy her. It was not that she'd found Mr. Willigill ineffectual (on the contrary, she'd been very impressed with his shrewdness and businesslike demeanor) but that she could hardly bear to be just sitting about waiting for him to report. She believed that she had to be doing something *herself*; if she remained inactive, she'd feel she was betraying Stanley.

Another problem that troubled her was her relationship with Derek. He had been consistently kind, generous and helpful, and in return she was rewarding him with dishonesty. Instead of thankfulness, she was giving him deceit. Instead of basking in the pleasure of his friendship, she was becoming gloomy with guilt. What would he feel, she couldn't help wondering, if he discovered that she'd been lying to him from the first moment they'd met? He would have every right to feel betrayed.

Something the Bow Street runner had said triggered these thoughts. The fellow had discovered all sorts of things about her family that she'd never told him. When she'd pressed Derek on the matter afterward, he'd admitted that the runner had looked up the family in the *Peerage*. It had been as easy as that. Well, what was to stop Derek himself from checking the *Peerage*? If he did, he would discover that there was no Addison Farrington in the family, and he would realize immediately that Addison was Ada! What would he feel *then*?

Perhaps it would be better for her to confess the truth to

127

him at once. After all, there was little reason to maintain the deceit. She was safely ensconced in his mother's house, where she would be safe from the molestation of strangers. From this point on, she could search for Stanley equally well as a boy or a girl. It was likely, of course, that Lady Rutledge would be angry when she learned of the deceit, but Ada felt sure she would understand and forgive her once her motives were explained.

Derek, however, might find it harder to understand. Having been taken in for so much longer than his mother had, Derek might very well feel a fool and be much less forgiving. And who could blame him? She and Derek had spent a great deal of time together during the past few days, time in which she'd had ample opportunity to reveal the truth to him. He'd have every right to be furious with her. And by this time Ada understood her own heart well enough to know that she would find it very painful to incur Derek's fury. His good opinion had become very important to her.

But if she were to be honest with herself, Derek's good opinion was not enough. There was more to this situation than what she'd so far admitted to herself. Almost from the first moment she'd met him, she'd been drawn to Derek in a way that was something apart from her need of his assistance. There was something between them, some attraction, that she'd been too preoccupied to analyze before. But last night, when he'd come to dinner looking so magnificent and gazing at her with that blood-tingling gleam in his eye, the realization had burst on her how very much she cared for him. So it was more than his good opinion that she wanted. She wanted his love. And that she could not have while he thought of her as a boy.

What was suddenly becoming very clear was that she wanted him to see her as a girl. The words rang in her mind with a crystalline conviction: *I want to be a girl for him!* The affectionate feelings that were growing inside her toward him could not grow *in him* if the present situation continued. Even now it might very well be too late. His vision of her as a male might be so firmly fixed in his mind that the initial impression could not be erased. The thought of her as a girl might very well revolt him. But *that* she would never know with certainty until she put the matter to the test.

That was it, then. This was the time. All reasoning pointed to it. All feelings pointed to it. She would tell him the truth, and as soon as possible!

She turned back toward Berkeley Street almost running. Her heart pounded with excitement, wild anticipation stirred in her breast. *Perhaps I should tell Lady Rutledge first,* she thought suddenly, a dramatic idea bursting upon her. With Lady Rutledge's help she could dress herself as a girl and show Derek her real self at their very next meeting! It was too bad about her hair, of course, but she might otherwise, with Lady Rutledge's help, make a very presentable girl. She could almost imagine the scene: Derek standing in his mother's hallway, at the bottom of the stairs, looking up, and she appearing at the top in a white Belladine silk underdress covered with a diaphanous silver half-robe. His eyes would widen in astonished admiration. She would pause and look fondly down at him while love would blossom in his breast . . .

She was breathless when she ran into the house, the lovely scene she'd just imagined lingering like music in her mind. Lymber, carrying an empty tea tray, almost collided with her in the hallway. "Where's her ladyship?" Ada asked excitedly. "I must see her at once."

"In the drawing room, Mr. Farrington," the butler said, "but she's—"

But Ada didn't wait for more. Without even trying to stride like a man, she flew down the corridor and burst through the drawing room doors without knocking. "Lady Rutledge, I have something of importance to tell—"

But her ladyship was not alone. Seated opposite her, on the other side of a heavily laden tea cart, were two of the most elegantly gowned ladies Ada had ever laid eyes on. One, the elder of the two, was dressed in purple and gold from her leather slippers to her jewelled turban. The younger, an amazingly beautiful young woman, was clad in white. Her white-plumed bonnet was tied with white satin, her gown—a shiny lustring—was so deeply flounced that it fell round her ankles and down on the carpet in graceful swirls. A white wool spencer trimmed with white fur was draped over her shoulders and a pair of long white gloves lay in her lap. *If only I could appear before Derek in a costume like that,* Ada thought enviously.

Lady Rutledge looked up at the intruder with a smile. "Ah, Mr. Farrington," she clarioned with what Ada took to be an air of relieved eagerness, as if she welcomed the interruption, "I was *wondering* what had become of you."

"I beg your pardon," Ada mumbled awkwardly. "I didn't realize I was intruding. I shall come back later, ma'am, when you're not busy."

"You are not intruding. Not at *all*, dear boy! I was just telling Lady Chadwick about you. Do come in and join us for tea. Lady Chadwick, Miss Cynthia Chadwick, may I present Mr. Addison Farrington of Suffolk?"

After the introductions were fully concluded (Ada finding them rather inordinately lengthy and formal), Ada was seated and provided with tea. She stirred her tea round the cup absently as conversation among the ladies resumed. Lady Rutledge explained to them that "this delightful young man" was her houseguest, a friend of her son's, who was visiting in town with the object of locating a missing brother.

Lady Chadwick turned her head slowly in Ada's direction, as if she had difficulty in performing so strenuous an exercise. "Missing? How unfortunate, Mr. Farrington," she said, her voice carefully modulated to express just the right amount of concern.

"Yes," Ada answered, "most unfortunate. You see, he's only eight."

"Oh, dear," the beautiful Miss Cynthia Chadwick murmured sympathetically, "How very dreadful! Did I understand her ladyship to mean he was *abducted*?"

"Yes, we believe so."

"And Derek is assisting you in searching for him?"

"Yes, Miss Chadwick. Since I'm not at all knowing in matters of this sort, and also completely unfamiliar with London, I would have been utterly at a loss without him. Lord Esterbrook has been more helpful to me than you can imagine."

"Then that explains why Cynthia has seen so little of Derek these last few days," Lady Chadwick remarked to her hostess, lifting her teacup to her lips with practiced perfection.

Lady Rutledge lowered her eyes. "Yes, I suppose it does. The search for little Stanley has occupied a great deal of his time."

"Then I do forgive him, of course," Cynthia Chadwick said, bestowing a gracious smile on both her ladyship and Ada. "One must recognize that it is more important to pursue a solution to so urgent a dilemma as yours, Mr. Farrington, than to pursue so selfish a goal as . . . er . . . courtship."

Ada felt her chest constrict. "Courtship?" she asked, choked.

"Perhaps, Cynthia," her mother chided stiffly, "It is inappropriate to speak of courtship in this place at this moment. It is an intimate matter, after all, and Mr. Farrington is not well known to us."

"No, no," Lady Rutledge put in, "You need not stand on ceremony in this house. And Addison—Mr. Farrington here —is becoming quite like one of the family, I assure you. So good a friend of Derek's must already know his situation in relation to Cynthia. Derek *has* spoken to you of his courtship of Miss Chadwick, hasn't he, Addison?"

Ada's blood drained from her face as she grasped the significance of what the ladies were speaking of. "Well, I . . . I . . ." she mumbled, benumbed.

"There, you see, Lady Chadwick?" Lady Rutledge insisted, interpreting Ada's mumble as an assent. "Of *course* Derek's spoken of Cynthia to his friend. How could he not?"

Lady Chadwick's head made an infinitesimal swivel in Ada's direction, and she nodded her head so that the purple plume on her turban waved gently. "I suppose it *is* only natural, when a man is besotted, to speak of the lady of his heart to his friend," she said, her objection to the subject of the conversation quite overcome.

"Indeed, Mama," Cynthia said, smiling complacently, "I would not use the word 'besotted.' Derek is not so uncontrolled in his emotions as that."

A discussion involving the choice of a more appropriate word ensued, but whether they eventually decided on "enamored" or "infatuated," Ada didn't care. She understood enough to perceive the end of her hopes. Derek was in love with the beautiful Cynthia, beside whom Ada, even in the finest gown, would not be noticed.

Her entire spirit seemed to sink into a hole of misery, and she was not aware of anything surrounding her until she felt someone press her shoulder. She looked up with a start to find Lady Chadwick standing above her, holding out her hand. "You'll come, of course," she was saying. "Any friend of Derek's is always welcome at our house."

Remembering abruptly that she was supposed to be a man, Ada jumped to her feet. "I thank you, Lady Chadwick," she muttered bewilderedly.

"Good," Lady Chadwick said, gliding slowly toward the door. "I shall send round a card for Mr. Farrington, Felicia. Thank you for a most pleasant afternoon."

"Oh, yes," Cynthia said, adjusting her spencer and following her mother, "a most pleasant afternoon indeed."

"You're quite welcome," Lady Rutledge said, rising. "But you needn't bother with a card for the boy, Lady Chadwick. Your personal invitation is surely sufficient."

Lady Chadwick looked back at her hostess with disapproval. "Oh, dear, no," she said, like a governess correcting a child's bad manners, "one never should consider an invitation to be truly extended without a card."

As Lady Rutledge swept after them to see them out, Ada heard her mutter under her breath, "Without a card, indeed! Deuced silly widgeon!"

Ada sank back down on her chair again as soon as the door had closed and tried to absorb the shock. Derek was in love with Another. That simple fact brought to an abrupt end all her prospects of joy. Her time here in London, which a moment ago had brimmed with excitement and the anticipation of love and fulfillment, now loomed ahead of her like a prison sentence, a dark nightmare in which she'd be aware at every turn that Derek was thinking about, dancing with, *courting* the lovely Cynthia. His pursuit of Cynthia was not something she wanted to watch. In fact, she could hardly bear thinking of it!

There was nothing left for her to look forward to now except to find Stanley and go back home to the country life she'd lived before. *Oh, Stanley,* she cried inside herself, *where are you? I need you! Please, Stanley, let me find you so that we can go home and forget this place!*

The drawing room door opened and Lady Rutledge came bustling in. "At last, Addison," she chirped happily, "we can be cozily by ourselves. Don't get up, dearest boy. Let's have another cup of tea while you reveal what it is you came in so eagerly to tell me."

"No, thank you, your ladyship," Ada said glumly. "I think I'd better go up to my room. I'm . . . I'm not feeling very well."

Her ladyship's face fell. "Oh, I'm so sorry. Is there anything I can get for you. A James powder? A tisane?"

"No, nothing. Don't worry about me, your ladyship. I shall be quite all right after a short rest. Will you excuse me?"

"Of course, Addison dear, of course. *Do* go ahead and lie down. And as soon as you're better, we can sit down together right here, and you can tell me what it was you wished to say earlier."

"It was nothing, ma'am. Nothing at all."

"But . . ." Lady Rutledge peered at her worriedly. ". . . but you said it was something important."

"Did I? I seem to have forgotten what it was I was going to say, so it couldn't have been anything important, could it? Please don't give the matter another thought."

With that, she bowed herself out of the room, having decided with all the firmness and determination of which she was capable that she would not reveal her true identity after all. If she was going to spend the rest of her time in London being miserable, she might as well be miserable as a boy.

Chapter Nineteen

The world changed perceptibly for Ada in the next two days. Her mood, which before meeting Miss Chadwick had been steadfastly optimistic about the prospects of finding Stanley (and which had been additionally buoyed up by the excitement of her growing familiarity with Derek), now fell down with a thump. There was no word from the Bow Street Runner, and the silence from that quarter dealt a severe blow to her optimism. Equally depressing, she'd seen very little of Derek in these two days, an absence which she interpreted to mean that he was busily engaged in advancing his "courtship." What was worse, the weather turned cold, and the heavy grey sky which hung over London like a blight seemed to press upon her spirit with a physical weight. And all she could do to alleviate the oppression of her surroundings and her mood was to pace about her room.

As if to rub salt in Ada's wounds, fate dealt the girl another blow. A day after the tea party, a footman delivered to Ada's hand a gilt-edged invitation from Lady Chadwick to a dinner to be held four days hence. She attempted to send a refusal, but Lady Rutledge pointed out that she'd already given the Chadwicks a verbal acceptance, so there was nothing for it but to go. Ada hated the thought of spending a long evening watching Derek pay court to his Cynthia, but the only prospect she had of escaping the ordeal was that Stanley would be found sooner, and she and her brother could leave London before the dinner would be held.

Lady Rutledge, noticing Addison's low spirits, tried to entice her guest into a more cheery frame of mind by suggesting outings or by trying to arrange festive little teas, but Addison Farrington was not at all receptive to her efforts. He invariably made excuses, very politely of course, and remained locked away in his room. Her ladyship wondered if he was still feeling unwell. She began to think seriously of calling in a doctor to take a look at him.

On the evening of the second day after the fateful tea with the Chadwick ladies, Lady Rutledge left the house to dine with friends. She had pleaded with Addison to escort her, but the moping houseguest had declined. Unwilling to force him into society when he seemed so sincerely disinclined, she reluctantly left him alone, ordering Lymber to "see to it that the boy eats a little something, even if it's only a bowl of barley soup."

Ada refused the soup and, telling Lymber that she would not be requiring anything else of him for the rest of the evening, curled up on her bed in her breeches and boots and pulled a coverlet over her. At least she was alone and could embrace her misery instead of having to hide it behind a cheerful facade. For one whole evening she would not have to make polite conversation. For one whole evening she would not have to behave with that energetic boyishness that had once been fun but was no longer. For one whole evening she could cry like a girl.

Two hours passed, during which she found neither consolation nor sleep. But at least she'd accomplished one thing during that time—she'd used up all her tears. She was about to undress and go properly to bed when she heard Lymber pounding at the door. "Mr. Farrington, Mr. Farrington!" he called. "Lord Esterbrook's come. He's downstairs in the drawing room."

Ada looked desperately round the darkened room, foolishly hoping that she might suddenly discover an exit of some sort which had escaped her notice before. But of course there was no exit. She would have to answer.

But what was Derek doing here at this hour, she wondered? It was surely after ten. Shocked at this late intrusion on her privacy, she threw off the coverlet, got out of bed and stomped to the door in annoyance. "Didn't you understand, Lymber, that I didn't wish to be disturbed?" she said, opening the door and glaring at the butler. "Why didn't you tell his lordship that Lady Rutledge is out for the evening?"

"It is not her ladyship that Lord Esterbrook has come to see. He wants to see *you*, Mr. Farrington. I told him you'd retired, but he says it's important."

He's probably come to tell me he's offered for the oh-so-proper Miss Chadwick, she warned herself sternly. But if he'd come especially to give her his news, she supposed she might as well hear it now as later. "Oh, very well, Lymber," she said with a sigh. "I'll put on my coat. Tell him I'll be right down."

She closed the door, lit a candle and looked at herself in the mirror. "Oh, dear heaven!" she gasped aloud. "I look a *sight*." And indeed her eyes were red and swollen, and her hair was tousled beyond redemption. She plunged her face into the icy water of the lavabo, towelled it dry and ran a brush through her hair. Then, with a last, helpless look in the mirror, she shrugged into her coat and ran downstairs.

In the doorway of the drawing room she paused. Derek was standing at the fireplace, one booted foot resting on the hearth and one arm resting on the mantel. His eyes were fixed on the fire. He had not removed his caped greatcoat, although he'd left it hanging carelessly open. Both in attire and attitude he was a perfect representation of the London Corinthian. He was so deep in thought that he didn't hear her come in. Her heart clenched at the sight of him. With the amber glow of the firelight on his face, he looked too appealing for her to bear. The pain in her chest was so intense at this sight of him that she wanted only to run away. *I'll face him tomorrow,* she told herself, backing stealthily out of the doorway. *Whatever he has to tell me can wait till tomorrow.*

But her movement must have caught his attention, because he looked up at that moment. "Addie?" he asked, peering through the darkness of the hallway to get a glimpse of her. "Come in, old fellow. I have good news."

"Have you?" She came back slowly to the doorway. "What is it?" she asked, bracing herself.

"I've had a message from Willy Willigill." He flashed her a broad smile. "He's *found the man with the wart!*"

For a moment Ada did not grasp the words, but when she did it was as if her blood had been suddenly infused with spirits. A warm glow seemed to burst through the gloom that had enveloped her. *"Derek!"* she gased, almost afraid to let herself believe what she'd heard. *"Truly?"*

He nodded and, seeing the light flare up in her eyes, instinctively held out her arms to her.

"Oh, *Derek!*" Without thinking, she flew across the room and flung herself into his arms. "Oh, my dear, I can scarcely *believe* it!" she cried.

He laughed joyfully, the pleasure of holding her close registering only on a level of his mind below the conscious. "Believe it, Addie, because it's quite true," he assured her. And, tightening his arms about her, he lifted her up in the air and whirled her about in delight.

At about the third turn, while she looked down at his face from a dizzying height, she suddenly realized that she was not behaving as she should. A *boy* would not have thrown herself at him. A *boy* would not be whirling about in the air this way. *What* had she *done?*

And he, looking up and seeing the abrupt change in her expression, came instantly to that same realization. His grin died, and slowly, very slowly, he lowered her to his chest and then set her on her feet. "I'm afraid I was a bit carried away," he said, dropping his arms to his sides.

She stepped back, away from him, and dropped her eyes. "I was, too," she murmured, throwing him a quick, sidelong glance.

"A kind of momentary aberration, I suppose, brought on by our relief," he offered, hoping she would accept this awkward explanation of what must seem to her as extremely peculiar behavior.

"Yes," she agreed.

"Temporary craziness. No need to refine on it."

"No, of course not," she said, relieved that she hadn't given herself away.

Derek waited for a moment to see if she would take this opportunity to tell him the truth. But when nothing more was forthcoming, he turned back to the fire and calmly informed her of the details of the note he'd received from the runner. "The fellow wrote only that he'd found the man. He said that the rest would be revealed tomorrow morning, when he intends to call at Portman Square and tell us the whole."

While he was explaining all this, Lady Rutledge—who'd come in a few moments earlier and had, unwittingly, caught sight of her son and his friend in a strange sort of embrace— stepped back from the drawing room doorway into the shadows of the corridor. Covering her mouth to keep from gasping, she turned and, hardly breathing, tiptoed on unsteady legs up the stairs.

Chapter Twenty

Lady Rutledge had a great deal to think about. The evidence of her eyes was too confusing to be meaningful. She warned herself sternly against jumping to hysterical conclusions. The scene she'd just witnessed required serious analysis before she could draw *any* conclusions.

She tottered into her bedroom and sank down on the bench at the foot of her bed, her mind in a whirl. When her abigail bustled in and began to undress her, Lady Rutledge went through the motions without even noticing what she was doing. The abigail chattered away, giving her usual scold about her ladyship's disdain for her health—"Ye'll catch yer death, my lady, one of these nights, going out in the cold with only yer spencer on yer shoulders, an' comin' in at all hours . . ."—but Lady Rutledge hardly heard her.

What she had seen downstairs was truly shocking, but she knew there must be some explanation that was eluding her. She knew her son too well to believe that he was one of those odd fellows who preferred alliances with other males. Her son was, if anything, too lusty in his pursuit of female liaisons. So what was he doing *embracing* a *boy*?

Was it the boy himself who was in some way the cause? The whole business of his peculiar arrival was mysterious. Where had Derek met him? If it was at Farrington Park, what had Derek been doing there in the first place? And when he'd brought the boy to London, why had he brought him here to Rutledge House instead of installing him in Portman Square? If there *was* something havey-cavey between them, wouldn't it have been more sensible to put him up there?

There had to be a reason why Derek wanted the Farrington

boy here with his mother. But what was it? The only difference between the two households was that Derek had only McTeague and a cook on his staff, whereas she had a staff of six. But a shortage of staff at Portman Square couldn't be the reason; McTeague had managed to handle guests before. The only possible reason was that Derek wanted the fellow under *his mother's protection*, and *that* would make sense only if the guest was a female.

Something clicked in her mind as soon as that thought came to her . . . a memory of something Derek had said the night he'd brought Addison home. *"Unless you can find me a girl like Addie,"* Derek had said, *"don't ever make any more matches for me."* A *girl* like Addie! *Girl* was his very word!

"Heavens!" she gasped aloud. "That must be *it!*"

"Goodness, ma'am," exclaimed the startled abigail who'd been in the act of placing a lacy nightcap on her mistress's head, "ye gave me a fright! What did ye say, my lady?"

"Nothing, Nance, nothing. Give me the cap. I'll put it on myself, while you go and get Lymber for me."

The abigail looked at her askance. *"Lymber*, my lady? *Now?"*

"Yes, please. Now. There's something I wish to ask him."

After the abigail left, Lady Rutledge sat down at her dressing table and stared into the mirror. Mr. Farrington, a *girl*? Was *that* the explanation? It did seem to explain a great deal. Now that she thought about it, she realized that Addison Farrington's features had decidedly feminine qualities. And his skin was really too smooth to be a man's. Yes, Addie Farrington must be a girl; her ladyship was convinced she was on the right track. But just to be absolutely certain, she would question Lymber to obtain the final evidence.

Her ladyship was still sitting at her dressing table, calmly rubbing cream of cucumber lotion on her face, when the butler presented himself. "You wanted to see me, my lady?" he asked, a slight lift of his eyebrow the only sign that he was surprised at being summoned to her ladyship's bedroom at this time of night.

"Yes, Lymber. I wanted to know if you've been shaving Mr. Farrington."

The butler, expertly trained not to show his feelings in his face, did not reveal how unexpected the question was. "*Shaving* him? Why, no, my lady. He's never asked me to."

"Never?"

"No, ma'am, never. Very independent, Mr. Farrington is. Never lets anyone do for him. Even puts on his boots himself."

"Is that so? Then you think he shaves himself, too?"

Lymber permitted himself a shrug. "I suppose he must, unless . . . well, if I may be permitted to observe, my lady, his skin is so boyish that he may not require frequent shaving."

"Yes, he does seem immature in that regard," her ladyship mused. "But are you telling me that he has *never* asked to be shaved? Do you at least supply him with shaving things?"

The butler shook his head. "No, ma'am, I never have."

"Well, perhaps McTeague comes over to shave him," her ladyship said thoughtfully. "After all, he did cut the boy's hair."

"That first morning, yes, he did. But he hasn't been here since, except once to deliver new clothes."

"I see." She turned from the mirror and looked up at her butler. "I expect you're right in your observation that the boy is still too young to need daily shaving," she said with a smile. "But in any case, Lymber, the subject is really not important."

"No, my lady. But do you wish me to supply the lad with shaving things in future?"

"Oh, no. Not unless he asks. Just forget the whole matter, will you?"

"Yes, certainly, my lady, if you wish me to."

"I do. Thank you, Lymber, that will be all." She turned back to her mirror and resumed creaming her skin. "And, Lymber," she added with studied casualness just as he was about to close the door, "you won't repeat any of this conversation to anyone, I hope."

The butler remained utterly impassive. "No, ma'am, of course not. Goodnight, my lady."

Lady Rutledge remained at her mirror, motionless, for a long time. She was trying to understand the significance of what she'd discovered. That Addison Farrington was a girl seemed certain, but the reason for the pretense remained a mystery. The solution to the mystery was not crucially important to Felicia Rutledge, hostess. But to Felicia Rutledge, *mother*, it was critical. She felt she *had* to know what *Derek's* part was in all this. He obviously knew that "his Addie" was a girl—he would not have placed her in his mother's care otherwise—but did Addie know he knew? And, most interesting question of all, did Derek *care* for the girl?

Her ladyship rose from the dressing table and began to pace about the room. If she was not mistaken in what she saw downstairs, Derek was in love at last. But what sort of coil was it that his heart had drawn him into?

There was a great deal in this matter that could cause trouble. If Derek loved this girl, what did that mean as far as Cynthia Chadwick was concerned? And what sort of girl *was* this Farrington chit to have enacted so shocking a deception? As a boy, Lady Rutledge had found "him" charming, but she didn't know if she would care for "her" at all as a girl. If Derek had serious intentions toward her, Lady Rutledge needed to learn a great deal more about the creature before she could be happy.

Should she discuss this matter with Derek? she wondered. Should she reveal openly that she knew the truth about Farrington's deception and unmask the girl at once? No, she decided, that might not be wise. If there was a good reason for the masquerade, she might unwittingly destroy well-built plans. It would not do to cause destruction out of ignorance.

All at once, her ladyship stopped her pacing. There *was* a source of information available to her that she could take advantage of *without* revealing anything of what she knew and without interfering with what was taking place. There was *one* place where adequate information about the girl could be found! Eagerly, she crossed the room to the washstand and carefully soaped the cucumber lotion from her hands. Then she sat herself at her writing desk, lit her argonne lamp and, with brow knit thoughtfully, prepared the nib of her pen. Should she do this? she wondered. Was she stepping beyond what her son would believe were the limits of motherly interference?

She was still vacillating as she withdrew a sheet of paper. After a moment, however, she took a decisive breath and dipped her pen in the inkwell. *Dear Lady Farrington*, she wrote, *This letter of inquiry from a person unknown to you may strike you as strange, but . . .*

Chapter Twenty-One

As they'd arranged the night before, Ada and Derek met with Willy Willigill at ten in the morning at the house in Portman Square. The three gathered in Derek's sitting room, where Mr. Willigill graciously consented this time to take a seat. In all other respects, however, he remained as determinedly businesslike as before, refusing to accept refreshment of any sort and rejecting all conversational overtures not relating to the case at hand. As soon as he was seated, he set his strange, rounded hat on one knee, removed his spectacles and notebook from his pocket and, after placing the spectacles on his nose, looked earnestly over them at Ada. "I'd best tell ye at once that the news ain't good," he said bluntly.

Ada's heart sank to her shoes. After the elation of the night before, his words were a cruel blow. "Oh, no!" she moaned.

Derek leaped angrily to his feet. "But I thought . . . your note said you found the man with the wart!"

The runner put up a restraining hand. "I found 'im, just like I said. But I didn't find Stanley, an' that's the long an' short of it. Do ye wish to 'ear me report, m' lord, or do ye prefer to rant an' rave a bit?"

Derek, still glowering, sank down on his chair again. "Go ahead," he ordered glumly.

The runner referred to his notes. "Mornin' of the twen'y-second, nosin' round St. Giles, I get wind of a man wi' a wart what runs a flash 'ouse."

"Flash house?" Ada asked. "What's that?"

The runner looked up from his notes. "Ye never 'eard tell of a flash 'ouse?"

"No, I haven't," Ada said, something in his manner making her feel suddenly very frightened.

"Explainin' it don't make a pretty tale," he said, looking over at Derek uneasily. "Per'aps I should tell it to his lordship alone, Mr. Farrington. Ye're a bit youngish to 'ear the perticklers."

"No! I *want* to hear them," she insisted.

Mr. Willigill turned to Derek and gave him a meaningful look. "I think, m' lord, that, considerin' Mr. Farrington's . . . er . . . *background*—'im bein' a country *boy* an' all—shouldn' you an' me could discuss the perticklers alone?"

Derek caught the message. The runner seemed to feel that a young girl like Addie might be too innocent to hear the ugly details. But, not knowing how to convince Addie to accept such protection, he hesitated. "Well, I—"

"Derek!" Ada drew herself up in offense. "I am not a *child*! And Stanley is *my* concern, not yours. Therefore, I *must* hear the particulars, even though I shan't like hearing them. I shall do my very best to . . . to bear up."

Derek sighed. "Very well, Willigill, go on. You needn't worry. Mr. Farrington is much more intrepid than he looks."

The runner frowned, took a deep breath and did as he was bid. "A flash 'ouse, Mr. Farrington, is, if ye want the truth, a 'ellish place. Usu'lly it's a deserted, ramshackle buildin', full o' rats an' vermin. But London is full of orphans an' 'omeless brats what would feel lucky to live in one of 'em. The man or woman what runs the 'ouse takes in a number of these brats who 'e thinks can earn brass for 'im. The boys 'e trains in thievin' an' pilferin' an' the art of pickin' pockets. The girls —some not more 'n thirteen—well, ye cin guess 'ow *they're* s'posed to earn their keep."

"Oh, my God!" Ada breathed, horrified. "How can such things be *permitted*?"

"Who's to stop it, Mr. Farrington? There ain't enough constables in all of London to deal wi' it. An' 'alf of *them* keep theirselves in brass takin' bribes from flash 'ouse coves. An' when ye *do* close one of those 'ouses in one place, they start up again in another. An' in the meantime, all ye've done is sent the poor tykes into the street."

"It's damnable!" Derek muttered. "A *damnable* situation! But are you saying, Willigill, that our man with the wart keeps one of these houses?"

"Aye, me lord, that's what I'm sayin'."

Ada clenched her hands tightly. "Then go on with your report, Mr. Willigill."

He looked back at his notebook. "Arfter checkin' through flash 'ouses on Grape Street an' High Holborn, I locate our pertickler 'ouse at number thirty-seven Tottenham Court Road at twelve-forty-five in the post meridiem. I keep watch. At one-twenty-two, a man exits front doorway, wart on nose, age near forty, height five feet nine, weight fifteen stone, fringe of brown 'air round large bald spot."

"That does agree with the gypsy's description," Derek offered.

The runner nodded before proceeding. "Two-thirty post meridiem, return wi' two constables, proceed to search premises. Some boodle found, but no sign of S. Farrington. Man wi' wart returns five-fifteen, identifies self as Phineas Fox. We interrogate suspect fer one hour ten minutes. Suspect denies known' gypsy or purchasin' child." He closed his notebook, sighed deeply and lowered his head.

Ada stared at him. "Is that *all*?"

"Aye, sir. There was nothin' else we could do."

"But you should have kept *searching*! If he's the man who purchased Stanley—and it certainly seems to be so—then there must be some sign of the boy *somewhere* on the premises!"

"I 'ad two good men wi' me, Mr. Farrington. An' we searched the premises for almost three hours. Yer brother ain't there."

Ada lifted her chin belligerently, hoping the belligerence would keep her from crying. "There must be *some* sign of him! I want to go and see the place for myself."

"No!" Derek burst out. "This is the outside of enough, Addie. Willigill knows his business, and if he didn't find anything, there is nothing to be found."

"You needn't take that lordly tone with *me*, my lord!" Ada said icily. "Willigill may know his business, but *I* know Stanley. There may be something I can recognize that he missed. I found the muffler, didn't I?"

"That has nothing to do with this. The gypsy camp wasn't a flash house. For you to enter that hell hole is out of the question!"

"'Is lordship's in the right of it, Mr. Farrington," the runner said firmly. "That ain't no place fer ye. But there ain't no need, yet, to lose 'ope. We ain't through, ye know. We cin still keep lookin'—"

"Where?"

"I figure there's two roads we cin follow. One, we keep watchin' Mr. Phineas Fox. Two, we look to see if there ain't *another* man wi' a wart."

Ada did not answer. The runner rose from his chair. "I'll take meself off, then, Mr. Farrington. Ye'll 'ear from me in due course."

"I'll see you out," Derek said, rising.

"I may as well go, too," Ada said, getting wearily to her feet.

"Oh, no, I'm not letting *you* out of my sight," Derek said from the doorway. "I know you, Addie Farrington! You think you'll go to that place by yourself the minute my back is turned. But you'll do no such thing. Just sit there and wait for me, do you hear? Don't move an *inch*! I'll be right back to give you a proper talking-to!"

Derek and the runner stepped into the corridor, and Derek carefully closed the door. The runner looked up at him with narrowed eyes. "Ye know I cin find me way, me lord, so I'm guessin' that ye 'ave something private to say to me."

"Only to ask if you've told us everything," he said, walking slowly down the corridor beside Willigill. "Are you *certain* there was no sign of Stanley in that house?"

"Aye, me lord, certain as I cin be. The girl might be right, of course. With so many rags an' scraps an' trinkets as a 'ouse full of brats can 'old, 'ow certain cin I be that I didn' miss reco'nizin' somethin' of the boy's?"

Derek stopped in his tracks. "Then perhaps we *should* take her there," he suggested worriedly.

"I wouldn' recommend it, me lord. It ain't a pleasant sight."

"I didn't suppose it would be. How many children does this man Fox keep there?"

"Cain't say fer certain. Twen'y or more."

"Twenty!" Derek stared at the little man, appalled.

"Twen'y ain't so many. I seen 'ouses wi' hundreds of 'em."

"*Hundreds!* Good God!"

"I ain't sayin' it ain't 'orrendous, me lord, but them brats is better off than the ones livin' on the streets."

Derek winced. "Do you think *Stanley* could be living on the streets?"

"Don' know, me lord. I ain't got a inklin' of what's come of that boy."

Derek ran his hand through his hair in despair. "Then, confound it, Willigill, let's take her to the damn house! It may be our last chance. She's a brave-hearted lass. She'll bear it."

"Are ye sure, me lord? Ye ain't never seen such a place yerself. It's stench an' filth an' depravity from top to bottom. Y're bound to see things there, things I wouldn' say in front of the lady."

"What things?"

"I told ye there's not on'y boys livin' there, ye remember. There's girls, too. Well, when ye walk in, ye cin see 'em layin' about t'gether, if ye know what I mean. I wouldn' wish that poor lass to see it."

Derek frowned thoughtfully. "No, nor would I. Perhaps if you and your men could go in first and . . . and clear it up a bit?"

The runner cocked his head, his eyes brightening. "I s'pose we could at that."

"Then come back with me, man, and let's tell her we're going. It's just as well, you know. The girl would not have let me rest otherwise."

Derek strode back down the hall, Willigill at his heels. But when they threw open the sitting room door, they discovered that the room was empty. Ada was gone. An open window, leading to the rear garden, told them at once how she'd escaped them. "Damnation!" Derek swore angrily. "She's taken off without us."

But the runner looked more worried than angry. "Then let's get a move on, me lord. We've got to catch 'er before she gets there. A flash 'ouse ain't no place fer a lady . . . an' fer a lady alone, it's the edge o' doom!"

Chapter Twenty-Two

Ada, repeating the address of the flash house in her mind to be
sure not to forget it, walked quickly away from Derek's
house. Derek was bound to come after her, so she had to get
away from Portman Square before she could permit herself to
stop and search for a hack. An icy rain was falling from an
almost-black sky, and she suspected that it might not be easy,
on such a day, to find a carriage to hire. But to her surprise,
she located an available hack almost at once. She climbed in,
gave the Tottenham Court address and sat back against the
cushions. The driver, however, refused to start. "That address
can't be right, sir," he said. "You wouldn't be goin' *there*. It
ain't a place for a proper gent."

"Nevertheless, that's where I'm going," Ada insisted, "so
get on your way, if you please."

When the carriage drew up at number thirty-seven, Ada
almost lost heart. The street was dingy and lined with vagrants
who were huddled under blankets or boxes or even newspa-
pers to protect themselves from the rain. Very few of them
bothered to look up at the young man descending from the
carriage, but when they did they seemed ominous and threatening. The house itself, which was very narrow and set back
from the street several feet farther than the two larger build-
ings on either side, was in complete shadow. It looked ab-
surdly forbidding, with its boarded-up windows and dirty
edifice, but Ada knew she had no choice but to go ahead with
her plan. Instructing the coachman to wait for her, she walked
gingerly into the shadows, approached the doorway and
knocked with her cane.

An endless moment passed before she heard a bolt being

pulled back. The door opened an inch and and eye appeared in the opening. "Well?" came a girl's voice.

"I'm here to see Mr. Fox," Ada said, hoping that her lack of confidence was not apparent in her voice.

"Mr. Fox ain't in."

"Let me in, please," Ada insisted. "I'll wait for him inside."

"Ye cin wait fer 'im out there," the girl said.

Ada held out a shilling. "Inside."

The door opened wider, and as soon as Ada stepped inside, the shilling was pulled from her hand. But she hardly noticed the act, for she was assaulted by the most dreadful, overpowering stench she'd ever experienced. It seemed to be compounded of one part burnt meat, one part rotten fish and two parts human excrement. For a moment she was afraid she would choke. Coughing and gasping, she reached for a pocket handkerchief and covered her nose, all the while aware that the door was being closed behind her and the bolt slipped into place. She turned to look at the girl who'd let her in, but she caught only a glimpse of a pair of dirty legs below a shabby skirt as the girl scurried away into the shadows.

When her eyes had adjusted themselves to the dimness of the place, Ada looked about her. She found herself standing in a square room whose only light came from the cracks between the boards that covered the two windows cut into the front wall. The room was evidently a sleeping area for many people, for there were a number of thin pallets and shreds of blankets tossed here and there on the uneven, rough-hewn floorboards, as well as a number of wooden bunks built three tiers high along the walls. There were no other furnishings of any kind. The room's small fireplace was unlit and emitted a dank, smoky odor of its own. There were no doors or corridors leading to other rooms—at least none that she could see—although there was a narrow staircase in the far corner, indicating that additional rooms might be found above.

She was aware of a few sleeping figures in the bunks, but most of them seemed to be unoccupied. In one of them, someone turned over and groaned. Another seemed to be occupied by more than one person, but it was really too dark to tell. But none of the occupants of the bunks took any notice of her. Nor could she find any sign of the little girl who'd let her in. Since the girl had not gone up the stairs, Ada couldn't help wondering through what secret passage the girl had disappeared. And if there *were* a secret passage, she asked herself, had Mr. Willigill found it? Could she permit herself to hope that, hidden away in some secret hole, was Stanley himself?

It was then that she noticed a blanket hanging on the wall to her left, the direction the girl had taken when she'd scurried off. Convinced that the blanket concealed a door, she gingerly crossed the room and pulled it aside. It didn't hide a door, but it *did* cover an opening in the wall which led to a smaller room beyond. The room, a kind of storeroom, had no windows at all. Its walls were lined with cupboards and stacks of bundled rags, and a trestle table with two benches stood in the center. A candle burning on the table and a coal fire smoldering in a small grate were the only sources of light. However, the light was sufficient for Ada to see the dirty little girl who'd let her in and an older boy on their knees in the far corner. They were hurriedly stuffing things away among the rags in one of the larger bundles. The girl had evidently warned the boy that there was an intruder in the house, and they were hiding their loot. Ada noticed that the girl, a scrawny, wild-haired creature of not more than twelve, was barefoot and bare-legged in spite of the chill in the house.

"Look, Nicky," the girl muttered, tapping the boy's shoulder and pointing to where Ada stood.

The boy turned round and gave Ada a measuring glance. Evidently deciding that the intruder was not large enough or forbidding enough to be threatening, he rose from his knees and advanced toward her. He was a wiry lad, as raggedly and filthily dressed as the girl, but at least he was wearing shoes. As he came closer to where she stood in the opening, Ada could see that he had close-set, sharp eyes, a flat nose and protruding chin. Almost as tall as Ada herself, he seemed to her to be about fifteen. "Didn' ye 'ear what Rosie tol' ye?" he asked with a sly sneer. "Mr. Fox ain't here."

"I know that," Ada said bravely, stepping through the opening into the room, "but perhaps I can talk to you instead."

The boy circled her, studying every particular of her person and dress. He seemed especially taken with the beaver she still had on her head. "Grand 'at, that," he remarked coolly.

"I'll give it to you if you answer my questions honestly," she offered.

"Will ye, now?" He completed his circle and perched on the end of the table facing her. "Ye might give it t' me whether I answer yer questions or not."

"No. You'd have to take it." Ada tapped the head of her cane against her palm suggestively. "And that might not be as easy as you think."

The boy leered. "Hah! Easy enough, I'd say. But what're yer questions? Le's see if they're somethin' I'd care t' answer."

"I want to know if you've seen a boy here during the past week. Small, about eight years old, with reddish-blond curly hair."

The boy's eyes narrowed. "*Now* I know what's brung ye! Y're the cove what sent the runner, blast yer 'ide!" And he got up and walked toward Ada with tightened fists.

Ada raised the cane. "No need for fisticuffs, fellow," she said with a steady calm she was far from feeling. "There are no runners with me now."

"Don't, Nicky," the girl said, scurrying up to him and grasping his arm. "'E's right. 'Tain't no good t' maul 'im. 'Twould on'y make trouble."

The boy, keeping his eyes on the intruder, nevertheless lowered his arms. He stared at Ada for a long moment and then, making a sudden swing, knocked the hat off her head. In a movement almost too quick to see, he dived for it and, backing away, placed it on his head in gleeful triumph. "See? I got it wivout answerin' no bleedin' questions."

"Very well, you've got it. But if you want to keep it, then tell me what I want to know."

"I think I want yer stick, too," the boy said cockily.

"No, you won't get the stick. You won't get anything else from me."

"No? Well, le's just see about that." And, fists raised again, he came toward Ada slowly.

Ada raised the cane threateningly, and the two began to circle each other, eyeing one another warily. "Nicky, leave off!" the girl said, placing herself in front of him. Then she

turned to Ada with hands on hips. "What's that li'l boy t'
you?" she asked.

Ada's heart leaped hopefully. "He's my brother. You *have*
seen him, haven't you?"

"We don' know nuthin' about 'im," the boy said, glaring at
the girl.

Ada ignored him. "Please tell me," she begged the girl.
"I'll make it worth your while."

"She don' know nuthin'!" the boy declared angrily. "An' if
ye think ye'll 'ave anythin' t' garnish Rosie wiv when *I'm*
through wiv ye, y're in fer a surprise."

He advanced toward her, more quickly this time, and
grabbed for her cane. Ada, however, also moved quickly and
swung its heavy head at him, catching him just below the left
shoulder and dealing him a solid blow. "Ow!" he cried out in
pain.

Recovering quickly, and wrathful at this momentary defeat,
the boy came toward her again and swung at her with tightened fist. This time he hit his mark, delivering a sharp blow to
her nose. Ada felt an astounding pain and cried out, but she
didn't permit herself to back away. She planted her feet sturdily apart and swung the cane again, connecting with his jaw
and causing him to stagger.

The girl screamed. Nicky, regaining his balance, let out a
stream of curses and, now fully enraged, moved toward Ada
again. The girl, beginning to blubber, threw herself on him.
"Nicky, *stop*! 'E's a *nob*, an' 'e's *bleedin*'! There'll be the
devil t' pay!"

"Keep yer sneezer out o' this!" Nicky snarled, trying to
push her aside.

But the girl held on to his arms tenaciously. "*Look* at 'im,"
she begged tearfully. "'E don' seem a bad sort. 'E don' mean
us no 'arm. 'E on'y wants t' find 'is *bruvver*!"

"'Old yer clapper, y' damn chubb!" Nicky cursed, shoving
her away with such force that the girl fell to the floor.

Ada, tasting the blood running from her nose, did not wait
for the boy to advance again. With heart pounding, she swung
her cane again at his head. He parried the thrust with his arm,
but not before the sharp, pointed ear of the ivory wolf's head
made a deep scratch right under his eye. Blood spurted out,

and Rosie, watching the scene through the greasy locks that
had tumbled over her eyes, screamed again. "*Stop!*" she cried
in terror. "Ye've cut 'is *eye!*"

Nicky backed away until he reached the table. Leaning
against it, he pressed his palm to his face. The blood seeped
through his fingers. "*Gawd!*" he whined, horrified. "Me eye's
bleedin'!"

Rosie leaped to her feet and ran to him, lifting her skirt and
pulling the hem toward his face. As soon as Ada realized that
Rosie intended to use her grimy skirt to staunch his blood, she
went to the girl and pressed her own handkerchief into the
girl's hand. Rosie stared down at the square of clean white
linen for a moment, and then, brushing the wild hair from her
face, threw Ada a look of grateful astonishment. "Thank ye,"
she mumbled.

"It's nothing," Ada answered, keeping her eyes on the
girl's face.

Rosie swabbed at Nicky's face. "Ye'll never get the blood
washed out o' this," she warned Ada.

"Never mind. It's only a handkerchief."

The girl paused in her ministrations and stared down at the
bloody linen, biting her lip in thought. Then she lifted her
head, fixed her eyes on Ada's face and took a deep breath.
"The ol' fox sold 'im to a sweep," she muttered and turned
quickly back to her job of mopping away the blood from
Nicky's cheek.

Ada's heart stopped. "*Wh-What* did you say?"

"What're yer *doin'*, blabbermouth?" Nicky shouted furiously. "*Thankin'* the damn bloke fer takin' out me eye?"

"Yer eye's not touched," the girl assured him. "on'y a cut
on yer cheek. Besides, that li'l tyke Stanley deserves a bit o'
luck. 'Ow would *you* like t' be sold fer a climbin' boy?"

"Climbing boy?" Ada echoed, her brain in so confused a
whirl that she didn't pay any heed to the sound of footsteps
behind her. "Is that something very dreadful?" she asked
Rosie, only a small part of her mind taking note of Rosie's
sudden turn and the look of fright that leaped into her eyes.
"Do you know to whom he was sold? *Please*, can you tell
me—?"

A sound behind her made her stiffen. Rosie was gaping at

something just behind Ada's shoulder, her eyes widening in horror. *"Don't—!"* the child screamed. But before Ada could turn, the blow fell—a blow on the back of her head so excruciatingly painful that flashes of lightning and sparks of glaring red flame seemed to explode in her brain. This was followed by a hideous sensation of falling . . . falling down a narrow, curving, black hole that became deeper and deeper and darker and darker until there was nothing to see or to hear or to feel except a kind of enveloping blackness. And when the blackness completely surrounded her, there was nothing left. Absolutely nothing at all.

Chapter Twenty-Three

Ada had no idea how much time had passed when a beam of dusty light intruded into her dark nothingness. At first she resisted looking at it, for it was more painful than the blackness had been. But once she recognized its existence, it wouldn't go away. Then she began to ask herself the question that everyone asks when returning to consciousness: *Where am I?* She could hear sounds, voices, footsteps running, but nothing was clear. The only clear thing in the world was the pain, a pain centered at the back of her skull and sending out aching waves that spread into her head and down all of her body. It was too dreadful for words. She shut her eyes to blot it all out.

"Addie? Addie, *speak* to me!"

Her mind leaped awake. She *knew* that voice. *Derek*! She tried to say his name, but the effort to move her lips seemed too great to undertake.

"Addie, please! Open your eyes or say something! I'm here now. Nothing will hurt you anymore, I promise. Oh, my love, *please*!"

Something in those words filtered through the pain like a beam of sunlight through a murky wood. "*What* . . . did you . . . say?" she whispered hoarsely.

"Addie!" It was an exclamation of joyful relief. "Oh, *Addie*!" he breathed, and she felt herself being gathered into his arms. She could even feel his cheek against her hair. *I must be dreaming*, she told herself, but, dream or not, she wanted to cling to the feeling. Her arms crept up, and she clasped her hands tightly round his neck. He responded by holding her tightly against him, so tightly that she couldn't breathe. "My *dearest*," he murmured into her ear, "I was so afraid . . . so absolutely terrified that I'd lost you. Oh, *God*! I couldn't *bear* to lose you . . . not now! Not without ever having said . . . having told you . . ."

But his voice failed him, and he fell silent. She could not speak either, feeling utterly lost in a strange, bewildering fog of pain and joy. *None of this is real,* she thought. *He couldn't be saying these things to a boy!* But before she could summon up the strength of mind to determine what was real and what was illusion, she felt the black fog creep up on her again. She couldn't hold it back. With a surrendering sigh, she let herself slip into the darkness again.

After an indeterminate time, she drifted back into consciousness. She felt him lift her chin. She opened her eyes and saw, as if through a mist, his face smiling down at her. "Derek?" she asked, wondering if, this time, she was waking from a dream.

"Yes, love," he smiled. "You've come back to us again."

There it was again, the word "love." But he couldn't have said it. She *was* dreaming. She lifted her head to try to see where they were, but her efforts were rewarded with so sharp a stab of pain that the yawning pit of black threatened to envelope her again. All she could do was groan and cling to Derek's shoulder for dear life.

"Don't try to sit up," he said softly. "It's all right. I'm going to take you home."

Then they *weren't* home. Were they still at the flash house? The fearful words seemed to trigger her memory, and the entire scene that had occurred before the blow flashed into her mind. *Stanley!* Did Derek *know* about Stanley? "No, *no*," she muttered incoherently through lips that were strangely dry and stiff. Afraid that she would soon be pulled back into the black pit, she clutched at his coat lapel. "We *can't* go . . . home! You don't know . . . about *Stanley*—!"

"Don't think about Stanley now, my dear. You have to rest . . ."

She tried to shake her head, but any movement she made was so painful that the black fog rolled closer. "*Derek*," she whispered as urgently as she could, "you don't understand. I've learned—"

"Ssh!" he said gently, placing two fingers on her lips. "It's all right. We're finished here. Willigill and I tore this place apart. I'm so sorry Addie, but Stanley's not here. However, Willigill doesn't think we should despair. We'll find him yet. Meanwhile, he's taken Fox into custody. That damnable miscreant won't break a pitcher over anyone's skull ever again!"

"Is that . . . what happened?"

"I'm afraid so. I wanted to kill him. Willigill's arrested him. He's taking the boy in, too. The one they call Nicky."

She tried to lift her head again. "Oh, but . . . Derek, not *Rosie*! You won't let them . . . take Rosie . . ." Her head began to pound, and she let it fall back against him, but she kept her urgent hold on his lapel. "She's a . . . kind little girl . . . really . . . and she told me—"

"Hush, my dear, hush. Don't upset yourself. I'll see to Rosie, whoever she is, but don't try to talk anymore."

"But please, Derek, you must . . . *listen*," she begged, peering at him earnestly through a fog of pain. "Oh, dear! I have a feeling . . . I'm going to . . . faint again. But before I do . . . I must tell you" . . . But her voice failed her and, feeling the fog approach, she shut her eyes.

"Tell me what, dearest?" he asked, cradling her head and rocking her gently.

More than anything in the world, she wanted to lift her hand and touch his cheek. But the dark fog in her brain was thickening, and she had to tell him what she'd learned before it overcame her. "Stanley . . . he was *here*!" she managed in a faint whisper. "The girl, Rosie . . . told me. Mr. Fox sold him . . . to a sweep!" With that last effort expended, she turned her head to his chest, burrowed in his arms and let the waves of blackness come. *Did I really hear him call me dearest?* she wondered as the black fog rolled in. Then all thought evaporated as she slipped down, down, down into the pit again.

Chapter Twenty-Four

Lady Rutledge had invited seventeen of her very best friends to her home for a card party. Three tables had been set up in the sitting room, and a light buffet was being readied in the drawing room to refresh the ladies after play had ended. Lymber, occupied with setting out the various crumpets, cakes and creams with which the ladies would soon satisfy their appetites, did not hear Lord Esterbrook come clumping into the entryway. Neither did any of the housemaids nor the footmen, all of whom were belowstairs taking tea.

Derek, carrying the still-unconscious Ada in his arms, looked about the empty hallway anxiously, hoping to find somebody—anybody!—to assist him. He was covered with dirt from his search through the flash house, his clothes and hair were in complete disarray and his temper—exacerbated by his alarm over Addie's condition—was at the breaking point. "*Damnation*," he muttered, "where *is* everyone?" But his only answer was the faint sound of laughter and the babble of female voices emanating from the sitting room.

Within the sitting room, the games were well in progress. Everyone was utterly absorbed in her cards when the door flew open with a crash. Eighteen turbaned or feathered heads lifted, and eighteen pair of eyes turned toward the sound. Eyebrows rose and mouths dropped opened at the sight that met their eyes, for there stood Derek, dirty and dishevelled, in the doorway, Addison Farrington drooping lifelessly in his grasp. "Mama," he barked, "I shall need you." Without another word, he abruptly turned on his heel and disappeared from view, having shown not the slightest recognition of, attention toward, nor interest in his mother's guests.

Lady Rutledge, paling in alarm, rose trembling from her

seat and ran from the room. The guests, astonished and confused, looked from one to the other wordlessly. At last, Mrs. Endicott, who was the mother of six and accustomed to emergencies, wondered aloud if she should go up and offer assistance. Lady Woolcott then asked if his lordship had been carrying a dead body. Then everyone began speaking at once, making remarks which varied from speculation about a possible murder to evaluation of the propriety of continuing the games in spite of the possible calamity upstairs and, more important, of helping themselves to refreshments in the absence of their hostess. On this point, Lady Chadwick, at least, had a decided opinion. "I, for one," she said, rising, "do not intend to play a *moment* longer nor to take so much as a *single sip* of tea. That Lady Rutledge should have left us without a *word* of explanation is an act of *rudeness*, whatever the cause. And for Lord Esterbrook to have shown himself before a group of ladies in *all his dirt* is positively *unforgiveable!*"

Upstairs, Derek was just placing Ada gingerly on her bed when his mother came running in. "Good heavens, Derek, what have you *done* to the girl?" she cried.

He wheeled about and gaped at his mother in astonishment. "*Girl?*"

"Yes, girl!" she snapped, pushing him aside and bending over her unconscious guest with motherly concern. "Do you take me for a fool? But we can discuss that later. Tell me what's *wrong* with her?"

"She was struck at the back of her head with a heavy piece of pottery. I found her completely unconscious. But she did come to her senses for awhile and spoke to me quite lucidly." He shut his eyes and rubbed his forehead with shaking fingers. "Oh, God, Mama, you don't think the blow could have been mortal, do you?"

"*Mortal!*" Her ladyship felt her blood run cold. But one look at her son's distraught expression made her realize that she had to say something encouraging. "Dear me, no!" she assured him. "At least it doesn't seem likely, especially since she's already wakened once." She knelt down beside the bed and peered at Ada closely. "Her color is pale, of course, but not waxen. And her breathing seems normal. Go down to

Lymber and tell him to fetch Dr. Simpson at once."

"Shouldn't we make her more comfortable first? Take off her boots? Loosen her neckerchief?"

"Yes, yes! I'll do that," she assured him, bending over Ada and smoothing back the hair from the girl's forehead tenderly. When she heard no sound of movement from her son, she looked up at him. "Go along, my dear, go along. There's no need to look like that, you know. I shan't leave her side, I promise."

He paused at the door. "What about your friends?" he asked. "I seem to have broken up a party."

"Oh, who cares for that? If they haven't had the sense to leave by this time, they soon will."

The doctor appeared within the hour. If he wondered why the young lady on the bed was dressed in man's clothing, he did not bother to remark on it. He was interested only in her medical condition. He lifted her eyelids, peered into her eyes and requested Derek to lift her so that he could examine the back of her head. He discovered a sizeable lump but could feel no actual break. "Contusions, not concussion," he said with cheerful confidence. "She'll come out of it soon enough. I could bring her round, but she'll have the devil of a headache when she wakes. Let her come out of it on her own. I'll leave some headache powders for her, and if they prove insufficient, you can give her some laudanum in milk. Cheer up, my lord. The chit'll be good as new in a week."

As soon as he departed, Derek sank down on his knees beside the bed and dropped his head on the coverlet, his whole body sagging in relief. His mother watched as his hand crept over the cover until it reached the girl's. He grasped it convulsively and held it fast. Lady Rutledge, touched to the heart, crept silently out of the room and left them alone.

She came downstairs expecting to find that all her guests had gone, but Lymber informed her that there were two "persons" awaiting her in the sitting room. She went in to find, not one of her card-players, but a peculiar little man in a peculiar round hat, accompanied by the scruffiest, dirtiest, most pathetic little girl she'd ever seen. Why, the child didn't even have shoes on her feet!

The man jumped up at her entrance. "Willy Willigill, Bow Street," he said, making a little bow. "An' you, ma'am, are Lady Rutledge, mother of 'is lordship, Viscount Esterbrook?"

"That's right," her ladyship said, brows upraised. "Bow Street, you say? Don't tell me you're a runner!"

"Aye, me lady, just so."

"Good heavens, am I to be arrested?"

"No, ma'am," he said without a trace of a smile to respond to her sally.

"Then, if you're not going to arrest me, please sit down and tell me why you've come."

"No, thank ye, ma'am. I cin state me business standin'. I've brung ye the little girl, y' see."

Lady Rutledge glanced over at the child, who was huddled in a chair chewing a filthy fingernail and looking terrified. "You've brung . . . brought her to *me*?"

"Aye, me lady. On orders of yer son. He tol' me, when he carried Miss . . . er, *Mr.* Farrington out o' the 'ouse on Tottenham Road, t' find a girl named Rosie an' bring 'er to you. This 'ere is Rosie."

"Indeed? Rosie who?"

"Cain't say, me lady. All I cin tell ye is that she 'as no fam'ly an' no 'ome neither, now that 'er flash 'ouse is closed down."

"Flash house? Are you telling me this *child* has been living in a den of *thieves*?"

"'Fraid so, ma'am."

Lady Rutledge shook her head. "I'm sorry to hear it, of course," she said kindly, "but what, pray, am *I* to do with her?"

The runner shrugged. "She was a real 'elp to us, y' see. In the matter of Stanley Farrington, the missin' boy. Admitted she seen Stanley and over'eard Fox sell 'im to a chimbley sweep fer three guineas. Mr. Farrington, he wanted t' reward 'er, I s'pose."

"Ah, I *see*," her ladyship said as understanding dawned. She walked across the room to where the child sat watching her in suspicious terror. "Goodness, child, stop chewing your nails! Well, Rosie, stand up and let me look at you. What's your surname?"

The girl stood up on her two naked, bowed legs and, hugging her arms closely to her chest, peeped up at her ladyship from under lowered lids. "I dunno, ma'am. Never 'ad no other name but Rosie."

"Well, we can pick one for you, I suppose. What do you think of" . . . She glanced over at Mr. Willigill for inspiration. . . . "of, well, Williams?"

"I like Farrin'ton better," the girl muttered.

"Do you, indeed?" Lady Rutledge laughed. "You'll have to ask Addie about that. Stand up, girl. How old are you? Ten?"

"Goin' on thirteen, ma'am, I figure."

"Do you think, if I keep you here, that you could work and earn your keep?"

"Work, ma'am?" The girl regarded her with utter disbelief. "'Ere?"

"Yes. In the kitchen. Helping cook in the scullery with the washing up and so forth."

The girl's eyes opened saucer-wide. "Do ye mean I could stay? In this 'ouse?"

"Of course in this house. Well? What do you say?"

"Oh, ma'am!" The girl breathed in a deep, blubbering breath, and then, with a suddenness that made Lady Rutledge jump, cast herself down before her ladyship and embraced her legs. "Oh, ma'am!"

Lady Rutledge stared at her in amazement. "Very well, Mr. Willigill, we'll keep her. But you, Rosie, get up at once! And don't ever let me see you do anything like that again. A simple bob and a thank-you will be quite sufficient!"

When Derek emerged from Ada's bedroom some hours later, he found his mother in the now-deserted sitting room, taking a solitary tea. The card tables and all other vestiges of her aborted party were gone. "I've quite ruined your day," he said from the doorway, "and probably your reputation, too."

She smiled up at him. "Is Addie all right?"

"Sleeping," he said, coming in and pulling up a chair beside her. "I think it's a normal sleep. However, despite Dr. Simpson's reassurances, I shall feel a great deal easier in my mind when she opens her eyes and says something."

Lady Rutledge put down her cup and folded her hands in

her lap. "Are you in love with the girl, Derek?" she asked bluntly.

"More than I ever thought possible. Are you shocked?"

"No, not at all. Why should I be?"

"Because I led you to believe she was a boy. Because she doesn't even know I know she's a girl. Because she's little more than half my age." He threw his mother a rueful grin. "I could probably give you a few dozen other reasons if I tried."

"None of those reasons sounds insurmountable, my dear," his mother said complacently. "Will you marry her?"

"I don't know. There is one insurmountable reason that may prevent it."

His mother nodded and sighed guiltily. "Yes, I know. Cynthia Chadwick."

"*Cynthia*? Good God, no! I realize I haven't extricated myself yet from that entanglement, but as soon as I have time to think I shall find a way."

"Then what *is* the insurmountable obstacle to your wedding your Addie?"

"She may not love me, you know," Derek said glumly.

"That would be an obstacle indeed," his mother agreed. "Why don't you ask her?"

"You mean, just go up to her and say, 'Addie, I've known from the first that you're a girl, so you may as well stop hiding behind those breeches and marry me'?"

"I see what you mean. It would be too abrupt to declare yourself before you've been able to know each other as man and maid."

"Exactly." He eyed his mother admiringly. "For a woman who has so little talent for matchmaking, Mama, you are showing remarkable perspicacity and understanding now. Have I been underestimating you? You were even shrewd enough to guess that Addison Farrington is a girl. How did you do it, ma'am?"

"Simple. I saw you hugging her the other night and, knowing my son, could reach no other conclusion." She picked up her teacup again and stirred the brew thoughtfully. "I unbound the strapping she uses to keep herself flat when I undressed her today, you know. When she wakes, she will know that her secret is a secret no longer."

His brows knit abruptly. "Oh, blast! I was hoping this accident would *not* force her to reveal herself."

"Oh? Why not, for heaven's sake. Didn't you just say that you wished you could know each other as man and woman?"

"Yes, but I wanted her to tell me the truth in her *own time* and of her *own accord!*"

"But why? What difference can it make?"

"A great deal, don't you see?" He got up and began to pace. "She's bound to be grateful to me for my aid in the search for her brother. But I want love, not gratitude. If she loves me, she'll *want* me to know she's a girl. But if it's only gratitude she feels, I think she'll find it easier never to let me know the truth."

"I don't understand. Why would it be easier?"

"For one thing, she'd never have to admit the dishonesty. And, more important, if she keeps behind the disguise, the man-woman question can be completely avoided. If she doesn't care for me as a maid does a man, all she need do is to thank me with boyish profusion and go home without ever letting me know that something beside gratitude is *possible* between us."

"Yes, I see. In that case, Derek, let me go upstairs and bind her up again. Perhaps we can all continue to pretend that we think she's a boy."

Derek paused in his pacing and stared at her hopefully. "Do you think we can? The only ones who know are you, McTeague, the runner and I. We've all managed to carry it off so far. I don't see why we can't keep it up."

"Neither do I," his mother declared, putting down her cup and rising purposefully.

"But, dash it all," her son said, his optimism faltering, "I said some things to her when I found her lying senseless on the floor of that miserable hole . . . things that must surely have given me away."

"Oh? What sort of things?'

Derek rubbed his chin in embarrassment. "Surely you can guess. The sort of foolish, romantic, ardent things a lovesick man is likely to babble when the girl he adores is lying wounded in his arms."

"But the girl was unconscious. Are you sure she heard you?"

"I don't know. She wasn't unconscious all the time."

"But even then she must have been dazed. I think it's quite possible that she didn't hear you. Let's chance it."

"Very well, Mama. Go up and bind her. And we'll see what we shall see."

Lady Rutledge hurried to the door. But there she paused and turned round to her son with a taunting grin. "Ardent, romantic and lovesick, eh? I never would have thought it of you, Derek. You've always pretended to be such an unsentimental type." She hurried out of the room, but her laughing voice floated back to him. "Ardent, romantic and lovesick! Derek, my dear, you are a *constant* surprise to me."

Chapter Twenty-Five

Ada opened her eyes and found herself back in her bedroom at Rutledge House. She wondered at first if she'd dreamed the whole incident at the flash house, but as soon as the thought passed through her mind she became conscious of a raging headache. It was evidently no dream, then, that she'd been struck on her head with a pitcher. She lifted a shaking hand to the bruised place at the back of her head and moaned.

Lady Rutledge, who'd been keeping watch, bent over her at once. "Ah, Addison, dear boy, you're awake! You don't know how glad I am to see you return to consciousness at last."

Ada blinked up at her. "At last?" she croaked. "How long have I—?"

Her ladyship beamed down at her fondly. "You slept the clock round three times over."

"Goodness! *Did* I?" She struggled to sit up. "Do you mean I slept through all of yesterday?"

"Yes, like a log." Lady Rutledge helped her up and stacked a mound of pillows behind her for support. "How are you feeling, Addison? A bit dizzy, I expect."

"I have the most appalling headache, ma'am," Ada answered, gingerly leaning back against the pillows, "but I seem to be sound otherwise."

"Yes, Dr. Simpson warned us about the headache," her ladyship said placidly. "I'll go and fix a headache powder for you."

As soon as she was alone, a dozen worries crowded into Ada's mind. Evidently Lady Rutledge still believed her to be a boy, but what about Derek? She glanced down at herself and discovered that she was still clad in shirt and breeches. She was surprised, but quite relieved, that no one had undressed her. They didn't wish to wake her, she supposed.

But she'd slept away a *day*! An entire day in which she could have begun to search for the chimney sweep who'd bought Stanley. How could she have permitted herself to do it? She had to get up from her bed at once. She raised her head, lifted her stockinged feet over the side of the bed and tried to rise, but the pain in her head was so severe that she fell back upon the pillows again. *Perhaps*, she told herself weakly, *I need just a bit more rest*.

She closed her eyes and let another memory rise to the surface of her mind: Derek, holding her in his arms and calling her "love" and "dearest." If the blow on her head was real, perhaps that, too, was real. *Could it be possible,* she wondered, *or is it only some sort of peculiar fantasy created by a bruised brain from wishful thinking?* Well, she would know soon enough. If, the next time she saw him, Derek still believed she was a boy, she would know she'd been mistaken and that everything she thought he'd said was only an illusion. His loverlike behavior was beginning to seem like an illusion already, for he was not here beside her. Wouldn't a lover be hovering over her, waiting for his beloved to open her eyes? If his words in her ear were *not* an illusion, where was he now?

As if to answer the question, Lymber entered the room with a glass of vile-looking liquid on a tray. "There's someone waiting to see you, Mr. Farrington," he said, handing her the glass. "Shall I send him up?"

Her heart leaped up into her throat. "Yes, of course, Lymber. At once."

She could barely drink the medicine down in her eagerness to see him. But the man who appeared in her doorway was not Derek. It was Mr. Willigill.

She swallowed her disappointment with the remainder of her medicine. "Come in, Mr. Willigill," she said, forcing a smile. "Do sit down."

"No, thank ye, Mr. Farrington," the runner said, his ferret-like face more dour than ever, "I won't be stayin' long. I on'y come t' say how sorry an' shamed I be."

"Shamed? But why?"

He twisted his hat round and round in his hands. "Willy

Willigill's not knowed as the rummest runner in the bizness fer nothin'. It ain't like me t' bungle a case."

"But you didn't bungle it, Willigill. You said Stanley wasn't there, and he wasn't."

"But 'e *had* been there. I shoulda knowed it. An' I shoulda never let ye in on the flash 'ouse address. If I 'ad me wits about me, ye never would 'ave been conked on the noggin." He came closer to the bed and peered down at her earnestly. "I'll make it up t' ye, Mr. Farrington. Ye 'ave me word. I'll find the boy if I 'ave t' chase down every sweep in London."

She smiled up at him warmly. "I know you will, Willigill. After all, you found the man with the wart. You *must* be the rummest runner in Bow Street to have done that. And you'll find Stanley too. I have every confidence in you."

She *did* have confidence in the fellow, she decided when she thought about the matter after he'd gone. It couldn't have been easy to have found the man Fox, yet he'd done it in two days. With any luck, he'd find the sweep, too. She had no idea how many chimney sweeps there were in London, but there couldn't be many more than there were men with warts. And Willigill was quite determined. He would find him.

The door opened again and a little girl holding an enormous tray stepped carefully into the room. "Cook said I could bring yer breakfast meself," she said proudly, setting the tray awkwardly on the bedside table.

Ada stared at her. The little girl was dressed like an ordinary housemaid in a black bombazine dress (which, because she was a child, came only to midcalf and thus revealed two thin, black-stockinged legs and two small feet shod in very new shoes), a starched white apron and a ruffled mobcap (set on a head of unruly but shiny-clean hair), but she was not quite ordinary. Ada had seen her before. "Good heavens!" she exclaimed, sitting up abruptly. "*Rosie*?"

The girl grinned widely. "It's me! Ain't I grand? An' it's all yer doin', Mr. Farrin'ton. I'm that grateful I could '*ug* ye, but 'er ladyship says I'm on'y t' give a bob an' a thank-ye. She says a bob an' a thank-ye is 'quite sufficient,' but it ain't really."

Ada laughed delightedly. "Yes, it is sufficient, really, but you can give me a hug anyway. Come here and sit down beside me, Rosie. I want to hear everything that's happened to you."

Rosie perched on the bed and began eagerly to relate her adventures, from the fearful experience of her first bath to the fitting of her new shoes. But she was interrupted by the sound of a knock at the door, followed by the entrance into the sick room of Lord Esterbrook himself. "Well, what have we here?" he asked in surprise at the unconventional scene that met his eye.

"This is Rosie," Ada explained as the child slid off the bed in fright. "Rosie, this is Lord Esterbrook, the gentleman who *really* deserves your thanks."

Rose made a little, bobbing curtsey, breathed a quick, "Thank-ye, me lord," and scurried from the room.

"I didn't know I was so terrifying to children," his lordship remarked, looking after her in amusement.

"I don't know how to thank you for finding her, Derek. It was very good of you."

"Nonsense, Addie. Don't talk fustian." He came up to the bed and gazed down at her. He noticed with relief that the look in her eyes—unlike the blurry, glazed, disoriented look she'd had when last seen—was bright and clear. He noticed, too, that her cheeks were turning pink under his gaze and that her breath was growing rapid. His presence was affecting her emotions, that much was clear, but it was not clear that *love* was the emotion involved. He wanted so much to gather her up in his arms that the yearning was like a physical pain in his chest. But she hadn't yet told him the truth, and he'd sworn to himself that he would wait until she did. So he clenched his fists behind him and held himself back. "You're looking better, my lad," he said with avuncular heartiness. "Almost like your old self."

Ada stared up at him for a moment but soon dropped her eyes. She had thought, for one heart-stopping instant, that he was going to take her in his arms. But it had turned out to be another example of the work of a disordered imagination. He was merely being fatherly. He'd even called her (good *God*, how she hated those words!) "my lad." "Yes, I'm . . . fine," she said, stoutly swallowing the tears that burned her throat. "Quite myself again."

But she was not feeling at all fine. She wanted to crawl back into that black hole and feel nothing. *I'm still a boy to him*, her heart cried in disappointment. *Everything I thought I'd heard was nothing more than imagination*. She was aware that he was still gazing down at her, so she tried to maintain the smile that had lit her face when he came in. But she couldn't do it. It was hard to smile—so very hard—when one's dreams were being swept away like brown dead leaves in the harsh, cold wind of reality.

Chapter Twenty-Six

By the following day, Ada was feeling well enough to leave her room. She forced herself to dress and go downstairs, but her motions were lethargic. The lethargy came not from weakness but from lack of heart. She suspected that it would be some time before she heard from Mr. Willigill, and the waiting was a strain. The longer she had to remain here in London, close to Derek and everything that reminded her of him, the greater would be her pain.

Her depression was worsened by the prospect of having to attend Lady Chadwick's fete on the following evening. She dreaded having to be present at the affair. How could she bear, in so weakened and dispirited a condition, having to watch Derek pay court to his beautiful Cynthia? She did, of course, consider the possibility of using her weakened condition as an excuse to beg off, for what could be a better excuse for not attending a formal social function than having been dealt a severe blow on the head? But on second thought she decided against employing that excuse. Lady Rutledge would not go off and leave her if she said she was not well enough to go, and Ada didn't wish to spoil Lady Rutledge's enjoyment of the evening.

It was in this gloomy state of mind that she left her room for the first time in three days. If she had any hope that her spirits would be revived by this activity, she was to be sorely disappointed. She found Derek with his mother in the sitting room, conversing in the most serious tones with a tall, elderly gentleman in the somber black coat of a clergyman. "I beg your pardon," she apologized, backing out the door awkwardly. "I didn't know—"

"It's all right, dear boy," Lady Rutledge assured her. "You

may join us if you wish. Mr. Coulter, this is Mr. Farrington. It is *his* brother we've been discussing."

"How do you do, Mr. Farrington?" the clergyman said, rising and extending his hand. "I am most sorry to hear of your brother's disappearance. You have my deepest sympathy."

Ada shook the extended hand but threw a desperately questioning look at Derek. *Why,* she wondered, *are they discussing Stanley with a clergyman? Has something dreadful happened?*

But Derek, seeming to read her mind, relieved it at once. "Mr. Coulter is the secretary of the Society for the Abolition of Climbing Boys," he explained. "I wrote to him yesterday, inquiring if they could offer us any assistance, and he was good enough to call on us. He has been describing to us the conditions under which these unfortunate children are employed."

"Perhaps, Derek, it would be better for Addison not to listen to this," his mother suggested. "Mr. Coulter's information, even though it is general and not specifically applicable to Stanley, is very disturbing nonetheless."

"Yes, Mama, you're quite right. Addie, why don't you go into the morning room and have breakfast? You needn't subject yourself to—"

But Ada shook her head. "You must stop trying to protect me, Derek. I am a . . . a man, after all. I must learn to face the truth, no matter how difficult." She pulled up a chair and sat down. "Do go on, Mr. Coulter."

"I was saying, Mr. Farrington, that for thirteen years, ever since we were organized in 1803, we have been trying to persuade the sweeps to use mechanical means to clean the chimneys—"

"By mechanical means," Derek explained to Ada in a whisper, "Mr. Coulter means long-handled brushes and other mechanisms of that sort."

"Yes," Mr. Coulter agreed, "but the sweeps aren't interested. They prefer to use boys, and the smaller the better. Of course, the practice is quite inhuman. I don't wish to dwell on the details and upset Mr. Farrington, but the horror of it must be apparent to anyone who gives the matter even a modicum of thought. The child has to inch his way up flues that are sometimes less than two bricks wide, their sides thick with soot and flaking mortar. The stuff sticks to their skins and falls into their eyes. The smell, the smoke, the dirt... well, you can *imagine* what it must feel like to a very young child. The official minimum age is eight, but we have heard of cases where sweeps have used boys as young as *four*."

"Oh, my God!" Lady Rutledge exclaimed.

"Yes, it is quite shocking. The boys are often covered with bruises and sores, and if the sweep is particularly unfeeling, he forces the child up the flue by setting straw on fire in the grate, so that untreated, painful burns are added to his other ills."

A low moan escaped from Ada's throat. Derek rose immediately and went to stand beside her chair, pressing a sympathetic hand on her shoulder.

The clergyman, quite impassioned on this subject (which he'd lectured on thousands of times in his efforts to educate an unfeeling public) would not be put off by the pallor of Ada's face. It was not often that he found an audience whose interest was so intense, and he could not resist the opportunity to impress them with the importance of his mission by offering more details than he had at first intended. "And in cases where a boy is kept at the work for several years," he continued, "his growth is stunted, his eyes are weakened and he becomes subject to coughs, asthma and other ills which I won't have the hardness of heart to mention in Mr. Farrington's presence."

"Good God, Mr. Coulter," Derek exclaimed, "can't anything be done to prevent such evils?"

"Those who *could* do something are amazingly indifferent," Mr. Coulter responded, not mincing words. "Have *you yourselves*, who must have your chimneys swept once a year or so, taken *any notice* of the poor wretches who come to clean them? Our society has urged members of Parliment *repeatedly* to pass legislation, but thus far we haven't had any success at all. All we can do, because of limited funds, is to try to intercede in those cases where abuse is particularly severe."

"You can count on us in future, Mr. Coulter, for a substantial contribution," Derek promised. "And we shall be happy to be of assistance to your society in any other way we can."

"Thank you, Lord Esterbrook. I shall call on you to fulfill that promise." He sighed and got to his feet. "I wish I could be of such assistance to *you*, but I fear that I have no specific information that would be of help to you. Unfortunately, there is no such thing as a registry of sweeps. There is nothing to be done but to track down as many as you can and make them trot out their helpers for your inspection." He crossed to the door, and then added before departing, "If anything comes to my ears that I think has any significance, I shall, of course, relay the information to you at once."

It took many minutes after the clergyman departed for anyone to speak. Imagining the lives led by the unfortunate children who were forced to climb inside chimneys day after day until they were stunted and deformed kept all three silently brooding. It was Derek who broke the silence. He knelt before Ada's chair and took her hand. "Don't look like that, Addie. We shall find Stanley before too much damage has been done to him, I promise you, if I have to hire an army and comb the city street by street!"

The heartfelt sympathy in his voice dealt the final blow to Ada's self-control. She turned her face to the back of the chair and burst into tears. Derek, had his mother not been in the room, would not have been able to keep himself from taking her in his arms, but as it was, he threw her a look that clearly begged her to give what comfort she could to the weeping girl and strode to the door. "I'll be back," he said over his shoulder as he crossed the threshold, "but not before I have some hopeful news. This deuced, fruitless search has gone on long enough!"

Chapter Twenty-Seven

Ada had only one hope of being spared having to attend the Chadwicks' dinner party: the hope that Stanley might be found before the hour came. But no word reached Rutledge House from either Derek or Willigill, and at sunset both Lady Rutledge and Ada retired to their rooms to change for the festivities. Lady Rutledge, fearful that Derek might forget the engagement entirely and thus incur the Chadwicks' everlasting enmity and the social disgrace that comes from being labelled an unmannerly boor, sent a footman round to Portman Square with a message to McTeague to be certain to remind his lordship to present himself at the Chadwicks' at eight sharp.

Both Lady Rutledge and Ada found the first hour in the Chadwicks' Egyptian-style drawing room a time of consternation, Lady Rutledge because there was no sign of Derek, and Ada because Cynthia, gowned in a magnificent peach-colored Florentine silk, looked absolutely ravishing. To make things even more difficult for Ada's peace of mind, Charlotte and Irene Moncrief were among the twenty guests. The moment Ada set foot in the room, the sisters advanced on her and began to flirt with her in a manner so lacking in subtlety that she was put to the blush, not only for herself (for she had no idea how a real gentleman would respond to such blatant advances) but in shame for all her sex.

Lady Rutledge was painfully aware that Derek's absence was causing difficulty for her hostess. She noticed that the Chadwicks' butler twice approached his mistress for a whispered consultation about the time dinner was to be served and twice was told to wait. The third time, Lady Chadwick came up to Lady Rutledge and asked icily but with perfect politeness if something had befallen her son. Lady Rutledge could

only stammer that she feared the search for Mr. Farrington's
lost brother, which Derek had undertaken to conduct person-
ally, must have reached a crisis. Lady Chadwick reddened in
chagrin and responded that, although the cause of his absence
was no doubt admirable, it in no way excused his thoughtless-
ness toward his hostess. "I'm afraid, Felicia," she added
stiffly, "that I can delay dinner no longer. I shall have to order
the butler to remove his place. I suppose that I shall never
again be able to face the world when it becomes known that I
placed *my* guests at a table set with an *uneven number*!"

Ada, having been inveigled into escorting Irene Moncrief in
to dinner, was somewhat relieved to learn that their places at the
table were far apart. She found herself sitting between two
elderly ladies whose names she did not catch and who showed
not the slightest interest in the young man placed between them.
She was thus free to look about her at the amazing room in which
the Chadwicks dined. It was as long as a ballroom and boasted
twin sideboards, one on each long wall, that extended the length
of the room. The table and chairs had ornately carved legs
trimmed with gold, and behind each chair stood a gold-liveried
footman in white gloves and powdered wig, waiting in impassive immobility to serve the soup. Three enormous crystal
chandeliers hung from the ceiling, the hundreds of candles they
carried casting a brilliant light upon the dozens of crystal goblets, epergnes, gold plate and gleaming china with which Lady
Chadwick crowded her table. Eight goblets and ten pieces of
gold flatware were lined up at each place, and the magnificent
silver-gilt serving plates bore an Imari design in green, pink and
gold. Ada, who was accustomed to some ostentation in her own
home since Lydia had become its mistress, was nevertheless
completely overwhelmed. It was hard to believe that even the
Regent could set a table as grand as this.

The first course had already been served when Derek strolled
in. Dressed impeccably in a black dinner coat and satin
breeches, his neckcloth folded into an admirable *trone d'amour*
and his hair brushed into gleaming curls, he looked neither
hurried nor distressed. With suave urbanity, he approached his
hostess, lifted her hand to his lips, murmured an apology that
was evidently so cleverly worded that she was left speechless,
nodded to a few acquaintances and took the place that the butler

and two footmen immediately set for him. His mother beamed at him from across the table. Certainly no one, not even the forbiddingly formal Lady Chadwick, could find fault with so flawless a performance. *And what's more,* Lady Rutledge laughed to herself, *the number of her settings is now even.*

Two other ladies at the table felt their hearts lift at his appearance. One was Ada, who thought she'd never seen anyone look so handsome and carry himself with such *savoir faire* in all her life. The other was Cynthia Chadwick, who had been terribly disappointed by his absence and, having felt no interest in either of her table partners, was utterly delighted at seeing the butler place the latecomer's chair beside hers.

For the rest of the meal, Ada had to endure the torture of witnessing the whispered exchanges that took place between Cynthia and Derek. By the time the Apricot Russe was served, she was ready to weep. However, by the time the desserts had been eaten, her mind was distracted from its gloomy contemplation of the progress of the romance between Cynthia and Derek by the sudden development of a new problem: what to do when the ladies got up to leave the gentlemen to their postprandial drinks.

The problem burst upon her consciousness when Lady Chadwick rose, tapped her large goblet with a spoon and said, "Shall we leave the gentlemen to their brandies, ladies, and repair to the music room?" Ada was about to rise with the other ladies when she remembered her disguise. *Dash it all,* she thought, *I can't go with the ladies!* She would have to remain in her seat while the ladies departed, that much was clear. But would she then be forced to stay with the gentlemen? This was a problem to which Ada had never before given a moment's thought. But she needed an answer, and *quickly,* for although she had no idea what the gentlemen talked about when there were no ladies present, she had little doubt that the subjects were not fit for a lady's ears.

For a moment she sat frozen to her chair, but when a moustached man leaned over to her and handed her a brandy bottle, she decided that she must act. She got up, walked as purposefully as possible to where Lord Chadwick sat at the head of the table (ignoring Derek's keen observation of her every moment) and asked to be excused. "After my accident, you see, my lord," she said, "I find that I cannot be still for very long. I should like very much to take a walk on your terrace, with your permission."

Lord Chadwick gave a stiff but kindly nod, and Ada quickly whisked herself from the room. She walked down a long corridor to the doors of the terrace, but as soon as she opened them, she was assaulted by a cold wind. Not wishing to subject herself to the violence of the elements, she closed the doors again and looked round for some place to hide. From somewhere to her right she could hear the sound of a piano. The sound was undoubtedly coming from the music room where the ladies were gathered. She wondered who was playing. It couldn't be one of the Moncrief girls, she reasoned, for the technique was too perfect; the Moncriefs were too flighty to have disciplined themselves so carefully. It might well be Cynthia herself who was playing, for the pianist was so preoccupied with playing the notes *correctly* that she had no room in her mind for any other aspect of the music. That would be Cynthia to the core.

Ada slipped by the door to the music room and went a little farther down the hall. She opened the next door she came to. It was the library, a large, panelled room lined with book-shelves and family portraits, and, best of all, a fire was burning cheerily in the fireplace. She stepped inside, closed the door and approached the fire. Its warmth made this room the most inviting of any she'd yet seen in this ostentatious house, and she pulled a wing chair close to the grate and sank into it.

She must have dozed off, for she was startled by the sound of the door opening. Before her mind had fully taken in what was happening, she heard Cynthia say, "Come in here, Derek, where we can be alone."

Ada froze in embarrassment. She must make her presence known at once, she urged herself. But how? What was the least awkward way to get up out of this chair and show herself? Whatever she did, everyone would be embarrassed. But no matter the embarrassment, it had to be done. She quickly considered alternatives. She could stand up and say, "No, hang it all, you're *not* alone," but that would seem too bold. She could say, "I'm dreadfully sorry," but that would make everyone feel awkward, and they might be impelled to urge her to stay. She could simply run from the room without saying anything, but that would be too dramatic.

While she vacillated, she heard the door close. "I don't think your mother would believe this private *tête-a-tête* to be at all proper, do you?" she heard Derek ask.

Oh, dear, Ada thought, *I'm too late. I've already heard too much. Perhaps it would be less embarrassing for all of us if I hid here until they finished.*

"Perhaps Mama would not approve," Cynthia said in her beautifully modulated voice, "but I think it necessary. You know, Derek, I have believed, from the first day we met, that you and I seemed to have an instant understanding of each other. And, if you remember, you said you thought so too."

"Yes," Derek said slowly, "I remember."

I think I want to die, Ada said to herself in agony, *but this is the sort of torture that eavesdroppers deserve.*

"I *thought* you would remember," Cynthia went on. "Our friendship has made remarkably speedy progress, don't you agree?"

There was a moment's hesitation. "Are you suggesting, Cynthia, that the progress was *too* speedy?" he asked carefully.

"No, no, not at all," she said. "I have been very . . . *pleased* at the progress. But I must warn you, Derek, that you are treading on thin ice as far as my parents are concerned."

"Indeed?" he asked interestedly. "In what way?"

"Your manners of late have seemed, well . . . too spontaneous."

"Spontaneous? Do you mean instinctive, unplanned? Is there something wrong with that?"

"Well, sometimes, if manners are too spontaneous, you know, they can appear to be—if you will forgive me for using the word—rude."

Cynthia is an utter fool, Ada thought in disgust. *How can a woman who is loved by someone like Derek find fault with, of all things, spontaneous manners?*

"Do your parents believe I've been rude to them?" Derek asked.

"I'm afraid they do. When you left Chadwick Manor so abruptly, for instance, they were quite appalled. We understood, of course, that you believed your mother to be ill but, even so, your departure could have been somewhat . . . gentler."

"I see. And there were other instances?"

"Yes. Mother tells me that when she attended a card party at your mother's house, you broke in on the ladies in the most deplorable way—"

"Yes, I suppose I did," Derek said shortly. "And is that all?"

"That would be quite enough to cause concern, would it not? But then tonight—"

"Tonight?"

"Your rather shocking lateness, you see—"

"Yes, I do see. Does this mean, Cynthia, that you wish me not to call on you again?"

Cynthia gasped. "Oh, *no*, Derek! I don't mean anything of the *kind*! I think of you with the very highest regard, you must know that. I mean these little comments only to make you aware . . . it would be most distressing to me if Mama and Papa did not hold you in as high regard as I do. After all—if I did not misunderstand some of the things you said to me—you are in hopes of one day calling them Mama and Papa, too—"

This was more than Ada could bear to hear. With a choking sound, she leaped from her chair. "I'm . . . *sorry*!" she burst out miserably. "I didn't mean to—!" She threw an agonized look from one to the other, covered her face with her hands and ran from the room.

Derek, startled, stared at the door for a brief moment but, when he realized what had happened, he had an inexplicable impulse to laugh. However, it took but one look at Cynthia's face, frozen with shock, to make him restrain himself. He would not laugh, he told himself, but he wouldn't remain to endure any more of this conversation, either. "I beg your pardon, Cynthia, but there is something I must take care of at once. Please excuse me. I promise I will come to you tomorrow, when we can continue this very interesting talk with calmer minds." And with a quick bow, he followed Ada from the room.

He found her in a small sitting room across the hall. She had cast herself upon a sofa and, with her face burrowed into a cushion, was sobbing her heart out. He perched beside her on the edge of the sofa and put a hand on her shoulder. "Good God,

Addie, the incident doesn't require such a flood," he said cheerfully. "You couldn't help it if we barged in and began to converse without making certain the room was unoccupied."

"I'm n-not c-c-crying about th-that," came a small, hoarse voice from the depths of the cushion.

"Then what the devil *are* you crying about?"

She sat up and wheeled on him. "I'm crying b-because you're going to w-wed that . . . that *r-ridiculous f-female!*"

Derek eyed her interestedly. "Why ridiculous?"

"Because she c-cares more for *p-propriety* than for *p-people*, that's why!"

"That's a very interesting analysis. So interesting that I believe I quite agree with it."

"You *do?*" She looked up at him wide-eyed. "Even though she is so very beautiful?"

"She no longer seems so very beautiful to me."

"Then, Derek . . . *why* are you going to . . . to *m-marry* her?"

"Who said I was?"

"*She* did! I heard her say you'll one day c-call her p-parents Mama and P-Papa."

Derek sat back against the cushions and stretched out his legs comfortably. "Eavesdroppers seldom understand what they hear," he said pompously.

She stared at him in bewilderment. "Then . . . you're *not*—?"

"Not if I can help it."

"But Derek," she persisted, "*how* can you not—?"

"You, my dear, are being too blastedly inquisitive. As of this moment, I have said all I intend to say on that subject." He pulled a handkerchief from his pocket and handed it to her. "Here. Do you think you can dry your eyes now?"

"Yes, thank you," she sniffed, dabbing at her cheeks. At that moment it occurred to her that no boy of nineteen would ever have behaved as she just had. She gave Derek a sidelong, uneasy glance. "Hang it all, I haven't been acting in a . . . a very manly way, have I?"

"No, *hang it all*, you haven't," he laughed, hoping that the moment for her confession was at hand. "You shed some tears yesterday, too, if I recall. For a fellow of your age, you seem unusually prone to tears. In fact, for a nineteen-year-old, your behavior has been decidedly peculiar. Do you think you can explain yourself?"

She twisted her fingers together nervously. "I have an explanation, but I . . . I don't think you'd like to hear it."

His pulse began to race, and he sat erect in eager expectation. "Yes, I would," he urged. "Try me!"

"No, I can't tell you. It would . . . change everything. *Spoil* everything."

"Are you sure, Addie? Perhaps it would change things for the better."

She lowered her head and shook it adamantly. "No, it wouldn't. Don't ask me any more."

But Derek feared that if he failed to cajole a confession from her now, he never would. He therefore used the most effective bait he had. "What if I told you some news. Some very good news that would make you very happy indeed. Would you tell me then?"

Her head came up at once. "Derek! Is there some news about *Stanley*?"

He grinned at her. "That's why I was late. I met with Willigill. Now, don't set your hopes too high, for they've been dashed too often, but we have reason to believe we've found the sweep. With the description of the fellow that Rosie gave us, Willigill has managed to track down a sweep of that description to a neighborhood in Cheapside. We'll know tomorrow for certain, but Willigill says there's every reason for optimism."

"Oh, *Derek*!" Ada breathed joyfully, gazing up at him with utter adoration.

The look in her face undid him. He stared down at those tear-laden, green-grey eyes, the streaked cheeks, the slightly swollen lips, and the last of his self-control ebbed away. It no longer seemed to matter if she told him the truth or not. He loved her, and he could no more keep from embracing her than he could keep from breathing. He gathered her into his arms and lifted her chin. He lost all sense of the passage of time as he watched the look in her eyes turn to wonder. Her lips opened slightly and a little, gasping breath constricted her throat. But before it could escape from her mouth, he bent his head and kissed her hungrily.

With a little shiver, she slipped her arms about his neck, her body bending to the pressure of his arms. She could not think of anything but the exquisite bliss of being in his arms. Never had she felt so soft, so pliant, so utterly female. Never had she felt so close, so much at one, with another living being. She wanted the moment never to end.

But of course the moment ended. Thought came flying back into her brain, and as soon as he loosed her, she stared into his eyes in horror. "What are we *doing*?" she whispered hoarsely.

"Perhaps you'd better tell *me*," he said with an amused twinkle. "Have I kissed a boy?"

Her eyes widened in shock. As if a balloon had burst in her brain, she suddenly understood. "You *knew*!" she gasped, the blood ebbing from her cheeks. "You've known *all along*!"

"Yes, but—" The delight that the embrace had kindled in his chest was doused at once by the angry intensity of her voice. "Yes, I've known all along," he said in bewilderment, "but why does that upset you so?"

She rose slowly and backed away from him, as if he'd suddenly become a leper. "How *could* you?" she asked, trembling in fury. "It's been a huge *joke*! *All* of it! All this time, you've been laughing . . . making a *fool* of me!"

"Addie, that's not so!" He got up, took a step toward her and reached out his arms. "You *can't* believe that I—!"

"Don't touch me!" she cried, holding up her hands as if to fend him off. "I never want to speak to you . . . or see you . . . ever again!" She ran from the room, raced along the corridor and sped down the long flight of stairs that led to the Chadwicks' doorway. Ignoring the gaping looks of the footmen stationed at the bottom of the staircase, she flew by them out the door and down the street, leaving behind the hateful, ostentatious house that she hoped she would never have to lay eyes on again, ever, as long as she lived.

Chapter Twenty-Eight

Ada blundered down the dark streets, turning corners and crossing roads without knowing where she was going. She had just been through the most humiliating night of her life, and she was learning that humiliation is perhaps the most painful of all human emotions. The thought that Derek had seen through her disguise and had been laughing at her all this time was devastating. She must have seemed ridiculous indeed, prancing about in breeches and saying "hang it all" at the least provocation. How could he help but think her a fool? And how many others had seen through her, she wondered? Lady Rutledge? Willigill? Lymber? She felt so embarrassed that she wanted nothing more than to hide in a coal hole and never come out.

After about half an hour, Ada's storm of self-flagellation subsided, and she began to wonder where she was. The night was very dark, and she shivered with a sudden chill. Nothing looked familiar. She had no sense of the direction she'd taken from Chadwick House and, besides, she certainly didn't want to go back there even if she *could* find the way. But where *was* she to go? Back to Lady Rutledge's? Endure the added humiliation of facing her? She didn't see what else she could do, short of spending the night on the street. She would have to go back, at least until tomorrow, when there might be word of Stanley. That hope was the only bright spot in her dour, blighted future.

She turned a corner and then another, hoping to blunder upon some familiar landmark. When she turned a third, she blundered into a tall, caped man. "S-Sorry," she muttered, keeping her head averted.

He completely startled her by grasping her shoulders and shaking her furiously. "What do you think you're about, you wet-goose?" he shouted. "This is London, not Farrington Park! And it's after midnight! Don't you yet, after all you've seen, have any idea what can happen to an unescorted female on the streets at night?"

"Derek!" she breathed in relief.

"Yes, Derek, fortunate for you!" he snapped between clenched teeth. "I've been half out of my mind looking for you!"

"There was no need," she said, recovering both her equilibrium and her wounded pride. "I am dressed as a man, after all. And though the disguise may not have fooled you, it would probably fool any passing strangers on the street . . . in the dark."

His grip on her arms tightened, and he looked as if he'd have liked to throttle her. But he merely compressed his lips and restrained himself. "Your disguise, ma'am, is not a subject to be pursuing on a dark, windy street in the middle of the night. We'll talk about it tomorrow. Get in the carriage there."

"I won't!" she cried, pulling her arms from his grip. "I've had enough of your ordering me about!"

He put a hand to his forehead and expelled an exasperated breath. "You, Addie Farrington, are the most provoking, irksome, irritating female I've encountered in all my thirty-two years! *Get in the carriage!* It isn't *mine*, confound it, it's *mama's*. My own is waiting for me down the street. If there's a grain of sense left in that addled brain of yours, you'll climb up and go home with her. I think we can all use a night's repose before we begin to sort things out."

"Very well, I'll go. I don't wish to keep Lady Rutledge waiting in the cold. But there's nothing to sort out. As soon as Stanley is restored to me, I'm going *h-home*!"

"As you wish, ma'am," he said, handing her up. "I'm quite through arguing with you."

She climbed up into the carriage and dropped into the seat opposite her ladyship. Derek muttered a tight goodnight and slammed the door. After a moment of awkward silence, the carriage began to move. "Well, Addie," Lady Rutledge said calmly, "from what Derek tells me, you've had an eventful evening."

"I suppose that's one way to describe it," Ada muttered, looking across at Lady Rutledge uneasily. "Did he tell you . . . about me?"

"About your being a girl? He didn't have to. I guessed it several days ago."

"Did you?" She groaned in self-disgust. "I must have played the part very badly."

"Not at all. You did very well indeed. I only guessed when it occurred to me that my son was showing signs of being in love with a boy."

"In *love*—?" Ada peered at her ladyship suspiciously. "Derek isn't in love with me. How could he be? He's spent the last ten days laughing at me behind my back."

"Is that what you think, my dear? Then perhaps you ought to think again. Do you know what my son has been doing today? He's been closeted with Mr. Coulter, making plans to build a special school for orphaned boys who've been abused by chimney sweeps."

"Has he, Lady Rutledge?" Ada murmured, awestruck. "That is a very noble undertaking. You must be proud of Derek."

"Yes, very proud. But very surprised, too. That's why I'm convinced that he's in love with you. Very much in love."

Ada wrinkled her brow in confusion. "You say you're *surprised*, Lady Rutledge. But why? I don't find it surprising. From the first I've realized that Derek is very kind to . . . to anyone in trouble. I don't see why that has anything to do with being in love with me."

"Don't you, my dear? Well, I don't deny that Derek has a good heart. But before he met you, he never bothered his head about those in trouble. To be perfectly honest with you, Addie, I will admit that before he brought you home to me, my beloved son was a *rake*. A dyed-in-the-wool rake."

"Oh, my lady, I don't think—"

"Then *do* think, my dear. Think about this: When a confirmed rake so mends his way—and in a mere ten days!—that he becomes a . . . a man of *benevolence*, well, there must be some explanation. And the only explanation I can think of is love . . . the love of a good woman." Lady Rutledge smiled broadly at the wide-eyed girl opposite her. "And if that woman happens to be dressed in a pair of men's breeches, I don't think it makes much difference in the long run, do you?"

Chapter Twenty-Nine

The following morning, Lymber found much to complain of. In the first place, both her ladyship and her guest, the Farrington fellow, were sleeping late, and the butler was hard-pressed to keep breakfast warm for them. In the second place, the door-knockers, front and back, kept pounding. First, it was the back door, where Lymber discovered a chimney sweep, with two dirty little helpers in tow, waiting on the doorstep. The fellow claimed that he'd been sent by Lord Esterbrook to clean "all the chimbleys" of Rutledge House. Lymber, muttering that *he* hadn't been informed that the chimneys would be swept today, nevertheless admitted them and started them off to work on the kitchen flues.

No sooner had that been done when the front knocker sounded. This time it was a well-dressed couple who claimed to be Lord and Lady Farrington. They said they'd come all the way from Suffolk (at great personal sacrifice, the gentleman muttered irritably, since he had much estate business to conduct at home, and the lady was, quite obviously, in a "delicate" condition) in response to a letter they'd received from Lady Rutledge. "I'm sorry, Lord Farrington," Lymber told the gentleman, "but Lady Rutledge is still abed. And, if my assumption is correct, that you wish to see young Mr. Farrington, too, I'm afraid he hasn't come down yet, either."

Lord and Lady Farrington exchanged glances. "Did you say young *Mr.* Farrington?" Lord Farrington inquired.

"Yes, my lord. Mr. Addison Farrington."

"But there *is* no Mr. Addison Farrington," Lady Farrington stated with finality.

"It is not my place to contradict a lady, madam," Lymber

said with aloof condescension, "but there *is* a Mr. Addison Farrington residing in this house."

"I see," Mr. Farrington said, exchanging another glance with his wife. "Then, I would like very much to speak with him, please."

"As I said, my lord, he hasn't yet come down."

"Then, my good man, Lady Farrington and I will wait!" And, carefully assisting his huge-bellied wife to cross the threshold, Lord Farrington led her down the hall to the drawing room in Lymber's wake.

Then the rear knocker sounded again. This time it was McTeague. "I have something for Mr. Farrington," he explained to the butler, indicating a large box he carried under his arm.

"More clothes, eh?" Lymber queried, admitting him. "Well, go on up. You know the way."

McTeague took the stairs two at a time and tapped at Ada's door. "It's me, McTeague," he announced loudly. "Can I come in?"

"Yes, very well," came a croaking voice from within.

He entered to find her sitting up in bed, red-eyed, dishevelled and miserable. "Good mornin', Miss," he said cheerily.

"*Miss*?" She stared at him glumly. "You, too, McTeague?"

"Aye, I knew about ye from the first, Miss. We have no secrets, his lordship an' me."

"How very nice for you," she said icily. "I suppose it was all very entertaining for you, fitting me up with clothes and laughing while I struggled to get you out of the room while I dressed."

"Aye, begorra, it was that!" McTeague grinned. "I'll have to credit ye, though. Ye carried it off in splendid style."

"Oh, yes, splendid indeed. A splendid *dupe*! A perfectly splendid laughingstock for the two of you."

The valet raised his brows. "A bit twitty this mornin', are we, Miss? Under the weather? Blue devilled? Well, I have somethin' here to cheer ye. Look! His lordship sent it." And he placed the box on the bed beside her.

"If his lordship sent it, I don't want it," she said, pouting. "Take it away, McTeague."

"Sure, an' yer not goin' to poker up, are ye? Ye can take a

look at it, can't ye? Especially after his lordship went t' so much trouble t' procure it."

Ada eyed the box from the corner of her eye. "What is it? Another coat? Cut by Weston this time, or Nugee?"

McTeague beamed at her proudly. "Ye've learned men's fashions, I'll grant ye that. An' so quick, too! But that ain't a coat. Whyn't ye take a peep?"

Ada couldn't resist. She opened the box and rummaged through the sheets and sheets of tissue-thin paper that surrounded the contents. When she'd uncovered it at last, she gasped. It was a dress . . . an absolutely beautiful dress of so lustrous a green jacquard that it gleamed like a jewel.

"Well?" McTeague prodded eagerly. "What do ye think of it?"

"It's . . . lovely," she said softly, staring at it with yearning.

"Then put it on, Miss, put it on! Don't worry. I'll go down an' take me usual cup of coffee."

"No, McTeague," she sighed, "take it back. I can't take it. I don't want him to . . . to think I've forgiven him."

"No?" He cocked his head, studying her carefully. "Why not, may I ask?"

"Because he made a fool of me, that's why."

"Nay, lass, how can ye think it? The man's crazy fer ye."

"Don't be ridiculous, McTeague. What makes you think that?"

The valet grinned at her and strolled to the door. "I don't think it, Miss, I *know* it. An' if ye don't believe me, just ask him to show ye his watch."

"His *watch*?" she asked, looking at him dubiously.

"Aye. Dress yerself, Miss, an' come down. He'll be here shortly, I expect. Then ask t' see his watch an' snap open the lid. I'll wager two sovereigns ye'll believe me then. What do you say? Is that a wager?"

A small, hopeful gleam flickered to light in her eyes. "No, McTeague, I won't wager, because—although I don't know how—you've managed to make me believe that it is possible . . . just possible . . . that I might lose!"

Downstairs, Lymber was forced to answer the front door again. Two more callers stood on the doorstep: Lady Chad-

wick and her daughter, Miss Cynthia Chadwick. "Her ladyship has not yet come down," Lymber informed them.

"We're here to see Lord Esterbrook," Lady Chadwick said
stiffly. "We understand he is calling on his mother."

"I'm sorry, Lady Chadwick, but he is not here."

"Is he expected?"

"I have not been so informed, ma'am. But he often drops
by at this hour."

"Then we will wait," Lady Chadwick said, brushing by
him. "Come, Cynthia."

Lymber led them into the drawing room and introduced
them to the other visitors who were patiently waiting for their
hostess to make an appearance. When they were all made
known to each other and had taken their seats, Lymber left
them to their own devices. Lady Chadwick unbent sufficiently
to nod politely to the couple seated across the room and remark that it was such a shame that the weather was so chill.

"Yes, indeed," said Lady Farrington, eager to escape the
boredom of being immersed in her own concerns by engaging
in a little conversation. "It is even chilly in this room. I
wonder why there's no fire in the grate."

"It is rather shocking," Lady Chadwick agreed. "I always
tell *my* staff that fires must be kept burning in all the rooms,
even when they are unoccupied."

"Yes, so do I," Lady Farrington said. "I only wish one
could keep a fire going in one's carriage. I found our drive
down from Suffolk to be most unpleasant, with the wind
whistling in the windows in that dreadful way."

"Yes, carriages can be so draughty when the weather is
cold," Lady Chadwick said.

"And, you know," Lady Farrington added, "in my condition, one must be so careful not to contract a chill."

"Mmm," Lady Chadwick intoned in place of an assent and
turned her head away, effectively indicating that she did not
intend to continue the conversation. The lady on the other side
of the room had proved herself a vulgarian, and Lady Chadwick would endure no other communication with her. (The
solecism Lady Farrington had committed was a reference to
her "condition"; Lady Chadwick did not approve of any public
recognition of, or allusion to, so private and intimate a matter,

no matter how obvious.) Lady Chadwick, her sensibilities offended, therefore fixed her eyes on the portrait over the fireplace, folded her hands in her lap and withdrew into a haughty silence.

Lady Farrington, sensing that she'd been put down, whispered to her husband that she feared she might be getting nervous. Her husband patted her hand and assured her that there was nothing whatever to be nervous about.

The silence was threatening to become positively embarrassing by the time Lady Rutledge finally appeared in the doorway. Her appearance was another blow to Lady Chadwick's sensibilities, for she was very casually dressed in a flounced morning gown and lace cap. "Good morning," she said cheerfully, entering in a flurry of ruffles and ribbons. "I do apologize for keeping you waiting. I was not expecting callers this morning. Lady Chadwick! Cynthia! How delightful of you to call! I would have expected you to be still abed, after your exertions of last night." She turned her beaming smile on the Farringtons. "My lord! Lady Farrington! My butler told me you had come. How very good of you! Have you been introduced to the Chadwicks? Lady Chadwick gave so magnificent a dinner party last night that I don't know how she has the energy to be up and about so early today."

"It *is* after eleven," Lady Chadwick pointed out coldly.

"We were hoping to see Derek . . . Lord Esterbrook," Cynthia explained hastily. "Is he expected here this morning, Lady Rutledge?"

Before Lady Rutledge could reply, Lionel Farrington rose in magisterial annoyance, his patience at an end. "Lady Rutledge, I don't like to interrupt, but I hope you will permit me to state my business without roundaboutation or further delay. My wife and I have been travelling for two days, you see, and we have not yet stopped at our hotel. To be brief, ma'am, my mother received a letter from you regarding my sister, and we found it so puzzling that we've come to ask you about it."

"Oh, dear me, my lord," Lady Rutledge said apologetically, "I never meant to cause such trouble. You never should have bothered to make such a long journey, with your wife in her condition—you *are* expecting, momentarily, are you not, ma'am?—just to satisfy my curiosity about the family. It really was *too* good of you."

"We did not make the journey to satisfy *your* curiosity, my lady, but our own. You asked about my sister, did you not? Well, since my sister has been missing from her home for almost a fortnight—"

"Eleven days, to be precise," Lady Farrington put in, pursing her mouth in disapproval. "Eleven days, without any word from her except a cursory note in which she said nothing but that she was well and safe."

"Yes, exactly," Lord Farrington continued, biting his lip to keep from revealing his irritation at his wife's interruption. "That's why we've come, you see. We couldn't help wondering why you wrote to my mother about her at just this time. Can you have seen her lately, ma'am?"

"Then you *have* a sister?" Lady Rutledge asked airily. "I only wrote because I was not sure."

"Yes, but there must be more to it than that," Lionel insisted. "What made you curious about her in the first place?"

"No special reason," Lady Rutledge said, trying as best she could to avoid giving Ada's relatives any information until she could talk to the girl herself. "I was just thinking about my friend, the late Edward Farrington, your father, whom I used to know years ago, and I wondered if he had a daughter. It occurred to me that, if he had, I might like to invite her to me here in London, and even *present* her, if she should wish it."

"Present her?" Lydia asked in astonishment. "Why on earth would you wish to do that?"

"Perhaps," said Derek sarcastically from the doorway, where he'd stood listening for the past few minutes, "because her own family was not kind enough to do it themselves."

"Oh?" Lionel demanded in offense. "And who might you be?"

"Whoever he is, Lionel, dearest," his wife whispered loudly enough for everyone to hear, "don't lose your temper. I am on the verge of becoming nervous."

Lady Rutledge heaved a relieved sigh at the sight of her son. "May I present my son, Lord Esterbrook? Derek, here are Lady Farrington and Lord Farrington, come all the way from Suffolk to ask about their sister. It seems she's been missing for a fortnight."

"Didn't you get a letter from her, explaining that she was safe?" Derek asked curiously.

"A brief note, yes, but with no hint of her whereabouts. "You know her, then, I gather," Lionel said angrily, taking a threatening step in Derek's direction. "If you've had anything to do with her disappearance, Esterbrook, I'll have the law on you!"

"Will you, indeed? And what about you, Farrington? Your sister disappears for a fortnight, and only after my mother writes you a letter—which reminds me, mama, that I will have a word or two to say to you, too—do you trouble yourself to come looking for her! What sort of brother are you?"

Lionel reddened to the ears. "Who are you, my lord, to question my conduct? Even a member of the family wouldn't have the temerity—!"

"Even a *stranger* might have the temerity to inquire what possesses a brother to permit his sister to disappear and not even make the slightest push to look for her for almost a fortnight!"

"I . . . I had no idea where to look," Lionel said defensively.

"Your sister had no idea where to look for Stanley, either, but that didn't keep her from trying."

"Good heavens, Lionel," gasped his wife, "how do they know about Stanley?"

Cynthia, who had not been following the conversation with very great interest (having something much more personal on her mind), suddenly snapped to attention. "Stanley? Are you speaking of Mr. Farrington's little lost brother?" she asked curiously. "I thought it was *he* who was looking for Stanley."

"This is all very confusing," Lionel said, pulling out a handkerchief and mopping his brow. "Who *is* this Mr. Farrington?"

"I am becoming very nervous," Lydia Farrington moaned, placing her hands on her stomach as if to calm the baby. "In my condition, I do not think it is healthy to be nervous."

Lady Chadwick looked down her nose in revulsion at so vulgar a comment. "Cynthia, my love," she said, "all this has nothing to do with us. Perhaps we should state our business and take our leave."

Derek turned to her at once and made a quick bow. "You are quite right, Lady Chadwick. Forgive me for being distracted from greeting you by this . . . er . . . family matter. Lymber tells me that you wish to see me?"

"Yes, we do," Lady Chadwick said, rising. "I would have preferred to speak of this in private, but under the circumstances I hope you'll permit me to say what I came to say now. I can excuse myself this lack of manners by reasoning that you would tell your mother the substance of our conversation in any case, and the subject cannot matter to the Farringtons. Do I have your permission to proceed?"

"Of course, ma'am," Derek assured her. "I'm all ears."

"I wish you to know, my lord, that Lord Chadwick and I looked with favor on your suit for Cynthia's hand at first, for you had everything to recommend you in all the important aspects: family, position, personal charm and, most important, Cynthia's high regard for you."

"Thank you, your ladyship," Derek said drily, "but I seem to hear a 'but' coming up in that sentence."

"Yes, I'm afraid there is a but. Of late we have been troubled by a certain . . . er . . . "

"Spontaneity?" Derek offered.

"Carelessness, I think, would be the more appropriate word. A carelessness in your demeanor that Lord Chadwick and I cannot like. Not only did you depart from Chadwick Manor with shocking abruptness, startle a roomful of ladies at your mother's own party by appearing on her doorstep in soiled clothes and present yourself at my dinner last night one hour and twenty minutes late, but then, I'm told, you cut short an intimate interview with my daughter without so much as a by-your-leave!"

"Lady Chadwick!" Lady Rutledge said in outrage. "Are you calling my son *rude*? How dare you come to *my* house to insult my son in front of my nose!"

"Mama," Derek said sternly, "please be still! I agreed to permit you to *listen* to this interview, but I did *not* agree to let you speak. Go on, please, Lady Chadwick."

"I did not use the word 'rude,' you know. But if the shoe fits—"

"Lady Chadwick, *really!*" Derek's mother bristled.

"Mama, I *warn* you—" Derek snapped.

Lady Rutledge met her son's eyes, and the truth suddenly dawned on her. This was the interview Derek had been hoping for. If the Chadwicks withdrew from the entanglement, then Derek would not have to. She turned to Lady Chadwick and lowered her eyes meekly. "I beg your pardon," she said. "Please go on."

"It seems to us, Lord Esterbrook, that, in spite of the regard in which my daughter holds you, your conduct does not meet the standards that Cynthia's father and I require for our daughter. We therefore must regretfully request that you no longer call on her or communicate with her in any way."

"Unless, Derek," Cynthia added with as much desperation as her excellent breeding permitted, "you have some *explanation* of your behavior that would permit mama to make a less censorious interpretation of it?"

"I am sorry, Cynthia," he answered, "but I haven't—"

"Good morning," came a new and decidedly cheerful voice. Everyone looked up to see a vision in green jacquard standing in the doorway. Ada was truly lovely in the dress Derek had chosen for her. The long tight sleeves that puffed out on top accented the deeply cut neck that revealed a tantalizing glimpse of her feminine curves, and the high waist was gathered at the center and unfolded just below to fall in a graceful sweep of fabric to the hem. The color accented the green in her eyes, and her boyish haircut was softened by being brushed high over her forehead in a sweeping wave. No one in the room could have doubted that they were staring at a very lovely woman.

Lady Rutledge wanted to crow in delight. Lydia Farrington wanted to ask who the young beauty was. Cynthia, who was accustomed to thinking of herself as the most beautiful girl in any gathering, was smitten with jealousy. And Lionel, who recognized Ada at once, wanted to grasp her by the throat and throttle her for all the trouble she'd caused him. But, strangely, no one moved or uttered a sound, because Ada was staring at Derek with so starry-eyed an intensity that they sensed she was not aware of the presence of anyone else. Derek, too, was utterly captivated by the sight of his Addie in girl's garb. It seemed to him that she was almost luminous, as if she were somehow lit from within.

For a long moment no one breathed. But neither Derek nor Ada noticed, because, for them, the rest of the world had faded from their consciousness. As if they were completely alone, Derek took a step toward her. "Will *you* think me rude, Addie, if I say, quite spontaneously, that you're breathtaking?"

"Not rude," she said, smiling at him. "Just silly."

"Not silly," he retorted. "Just besotted."

She glanced up at him quizzically. "Is that really so? Are you *truly* besotted?"

"How long, ma'am, are you going to keep doubting my word?" he demanded.

"Until you show me your watch."

His eyebrows rose suspiciously. "My *watch*?"

"Yes, please," she said, putting out her hand.

He shrugged, nonplussed, pulled the watch from his waistcoat pocket, undid the hook and handed it to her. She fumbled awkwardly with the little catch, but in a moment the lid flew open, and she stared down at the long strand of red-gold hair that had been curled round and round until it fit perfectly into the circumference of the watch-lid. "Derek?" she whispered, awestruck. "Is it mine?"

"Of course, you goose. I found it in a basket at the Green Gander. I saw you there that day, with your long hair hanging down your back. I think I've loved you from that moment on."

"Even with my hair like this?"

"Especially with your hair like this."

She came up close to him, tucked his watch back in his pocket and peeped up at him shyly. "Then the things I thought I heard you say to me in the flash house . . . you really did say them?"

"I'll say them again, if you still doubt it. Are you willing at last to say them to me?"

"Oh, Derek!" she sighed and threw her arms round his neck, "I do love you so!"

With the spontaneity that was becoming quite natural to him, he pulled her to him and kissed her as passionately as if they were alone.

But they weren't alone. "How disgraceful," Lady Chadwick muttered, breaking the spell of silence. "I *told* you he was a rudesby, Cynthia. *Now* do you believe me?"

Cynthia stared at the couple locked in a blissful embrace. "Yes, Mama," she said glumly.

"Who is that creature?" Lady Chadwick asked curiously. "Mr. Farrington's twin?"

"Why, I think . . ." Lydia Farrington squinted at the lovers in disbelief. "Goodness gracious, Lionel, I think that's *Ada*!"

"Of course it's Ada," Lionel snapped. "And if she thinks I'm going to stand here and watch this utterly disgraceful behavior—!"

But before he could conclude his threat, there was a cough from the doorway, and Lymber entered hurriedly. "I beg pardon, my lady," Lymber said to Lady Rutledge, who was watching the lovers with a beaming smile, "but Mr. Willigill—" At that moment, following the direction of Lady Rutledge's glance, the butler caught sight of Ada in her green gown. For once his butlerish reserve failed him. "*Blimme!*" he exclaimed, aghast. "It's *Mr. Farrington*!"

But Derek had heard the butler announce the name Willigill, and awareness of the rest of the world came rushing back to his consciousness. "Never mind about *Miss* Farrington," he said, taking one arm from round his beloved and turning to the butler. "Send Willigill in, Lymber."

"Derek, do you think—?" Ada asked excitedly.

"I say, m' lord," Willigill said from the doorway, his eyes taking in a quick look at everyone in the room, "where's the sweep?"

Derek tensed at once. "Where's *who*?"

"The *chimbley sweep*! I tol' 'im to come 'ere this mornin'. I didn' tell 'im *why*, o' course. I jus' said Lord Esterbrook wanted the chimbleys cleaned at Rutledge 'ouse, an' that 'e was t' bring 'is 'elpers. Don't tell me 'e 'asn't come!"

"Damnation!" Derek swore. "Why didn't you tell me? We haven't gone and lost him, have we?"

"There *is* a sweep here, my lord," Lymber spoke up. "I think he's still in the kitchen."

"Then fetch him, man!" Derek ordered in relief. "Bring him here at once. And his helpers, too."

Lymber ran out at once. Ada, a gleam of hope leaping up inside here, clutched Derek's arm. "Do you think, my love, that we shall be lucky this time?" She looked round to see if Lady Rutledge was there to share the anticipation, and was suddenly struck by the number of people in the room. "Good heavens!" she gasped, coloring. "I didn't see—! *Lionel!*"

"Yes, you may well gasp, Miss!" her brother barked, stepping forward. "What on earth is the meaning of all this? Why did the butler call you *Mr.* Farrington? How is it that all these people know about Stanley? And why are you behaving in that shocking style with this . . . this arrogant, overbearing *clunch!*"

"Lionel," whined his wife, "I wish you will not shout. My nerves are all ajangle, and you know that cannot be good for the baby."

"And furthermore, Lord Farrington," Lady Rutledge declared, drawing herself up to her full height, "I've heard just about enough abuse of my son for one day! If you say one more word to denigrate him, I shall have to ask you to *leave this house.*"

Ada went up to her brother and put a hand on his arm. "Poor Lionel," she said gently. "I'm sorry I've caused all this uproar. But as soon as we've finished our business with the sweep, we shall all sit down with a lovely, soothing cup of tea, and I shall explain everything, I promise."

"I hope you can," muttered Lionel, somewhat mollified. "But what sort of business can you possibly have with a chim—?"

But the chimney sweep came in at that moment, dragging a soot-covered little boy behind him. "Ye wish t' see me, lor'?" the fellow asked.

Ada, drawing in a gasping breath, ran toward the child. But after three steps she stopped short. "But . . . *that* isn't Stanley!" The croak of her voice was all the evidence anyone needed to know the extent of her disappointment.

Derek turned to the sweep. "Isn't there another one?"

The sweep, suspecting by this time that there was something more at work here than simply cleaning the chimneys, took a step backward. "*Another* one, m' lor'?" he mumbled, edging toward the door.

"Yes, blast you! Lymber, how many boys did he bring with him?"

"Two, my lord. I remember that distinctly."

"Well, fellow?" Derek barked. "Where is he?"

The sweep blinked at Derek for a moment and then, with a sudden lunge, broke for the door. But Willigill was too quick for him. He caught him by the collar of his coat and, quicker than anyone could see, grasped his arms and twisted them behind his back. "Now, ye nip-shot, let's 'ear ye. Where's th'other one?"

"Right 'ere, blast yer 'ide," the sweep muttered.

"Here?" Derek brows knit in surprise. "In *this room*? How can that be? We would have seen him climb up."

"This fireplace 'ere's a double. Same openin' as the one in th' next room. I sent 'im up on that side, see?"

"Very well. Now get him down."

Willigill gave the sweep a shove in the right direction. The sweep, after a nervous glance over his shoulder, crossed to the fireplace and knocked with his fist against the wall over the mantel. Then he bent down and shouted up the flue, "Hoo, boy! Come down now!"

There was no response. The sweep took another look over his shoulder. Everyone in the room had risen from their chairs; their eyes fixed on him tensely. He turned and hammered on the wall again. "Did ye 'ear me, ye scamp?" he yelled. "Git down 'ere, *quick!*"

There was a scraping sound behind the wall and then a thump. A second thump, much louder than the first, was followed by a thin cry. And then, amid the sound of falling plaster and a cloud of soot, a little bundle came tumbling down from the flue and rolled out onto the hearth with a yowl of pain. Derek pushed the sweep aside, lifted the bundle— which, when the soot settled, turned out to be a boy—and set him on his feet. The boy was black with soot from top to toe except for two raw bruises, one on each bare knee, which seeped blood. Even the color of the child's hair could not be determined through the thick powdering of soot.

Kneeling beside him, Derek dusted some loose flakes of plaster from the boy's hair and cheeks and, turning him toward Ada, looked up at her with eyes aglow with hope. "Well, my love?"

Ada stared at the child for a moment, while no one in the room dared to breathe. Then, clasping her trembling hands to her breast, she dropped to her knees before the bewildered little boy. *"Stanley!"* she croaked.

Two white eyes in the child's blackened face blinked back at her. After a long moment, his chin began to quiver and his lips parted. "Ada?" he whispered, not quite believing.

She nodded, her hands clasped over her mouth to keep herself from crying out.

Everyone watched as two fat tears oozed from the boy's eyes and traced two pale tracks through the dirt of his cheeks. Little Stanley took one unsteady step toward the kneeling girl and peered at her closely. "Ada, ith it . . . really you?"

Ada lifted her arms to him. "Stanley, *dearest!*"

The child's face seemed to light up behind the soot. *"Ada!"* he gasped, flinging himself into her embrace. He threw his arms about her neck and clutched her tightly. "Ada, Ada, it'th *you!*" His little limbs trembled with excitement as he burrowed his face in her neck. "I *knew* you'd find me!" he cried joyfully as she rocked him in her arms. "I knew it all the time!"

Author's Note

Flash houses and climbing boys are not the creations of the author's imagination but were a very real fact of Regency life. Flash houses existed by the hundreds in London in the early nineteenth century. It was not until Sir Robert Peel established London's police force in 1829 that the flash houses began to disappear. Fagin's house, in Dickens's *Oliver Twist*, must have been one of the last survivors of that particular horror.

The use of little boys to clean chimneys was a horror that endured much longer. In 1817, a year after the setting of this book, a Select Committee of Parliament made a thorough study of the plight of climbing boys. They amassed enough evidence to give the members of Parliament what J. B. Priestley calls "a glimpse of Hell." But the indifferent members of the House of Lords defeated bills in both 1818 and 1819. Because of their lack of compassion, it was not until 1875, when the Chimney Sweepers Bill was finally passed, that England abolished its wretched practice of pushing little boys up chimneys.

E.M.